What People Are Saying About *Saving Grace*:

"Katie is the first character I have absolutely fallen in love with since Stephanie Plum! I'm hoping for a series!" Stephanie Hayes Swindell, reader

"Katie is someone who could be you, your sister, or your best friend — someone you can really connect to." Rene Riedlinger, reader

"*Saving Grace* is a remarkable debut novel. It is everything a good read should be, with an exotic setting, vivid characterization (including jumbies), authentic-sounding dialogue, and real emotion, all balanced with page-turning doses of action and suspense. Fun, witty, exciting, and unputdownable!" Rhonda Doyle Erb, editor and reader

"This book was worth every moment I spent savouring it, and I can't wait to read the next one." Joana James, author of *Finding Romeo* and reviewer for *Book Wormz*

Saving Grace

Pamela Fagan Hutchins

SkipJack Publishing books may be purchased for educational, business, or sales promotional use. For information, please write: Sales, SkipJack Publishing, P.O.B. 31160 Houston, TX 77231.

First U.S. Edition

Hutchins, Pamela Fagan

Saving Grace/by Pamela Fagan Hutchins

ISBN-13: 978-0988234802 (SkipJack Publishing)

Foreword

Saving Grace is a work of fiction. Period. Any resemblance to actual persons, places, things, or events is just a lucky coincidence.

To Eric
(of course)

Acknowledgments

Huge thanks to my editor Meghan Pinson, who managed to keep my ego intact without sacrificing her editorial integrity. Thanks of generous proportions to my critique partners, without whose encouragement and honesty I would not be publishing this book. The biggest thanks go to my Cruzans: husband Eric, friend Natalie, and house Annaly. They are the ones who inspired me to dream up stories in the islands. Eric gets an extra helping of thanks for plotting, critiquing, editing, listening, holding, encouraging, supporting, browbeating, and miscellaneous other roles, some of which aren't appropriate for publication.

Thanks also to princess of the universe Heidi Dorey for fantastic cover art. Heartfelt appreciation to Alayah for good eyes and a spirit of adventure.

Table of Contents

Chapter One

Last year sucked, and this one was already worse.

Last year, when my parents died in an "accident" on their Caribbean vacation, I'd been working too hard to listen to my instincts, which were screaming "bullshit" so loud I almost went deaf in my third ear. I was preparing for the biggest case of my career, so I sort of had an excuse that worked for me as long as I showed up for happy hour, but the truth was, I was obsessed with the private investigator assigned to my case.

Nick. Almost-divorced Nick. My new co-worker Nick who sometimes sent out vibes that he wanted to rip my Ann Taylor blouse off with his teeth, when he wasn't busy ignoring me.

But things had changed.

I'd just gotten the verdict back in my mega-trial, the Burnside wrongful termination case. My firm rarely took plaintiff cases, so I'd taken a big risk with this one—and won Mr. Burnside three million dollars, of which the firm got a third. That was the total opposite of suck.

After my coup at the Dallas courthouse, my paralegal Emily and I headed straight down I-20 to the hotel where our firm was on retreat in Shreveport, Louisiana. Shreveport is not on the top ten list for most company getaways, but our senior partner fancied himself a poker player, and loved Cajun food, jazz, and riverboat casinos. The retreat was a great excuse for Gino to indulge in a little Texas Hold 'Em between teambuilding and sensitivity sessions and still come off looking like a helluva guy, but it meant a three and a half hour drive each way. This wasn't a problem for Emily and me. We bridged both the paralegal-to-attorney gap and the co-worker-to-friend gap with ease, largely because neither of us did Dallas-fancy very well. Or at all.

Emily and I hustled inside for check-in at the Eldorado.

"Do you want a map of the ghost tours?" the front desk clerk asked us, her polyglot Texan-Cajun-Southern accent making tours sound like "turs."

"Why, thank you kindly, but no thanks," Emily drawled. In the ten years since she'd left, she still hadn't shaken Amarillo from her voice or given up barrel-racing horses.

I didn't believe in hocus pocus, either, but I wasn't a fan of casinos, which reeked of cigarette smoke and desperation. "Do y'all have karaoke or anything else but casinos onsite?"

"Yes, ma'am, we have a rooftop bar with karaoke, pool tables, and that kind of thing." The girl swiped at her bangs, then swung her head to put them back in the same place they'd been.

"That sounds more like it," I said to Emily.

"Karaoke," she said. "Again." She rolled her eyes. "Only if we can do tradesies halfway. I want to play blackjack."

After we deposited our bags in our rooms and freshened up, talking to each other on our cell phones the whole time we were apart, we joined our group. All of our co-workers broke into applause as we entered the conference room. News of our victory had preceded us. We curtsied, and I used both arms to do a Vanna White toward Emily. She returned the favor.

"Where's Nick?" I called out. "Come on up here."

Nick had left the courtroom when the jury went out to deliberate, so he'd beaten us here. He stood up from a table on the far side of the room, but didn't join us in front. I gave him a long distance Vanna White anyway.

The applause died down and some of my partners motioned for me to sit with them at a table near the entrance. I joined them and we all got to work writing a mission statement for the firm for the next fifteen minutes. Emily and I had arrived just in time for the first day's sessions to end.

When we broke, the group stampeded from the hotel to the docked barge that housed the casino. In Louisiana, gambling is only legal "on the water" or on tribal land. On impulse, I walked to the elevator instead of the casino. Just before the doors closed, a hand jammed between them and they bounced apart, and I found myself headed up to the hotel rooms with none other than Nick Kovacs.

"So, Helen, you're not a gambler either," he said as the elevator doors closed.

My stomach flipped. Cheesy, yes, but when he was in a good mood, Nick called me Helen—as in Helen of Troy.

I had promised to meet Emily for early blackjack before late karaoke, but he didn't need to know that. "I have the luck of the Irish," I said. "Gambling is dangerous for me."

He responded with dead silence. Each of us looked up, down, sideways, and anywhere but at each other, which was hard, since the elevator was mirrored above a gold handrail and wood paneling. There was a wee bit of tension in the air.

"I heard there's a pool table at the hotel bar, though, and I'd be up for that," I offered, throwing myself headlong into the void and holding my breath on the way down.

Dead silence again. Long, dead silence. The ground was going to hurt when I hit it.

Without making eye contact, Nick said, "OK, I'll meet you there in a few minutes."

Did he really say he'd meet me there? Just the two of us? Out together? *Oh my God, Katie, what have you done?*

The elevator doors dinged, and we headed in opposite directions to our rooms. It was too late to back out now.

I moved in a daze. Hyperventilating. Pits sweating. Heart pounding. My outfit was all wrong, so I ditched the Ann Taylor for some jeans, a structured white blouse, and, yes, I admit it, a multi-colored Jessica Simpson handbag and her coordinating orange platform sandals. White works well against my long, wavy red hair, which I unclipped and finger-combed over my shoulders. Not very attorney-like, but that was the point. Besides, I didn't even like being an attorney, so why would I want to look like one now?

Normally I am Katie Clean, but I settled on a quick brush of my teeth, a French shower, and lipstick. I considered calling Emily to tell her I was no-showing, but I knew she would understand when I explained later. I race-walked to the elevators and cursed them as they stopped on every other floor before the Rooftop Grotto.

Ding. Finally. I stopped to catch my breath. I counted to ten, took one last gulp for courage, and stepped under the dim lights above the stone-topped bar. I stood near a man whose masculinity I could feel pulsing from several feet away. Heat flamed in my cheeks. My engine raced. Just the man I'd come to see.

Nick was of Hungarian descent, and he had his gypsy ancestors to thank for his all-over darkness—eyes, hair, and skin—and sharp cheekbones. He had a muscular ranginess that I loved, but he wasn't traditionally handsome. His nose was large-ish and crooked from being broken too many times. He'd once told me that a surfboard to the mouth had given him his snaggled front tooth. But he was gorgeous in an undefined way, and I often saw from the quick glances of other women that I wasn't the only one in the room who noticed.

Now he noticed me. "Hi, Helen."

"Hi, Paris," I replied.

He snorted. "Oh, I am definitely not your Paris. Paris was a wimp."

"Hmmmmm. Menelaus, then?"

"Um, beer."

"I'm pretty sure there was no one named Beer in the story of Helen of Troy," I said, sniffing in a faux-superior way.

Nick spoke to the bartender. "St. Pauli Girl." He finally gave me the Nick grin, and the tension left over from our elevator ride disappeared. "Want one?"

I needed to gulp more than air for courage. "Amstel Light."

Nick placed the order. The bartender handed Nick two beers beaded with moisture, then shook water from his hands. Nick handed mine to me and I wrapped a napkin around it, lining up the edges with the military precision I adored. Nick sang under his breath, his head bobbing side to side. Honky-tonk Woman.

"I think I like you better in Shreveport than Dallas," I said.

"Thanks, I think. And I like seeing you happy. I guess it's been a tough year for you, losing your parents and all. Here's to that smile," he said, holding his beer aloft toward me.

The toast almost stopped my heart. He was spot-on about the tough part, but I did better when I kept the subject of my parents buried with them. I clinked his bottle but couldn't look at him while I did it. "Thanks, Nick, very much."

"Want to play pool?" he asked.

"Let's do it."

I was giddy, the sophomore girl out with the senior quarterback. We both loved music, so we talked about genres, bands (his old band, Stingray, and "real" bands), my minor in music at Baylor, and LSD, AKA lead-singer disease. Over a bucket of beers, we swapped stories about high school, and he told me he'd once rescued an injured booby.

"An injured booby?" I asked. "Implants or natural? Eight ball in corner pocket." I sank it.

He gathered the balls out of the pockets and positioned them in the rack while I ground my cue tip in blue chalk and blew off the excess. "You're so land-locked. A booby is a bird, Katie."

I rolled his use of my real name back and forth in my brain, enjoying how it felt.

"I was out surfing, and I found a booby that couldn't fly. I carried it back home and took care of it until I could set it free."

"Oh, my gosh! How bad did it smell? Did it peck you? I'll bet your Mom was thrilled!" I talked fast, in endless exclamation points. Embarrassing. I was a Valley Girl on acid, like Oh-My-Gawd. "It was in shock, so it was calm, but every day it got wilder. I was fourteen, and my mom was happy I wasn't in my room holding some girl's real booby, so she was fine with it. It smelled really bad after a few days, though."

I broke. Balls clacked and ricocheted in every direction, and a striped one tumbled into a side pocket. "Stripes," I called. "So, your mom had caught you before holding a girl's booby, huh?"

"Um, I didn't say that . . ." he said, and stuttered to a stop.

I was more smitten than ever.

"Damn, I Wish I Was Your Lover" was playing in the background. I hadn't heard that song in years. It got me thinking. For months, I had been fighting off the urge to slip my arms around Nick's neck and bite the back of it, but I was aware that most people would consider that inappropriate at work. Pretty small-minded of them, if you asked me. I eyed the large balcony outside the bar and thought that if I could just maneuver Nick out there, maybe I could make it happen.

My chances seemed good enough until one of our colleagues walked in. Tim was of counsel at the firm. "Of counsel" meant he was too old to be called an associate, but he wasn't a rainmaker. Plus, he wore his pants pulled up an inch too high in the waist. The firm would never make him a partner. Nick and

I locked eyes. Until now, we'd been two shortwave radios on the same channel, the signal crackling between us. But now the dial had turned to static and his eyes clouded over. He stiffened and moved subtly away from me.

He hailed Tim up. "Hey, Tim, over here."

Tim waved to us and walked across the smoky bar. Everything moved in slow motion as he came closer, step by ponderous step. His feet echoed as they hit the floor, reverberating *no . . . no . . . no . . .* Or maybe I was saying it aloud. I couldn't tell, but it made no difference.

"Hey, Tim, this is great. Grab a beer; let's play some pool."

Oh, please tell me Nick didn't just invite Tim to hang out with us. He could have given him a short "hey how ya doing have a nice night I was just leaving" shpiel, or anything else for that matter, but no, he had asked Tim to join us.

Tim and Nick looked at me for affirmation.

I entertained a fleeting fantasy in which I executed a perfect side kick to Tim's gut and he started rolling around on the floor with the dry heaves. What good were the thirteen years of karate my father had insisted on if I couldn't use it at times like these? "Every woman should be able to defend herself, Katie," Dad would say as he dropped me off at the dojo.

Maybe this wasn't technically a physical self-defense moment, but Tim's arrival had dashed my hopes for the whole neck-bite thing, and all that could have come after it. Wasn't that reason enough?

I cast out the image. "Actually, Tim, why don't you take over for me? I was in trial all week, and I'm exhausted. We have an early start tomorrow. It's the last day of our retreat, the grande finale for the Hailey & Hart team." I handed my pool cue to Tim.

Tim thought this was a fine idea. It was clear women scared him. If I had hoped for an argument from Nick, though, I didn't get one. He reverted to his outside-of-work "Katie who?" act.

All I got from him was "Goodnight," with neither a Helen nor a Katie tacked on.

I grabbed another Amstel Light from the bar for the plod back to my room.

Chapter Two

Fifteen minutes later, I'd liberated a bottle of wine from the mini-bar. I clutched my iPhone with an intent to text. Texting while intoxicated, never a good idea. I wish a cop had been there to cuff me—it would have saved me from what came next.

To Nick: "You dumped me for Tim. I'm lonely." I might as well have added, "Love, Your crazy stalker."

No response. I waited five minutes while I finished a glass of wine. I refilled my glass. I scrolled through Emily's three hundred texts asking where I was and responded to her with "Nick!!! So sorry. Talk to you later."

I sent another to Nick. "R u there? R u still with Tim?"

"Hey," was his reply.

Another text from Nick dinged seconds later. "We need to talk."

Good talk or bad talk, I wondered. Talk as a euphemism for not talking?

I responded to Nick, "K. Where, when?"

"Monday, office."

Gut punch. Rally, Katie, rally. Don't let the moment slip away. There's still a chance. "No fair. Now? Pick a place."

"Bad idea. Been drinking."

"I can handle it. Rm 632."

No answer. Think think think think think think think. He didn't say no. He didn't say yes. I could text back and ask for a clear answer, but it might be the wrong one. *Assume it's yes and get yourself together, girl.*

I inspected the spartan hotel room, the dismal tan comforter graying from too many times through industrial washers, the tan drapes discolored from the room's "smoker" years, a framed mass-production print of a riverboat hanging on metallicized wallpaper. It didn't show much promise for a romantic interlude. I cleaned up the best I could anyway, the room and me, and tried to steady myself for sober thought and behavior.

No Nick. I paced. I fussed. I checked for texts. And then, suddenly, I knew he was there, felt him with my extrasensory Nick perception.

I peered out my peephole. Yes, there he was, doing the same thing as me on the other side of the thick slab of wood. I couldn't open the door, though, or he would know I was standing there watching him.

He raised his hand to knock. He lowered it. He turned to walk away; he came back. He clawed his hand in a scrubbing motion through his hair and closed his eyes.

He knocked. I held my breath while I said a quick prayer. "Please God, help me not screw this up." Probably not the most well-conceived or -crafted prayer I'd ever uttered. I opened the door.

Neither of us spoke. I stepped back and he walked in, clutching a bar napkin in his left hand. His right hand raked through his hair again, a nervous tic I had never noticed before this evening.

I sat down on the bed. He sat in a chair by the window.

"You said we needed to talk," I prompted.

He focused on his crumpled napkin for a long time. When he looked up, he motioned back and forth between the two of us and said, "My life is way too complicated right now. I'm sorry, but this can't happen."

These words were not the ones I had hoped to hear. Maybe they were approximately the ones I'd expected to hear, but I'd remained hopeful until he said them. My face burned. Countdown to meltdown.

"By 'this,' I assume you're referring to some kind of 'thing' between you and me? Of course it can't. I'm a partner at the firm." I heard my voice from far away. Superior. Distant. "I know I can come across as a flirt, but I'm this way with everyone, Nick. Don't worry. I'm not coming on to you."

I could almost see the handprint on his face from the slap of my words.

"I heard you talking to Emily on your cell phone when you got here this afternoon."

This sounded ominous. "What are you talking about?"

"I walked past your room. Your door was propped open. I saw you. I heard you."

I protested, "How do you even know it was me?"

"I know your voice. You were talking about me. I heard my name. I'm sorry I eavesdropped, but I couldn't help it. I stopped and listened."

I started to cut in again, but he plowed on.

"You said," and, oh, how I didn't want to hear what came next, "that you couldn't believe how attracted to me you were. That you felt guilty because you thought about me more than work or what happened to your parents . . ." Nick stumbled over his words, struggling to get something out. "You told Emily you couldn't help that you were in love with me."

Oh God. Oh my. All that hot blood drained out of my face. I had said that on the phone to Emily. She'd called to make sure I was coming straight down to the session, and I'd turned the conversation to Nick. It was such a normal thing that I'd forgotten about it. Hell, it was so normal that she'd probably tuned it out. Suddenly I knew how drunk I was, and the room teetered.

I forced a glass-breaking laugh. "Yes, I mentioned your name, but that isn't what I said."

"Yes, it was," he interrupted. "I'm not a moron. I know what I heard."

"Well, you're misinterpreting it," I insisted. "I'm not after you, Nick. For all I know, you're still married. And we work together. I'm sorry if I made you uncomfortable. I'll try to not to do it again."

"You didn't make me uncomfortable." He stopped and dragged his hand through his hair a third time, staring down at the napkin again. The damn thing had writing on it. "It's just . . ." He sighed, and didn't go any further.

"Just what?"

No answer. I wish it was only alcohol that made me lash out with sarcasm next, but it wasn't.

"Why don't you consult your magic napkin to see what you should say?"

His face darkened. "That was rude."

I was just gathering steam. "Well, it seems like you came in here with your speech all written out. 'Put poor lovesick Katie in her place.'" I sucked in a breath and spat out, "I can't believe you had to make notes on a bar napkin."

"I'm not as good as you with words, Madam Lawyer. I wanted to get this right. Don't make fun of me for taking it seriously."

"Sorry for making you go to so much trouble." I wasn't sorry at the moment, and I suspect my tone made that quite clear. "By all means, finish reading your napkin."

He stood up. "There's nothing else on my napkin that we need to talk about."

Too late, I saw how awful I was acting. "Nick, I'm sorry. Forget I said that. I've had too much to drink. Shit, I drink too much lately, and I'm totally going to cut down. I hope this won't set our friendship back, and that we can go on normally at work. You know how I am. I'm way too forward, and I have a big mouth." I trailed off from my useless babbling and fought to keep eye contact with him.

My thoughts jumbled. How had I misread him so badly? I had always believed that deep down he was as attracted to me—not merely on a physical level—as I was to him. That if I gave him the right opening and nudge, he would sweep me off my feet and into his magic carriage, away to happily ever after.

How ridiculous that was. I wasn't Cinderella. I was Glenn Close with the boiled bunny. And he was Michael Douglas searching for a way to escape.

I didn't know how to make it better. His eyes grew more hostile by the second. Without another word to me, he stomped out with that damn wadded-up napkin.

Chapter Three

I woke up with a vicious hangover that was as much from humiliation as Amstel Light and mini-bar wine, and remembered Nick in my room, and the way I had acted. It seemed unlikely that it could have gone much worse, but at least I hadn't met him naked at the door with a rose in my teeth. I would get up and pull myself together. I would be alluring in my moss-green Ellen Tracy sweater set. I would fix this.

But first I would check my texts because my phone was buzzing. At this early hour?

"Where the HELL r u?" It was Emily.

"?? Getting ready."

This stretched the truth, but the cardinal rule of texting is to keep it short, so I omitted the telling details.

"We started. Hurry your azz!"

Maybe it wasn't as early as I thought. "On my way."

Well, beautiful and together were out of the question now, although I don't know if I could have achieved them under the circumstances, no matter how much time I had. I scrabbled myself together in accordance with hygienic and aesthetic minimums and joined the teambuilding session, day two of two. I hoped I could fake it well enough to fool my co-workers.

I paused outside the open door to the conference room and listened to the presenter. The firm had hired a touchy-feely consultant to help us resolve any issues we had with each other in a positive, constructive way.

"Good luck with that," I thought. I wondered if he'd help me with my "I want to sleep with my possibly-still-married co-worker who oh yeah by the way hates me" issue.

This was not a kumbaya type of session, though; the consultant was actually quite good. Today we were learning how to talk about what we needed more of and less of from each other. He instructed us to partner up with the person with whom we most needed an effective working relationship.

I breached the entrance to the garishly floral conference room. Within seconds, the pairing off was almost complete. I scanned the room for Emily's big
blonde Texas hair, hoping she had waited for me, but she was with the lead
paralegal, taking the activity way too seriously. I glared at her and she shrugged
with eyebrows raised, as if to say, "It ain't my fault if you stand me up and then
can't drag yourself out of bed until noon." I harrumphed and searched the
room for a partner.

As I scanned the space, Nick's flat eyes slowly locked onto mine. Not good.
I, too, kept my face expressionless, a gargantuan effort considering that last
night's mini-bar trail mix wanted back out. I started to turn away, then realized
he was walking toward me. I expected him to move past me, until he didn't.

He said nothing, so I spoke. I couldn't help it. I always led. No wonder my
big brother told me I pushed men away.

"So, you want some more of this?" I tried a self-deprecating smile.

He didn't smile back. "It seems like the best way to get 'this' cleared up, so
we'll have an understanding before we get back to the office." He waggled his
hand back and forth between us. It reminded me of last night, and not in a
good way.

We took a seat. The flowers on the wallpaper and the floor weren't doing a
lot to cheer me up. The vines in the carpet suddenly reached up and bound me
to my chair by the ankles. *No, you blockhead, that's your imagination and too much
booze.* Ugh. Unnerving. I rubbed my hands on my forearms, trying to smooth
out my goose bumps.

Nick read the instructions aloud. We would take turns going through a list
of exercises. First, we would tell each other the things we appreciated; next, the
things we needed more or less of; and finally, what we were committed to do
more or less of for each other. In case we forgot these instructions, they were
block-printed in bold colored marker on flip charts all around the room. *I
appreciate you, posters, for breaking up this flowery nightmare,* I thought.

"You go first, Nick. I think you need to remember what you appreciate
about me." I said it in a playful tone.

He didn't reciprocate, nor did he hesitate. "I appreciate that you are a professional who does a good job and works hard. You are important to the firm."
Not exactly warm.

"Thank you, Nick. Anything else? You can keep the compliments coming if you want." I tried another smile, head tilted to the right. My best tilt.

"That's it."

This was going swell.

"OK, then, what I appreciate about you is . . . ," while he was taking the strictly professional route, I refused to be so impersonal, ". . . your creativity and insight, and how well we worked together on the Burnside case." I channeled B.S.-speak from the atmosphere, a legal version of a bad Dr. Phil episode. "And I appreciate that you don't have a bar napkin with you today." *Hint, hint— Nick, let's get past this.*

No chance. "Now we do the next part, more and less of." He ran his hands through his hair. Uh oh. "What I want you to do more of is let Gino know when you need support from me, and he and I will work it out. What I want you to do less of is," he hesitated, then said, "corner me."

Did I hear that wrong, or had Nick just dumped me? And accused me of stalking him? In so many words. Even after the difficult end to our evening, the professional dropkick seemed extreme. Was he suggesting I had sexually harassed him? I went from zero to sixty on the rage meter in less than a second. Oops.

"You don't want to work with me anymore? I CORNER you? We have one hard personal conversation, and you refuse to work with me?"

"Can you please keep your voice down?" he hissed. I threw up my hands. He took that as a yes and went on. "I just want to minimize our contact," he said. His voice matched his eyes.

"That's absurd." Nick's hand went up, and I ratcheted back my volume. "We're a great team. It's a huge benefit to this firm when we work together. I don't understand why you're doing this. Is it all because of last night?"

One hundred eyes were watching me crumble into emotional rubble. No, that was just paranoia. My hands reached for my collar and tried to tug it open further.

"I'm not going to talk about why. I just need some space. If you've got a problem with me, you need to take it to Gino."

Decision and self-control time. If I made a bigger scene, I'd embarrass him, and then I would never be able to fix it. I had spent half of last night reconciling myself to there never being an "us," no Nick and Katie. I disliked practicing law, but in the last year, I had loved working with Nick. Working with him was better than nothing. It might even be enough. But if he took that away, all I'd have left was me and the thoughts I didn't want to think.

I had to be realistic, too. I *was* important to the firm, but Nick's soon-to-be-ex-father-in-law was our biggest client. This rift had to stay between Nick and me. There would be no "going to Gino" for me. Besides, what would I say to him? "Gino, Nick won't work with me because he thinks I want to sleep with him. Make him be nice to me or I'll throw a temper tantrum."

I spoke in measured words. "I guess I have no choice. I will honor your wishes, but let me be one hundred percent clear: This is your decision. I don't understand it, and it's not what I want. I also promise to be honest with you. I'll start that right now." It seemed like a good place to start, since I'd lied to him last night and he knew it. "This hurts me. You're treating me like you hate me. We had a regrettable moment this weekend. I think we should talk about this again back at the office."

"I won't feel any differently there," Nick said. He stood halfway up, but I stopped him.

"Hold on. I get to say what I would like you to do more and less of."

He sat back down. I ignored the stabbing pain in my stomach and spoke. "I would like you to do more keeping an open mind and less judging and making knee-jerk decisions."

"OK."

"OK, you commit to that?"

"OK, I heard you."

We stared at each other for several more seconds. Then Nick got up. The feet of his chair made a horrible "shcreek" noise against the steel-wool hotel carpet. I cringed. My cringe timing was bad, based on the tightening of his lips and brows. He stalked off.

I stayed rooted to my chair.

A little while later—seconds? minutes?—Emily interrupted my impression of a block of ice.

"Earth to Katie. It's break time. Are you coming?" she asked. Her voice was snippy, but less so than her texts earlier.

I glanced up at her. She was all long legs, in cowboy boots and blue jeans that she had topped with a Gap denim jacket and purple cotton-knit shirt. "Um, thanks, no, I'll meet you back in here," I said.

Emily walked out of the conference room with a group of paralegals. I bee-lined for the bar. What drink was respectable at ten a.m.? I ordered a Bloody Mary, a drink I'd never tried. Who knew how good Bloody Marys were? The first one worked well for me, so I got another. With the help of my new friend Bloody Mary, I decided I could repair things with Nick. Only I couldn't find him.

When we returned from break, I cornered Emily. "Have you seen Nick?" I asked her.

Emily sighed. "He left. I heard him tell Gino he had a family emergency."

A bust.

The rest of the day passed. I don't remember much of it. I think I made appropriate facial expressions and comments when required. Or maybe I didn't. My washing-machine mind was churning with thoughts of Nick.

Sometime that afternoon, Emily drove me home in my practical old silver Accord. The day became the night, and the night became more of the day, and when I woke up the next day to the sound of my brother's voice, I was sprawled across my living room couch.

Chapter Four

"You have any better excuse for not returning my calls than this?" Collin said in a stern big-brother tone. I forced my eyes open long enough to see him gesturing around the living room of my once-beautiful apartment. Collin was my Irish twin, my elder by eleven months. We finished high school the same year, though, because my dad, a good Texan, had insisted on holding Collin back a year to help him gain a size advantage on the football field. Thus we had been classmates as well as siblings. Even so, Collin had always acted paternal toward me, especially in the past year after we'd lost Mom and Dad.

I opened my eyes a slit, enough to see the mess. I supposed it didn't look good. I'm usually particular to a fault about my surroundings. Collin has always called me OCD, but I don't agree. I vacuum backwards because I don't like how footprints look on the rug. I arrange my clothes by season and subcategorize them by function and color, because who doesn't? And while not everyone combs the fringe on their throw pillows, I think they should. Tangled fringe. The horror. Those last few weeks, though? Well, not so much.

There were—gasp—fast food wrappers on the kitchen table and a couple of empty V8 and Ketel One vodka bottles out on the counter. It wasn't unsanitary by Dennis the Menace standards, but, if you knew me as well as my brother did, it was troubling. My PJs were yesterday's work clothes, and the clothes from the days before lay in an undrycleaned heap beside the couch—the couch on which the throw pillow fringe was taunting me with knots and clumps. The television blared Bon Jovi's "Runaway" over a Direct TV '80s rock music station. An almost-drained Bloody Mary mocked me from the coffee table, where it sat by my red Vaio laptop, a bottle of Excedrin, and my iPhone.

I sat up in as dignified a manner as I could manage and smoothed out my clothes. "Why didn't I hear the alarm when you came in?" I asked him. Collin had a set of keys to my place, but my alarm should have beeped when he opened the door.

Bluntly, Collin said, "I guess you were too drunk to remember to set it. Or maybe you had a visitor that left late?"

He looked around for a second glass, but I'd been drinking alone. Collin started picking up my mess.

"Collin, I'll do that," I said.

"Nope. You go freshen up," he said. "I'm taking you to breakfast. That's an order."

I stared at him woefully. He was wearing his usual 501 jeans with a Hooters t-shirt, and he radiated "I've got no problems." I didn't want to go to breakfast with him. I wanted to curl into the fetal position. I wanted to sleep and be alone. I wanted to be so still that I didn't exist.

He looked at me, motionless on the couch, and something he saw made him put down the trash and come back over to me. Taking my hand, he pulled me to my feet. He held my stiff body in a bear hug, rocking me gently for a moment. Uh oh. At first, I tried to hold it in, but then I folded and sobbed on his big shoulder. Sobs became snorts, then hiccups, then shuddering breaths. He tilted my head back with a big thumb under my chin and looked into my eyes, appraising me.

"Go take a hot shower. We'll eat somewhere casual, but I'm leaving—with you in the car—in twenty minutes." He chucked the side of my chin with his knuckles. "Chop chop. You know I'll come in after you if I have to. Don't make me do it."

With a soft push, he sent me down the hall to my bathroom, and then I heard him resume cleaning. Tears rolled down my nose and cheeks. Ye gads, I would have to drink gallons of water at breakfast, because at the rate I was crying and with the amount of vodka I had consumed last night, I was on the brink of a major dehydration headache.

Forty-five minutes later, we took our seats in the Mockingbird Lane IHOP. It was a favorite place from our childhood, but today I noticed that it had a lot of garish orange in its décor, and I liked it a little less because of it. Collin surprised me when he requested a table for three, but I didn't expend the energy to question him. I understood when I saw Emily's pageant hair at the hostess stand. She walked toward us in pleated navy-blue pants and a silky yellow shirt cinched with a leather belt that matched her brown pumps.

"Hi, Katie." She looked at me for a moment, then averted her eyes.

I lifted a limp hand in greeting. Great. Another person to see me in this state. I had shunned my image in the mirror before I left the condo, but the brief glimpse I got was enough. Wet ponytail. An old track suit and t-shirt. Puffy-eyed and sallow. Ick.

We avoided talking by staring at our menus until the middle-aged waitress, who really should have worn a one-size-larger uniform, came for our order. My stomach muscles tightened as she walked away. I almost stopped her to add an orange juice I didn't want to my order, but I didn't. No use delaying the inevitable. Collin had assembled us for a reason, and something unpleasant cometh.

"Emily and I have been talking, and she filled me in on what's happening with you," Collin said.

I hoped Emily had held some of it back, but I couldn't fault her for caring about me. Or caving in to Collin. He was a cop, in the fine tradition of our father, and he'd never met a witness he couldn't crack, he liked to say.

Collin kept the floor. "We're worried about you. You're messed up. You're hurting yourself."

He looked at Emily for confirmation and she stared at the white Formica tabletop. If I knew Collin, he'd dragged her into this little intervention, and if I knew Em, she was reluctant as hell. Emily was self-confident, but boat rocking was not her style.

I didn't have the strength to fight Collin on this, and I didn't actually disagree with him. I was a train wreck right now, for sure. He had me at one of those rare moments when the tough-talking woman wasn't around to defend the fragile girl inside me. She was probably still sprawled across my couch nursing her hangover.

"You're right," I confessed. The words were dust on my dry tongue. "I need to get myself together."

"I think you should go to rehab." Collin's words sounded harsh, because that's the only way words like "go to rehab" can sound.

So this was how Amy Winehouse felt. And she was dead now. Something to think about it. Except I wasn't Amy Winehouse.

"I've been in the dumps, yes, and I've been drinking too much, but only for a few weeks. I don't think that warrants rehab." The thought of talking about my problems with all of those alcoholic people made me claustrophobic. AA may work for most people, but I don't do group activities very well. Besides, I was not an alcoholic.

"These last three weeks were especially bad, but you've been on this road for much longer than that," Collin said. "Like a year. Can you cut back or stop? I'll bet you've already tried that, haven't you?" I avoided his eyes. "And I'll bet it didn't work."

"No, asshole, I haven't," I almost said. Almost. Instead, I said, "I haven't tried. I know I can, when I'm ready."

My cheddar omelet came, but I wasn't hungry. None of us touched our food.

"I admit that I'd have trouble stopping here in Dallas if I did try. When I do try. But I know that if I could get out of my life for a few weeks, I could get this under control. I'm willing to start with that. Rehab's not for me. Maybe if you're pulling me out of a gutter someday, but not now."

"Fine. I'll give you one chance, sis, so make it count. Do you have anything in mind?" Collin asked.

I sucked in as much air as I could get, then forcibly exhaled until my stomach collapsed in. "St. Marcos. I need to get some closure on what happened to Mom and Dad." I started to cry, then swallowed it. I opened my mouth to speak, and the tears started again.

"Are you sure?" Collin asked.

I nodded and used the clean side of my paper napkin to wipe my eyes. As I looked up, a young black woman caught my eye, partly because she was staring at me, and partly because she was barefoot in IHOP and her clothing looked a hundred and fifty years out of place. Now *she* had a problem. Drugs, from the look of it. A total rehab candidate. Not me. I wiped my eyes again and when I opened them, she was gone. Nothing there at all. I was going nuts. I gulped air.

I desperately needed to get away. This trip, this solo rehab or mini-sabbatical or whatever it was, would be a godsend.

And so we agreed that I would go. Immediately. As in tomorrow. Yikes. A little sooner than I'd anticipated, but Collin insisted, and Emily promised to help me make it happen. Collin and I shook on it when he dropped me back at my condo, and Emily was right behind us.

Emily and I rolled into work at Hailey & Hart mid-morning, after I had changed into a work-acceptable cream-colored summer pant suit. We didn't get much done other than booking my trip and clearing my schedule for it. I talked to Gino about the vacation days, expecting him to argue with me, but he didn't. He patted my hand. Ugh.

"Time off will do you a world of good," he said. "You've worked hard this year under difficult circumstances, and you need to recharge and bring your best self back."

Great. That was boss-speak for "you're a hot mess, get the frick out of here." Well, I was. A humiliated hot mess. Tomorrow wasn't sounding too soon to get away from that after all.

At Collin's request, Emily babysat me overnight, leaving her husband home alone. Emily was a far better friend than I deserved, but once upon a time, I had played her role when Rich temporarily broke off their engagement. Life in balance.

Late in the evening, I finally mentioned the name no one had uttered all day. "If Nick asks where I am, please give him the sanitized version."

Emily was sitting at a barstool, and I was standing across the counter in my kitchen. She leaned toward me. "Don't even go there. Nick has acted like friggin' Heathcliff to you ever since Shreveport. Come on, girl. Let it go."

I was getting a lot of veiled messages today. This one was "he's just not that into you." Ouch, but she was right.

But could I leave my feelings about him here and truly go off to St. Marcos with a clear head? I tossed and turned in my bed all night, buffeted between images of my parents and Nick.

Chapter Five

"Please turn off and stow away all electronic devices at this time," came the voice of the flight attendant over American Airlines' P.A. system. Crap. I was writing an email to Emily promising her a rib-eye dinner from Del Frisco's, my treat, if she'd remove the leftover sushi from my refrigerator, but I had enough time to hit Send.

I had tucked myself into my first-class upgrade seat on the way to St. Marcos with my essentials around me: passport, red Vaio laptop, iPhone in its zebra-print Otter Box. I know Dell and Blackberry are the technologies of choice for most attorneys, but I liked to flatter myself that I was not like everybody else. Of course, lately I was living up to the worst of the attorney stereotypes: the hard-drinking one. Bad on me.

The email I'd sent yesterday to my non-work friends explained my sudden disappearance as a vacation. They could picture me sipping piña coladas on the beach and dancing the nights away to calypso music with a sexy West Indian man, getting my groove back like Stella. Emily would take care of a similar work announcement for me this morning.

Speaking of West Indian men, the slightly paunchy one next to me in first class was trying to read my screen. I turned it farther away from him. Where were his first-class manners, anyway?

I turned my attention back to my email. Shouldn't I tell Nick myself? Maybe he had acted Heathcliff-ish, but up until Shreveport, I would have sent him a flirty note about my trip. If he disappeared, I would want to know why. Ipso facto, wouldn't he? Under the grip of this logic lapse, I shot off a quick email to him.

To: nick.kovacs@haileyhart.com
From: katie.connell@haileyhart.com
Subject: Travel
Nick:

I am letting you know, on the off chance you notice I'm gone, that I'm on a Caribbean vacation. Back in a week. Emily will shepherd my cases while I am out. And Nick, I am sorry. For everything.

Katie

I had promised him I'd tell him the truth from Shreveport forward. Well, I was mostly honest, because this was sort of a vacation. I closed my eyes with my finger on Send, wavering.

"Ma'am, you'll have to turn that off and put it away now." The gray-haired flight attendant leaned down, a taut smile on her face. How she must hate repeating those words over and over and over each day to people like me who would lie, cheat, and steal to sneak a few more precious seconds of airtime before takeoff. I was a good girl this time, though.

"No problem," I said. I hit Send and turned my screen off. Well, sort of a good girl. I readjusted in my seat, pulling my purple maxi-dress out of an uncomfortable twist under my legs.

"My name's Guy," the man next to me said. He offered his hand.

Nooo. I wanted to sleep. I took his hand—his very soft hand, Vaseline Intensive Care soft—and said, "Katie. Nice to meet you," then broke eye contact. I leaned my head back. "Don't think about dandruff, lice, and other head-borne nastiness," I told myself. I immediately could think of nothing but.

A toddler screamed. I craned my head around my seatback to find the culprit. A young father was traveling alone with a child in the first row of coach. This didn't bode well.

The flight attendant was back. Her skin looked younger than her hair, and her eyes were bright. "May I get you a beverage before we take off, ma'am?"

I was anxious after sending that email to Nick. *L'enfant terrible* and the potential lice issue grated on my nerves. I was heading off to conquer demons and confront personal issues in a foreign environment. Even a responsible drinker would order a cocktail in first class under these conditions.

"Bloody Mary," someone said. Me. Oops.

"Absolutely, ma'am."

Well, I wasn't at the resort, I wasn't even on St. Marcos yet. If you really thought about it, this was the countdown, but the ball hadn't dropped. I didn't need to take a break from drinking until I got there. Besides, what were flight upgrades to first class for if not the free drinks? Sure, they served you a micro-waved bowl of mixed nuts and handed you a hot hand towel with a pair of kitchen tongs, maybe they even gave you a gooey chocolate chip cookie if you were lucky, but the booze was what it was all about.

"Make that two," my new friend Guy said. He leaned slightly toward me and said, "That just sounded perfect. I've been in Los Angeles to meet with television producers about filming a show on St. Marcos. Most tiring."

"Isn't that nice," I said.

When we landed on St. Marcos, I still felt tipsy-good from my in-flight liba-tions. I wished Guy a fond farewell and lied about both my last name and the resort at which I was staying, to ensure I wouldn't accidentally see him again.

I took a seat in the taxi-van for the Peacock Flower Resort, bobbing my head appreciatively to the beat of Bob Marley's "I Shot the Sheriff." When I arrived at the hotel, it was even more beautiful than I'd imagined. It stood proudly, pink stucco, two stories, surrounded by royal palms. I could see why my parents had loved staying here. As I breezed through the entrance, the doorman handed me a clear plastic glass of rum punch with a big chunk of pineapple on the side. Fruit. Dinner. The people here were perfectly lovely.

I checked in and the front desk clerk sent the nicest young man to assist me to my room. He refreshed my rum punch before we set out. "Long, thirsty walk to your room, miss," he said with a wink. His accent was delicious.

My room was right on the beach, but tucked back into a grove of palm trees for privacy.

"A lot of famous people stay in this room." He looked at me intently. "Should I know you? You're awfully beautiful, miss. Are you a model?"

I chose to overlook the fact that he was making this comment only mo-ments before he left me in my room, so it was ideally timed to coincide with my decision about tipping. I said, "Why, thank you," and pressed a twenty-dollar bill into his hand. He half-bowed appreciatively and wished me a "pleasant good afternoon."

I surveyed my surroundings. Ah, good, the desk area was just right. I put my purse on the floor beside it and squared my laptop perfectly, just the way I like it. I checked my phone. It had lost its charge. I pawed through my laptop bag for the phone charger and plugged it in. God knows how much time I'd lost waiting for messages with a dead mobile. Probably right when Nick would have emailed me back, too. I unpacked while the phone gathered enough juice for a connection.

I continued my self-tour of the suite. The resort's website had claimed the bathtub was big enough for two, and it was as billed. Large enough to hold me and my evil sharp-tongued alter ego who drank too much. Earth-hued marble tiles of varying shades, textures, sizes, shapes and patterns filled the bathroom. It should have been too much, but it wasn't. It was stunning.

The muted tropical palette of the rest of the suite set off the natural tones of the bathroom beautifully. It was the best of outdoors brought softly inside. The furniture and ceiling fan were bamboo, the linens an ivory pinstripe Egyptian cotton of what felt like 1000 thread count, covered by a fluffy cream-colored duvet. I couldn't wait to get in and roll around in those sheets, to rub crisp cotton on my skin. Most of the color in the room—brilliant yellows, palmetto greens, and fuchsia—came from fresh cuttings of local plants and flowers.

A set of French doors opened from the bedroom onto a patio tiled with almond-colored travertine pavers. The patio spilled out onto a short lawn dotted with coconut palms that ended with private beach access. Beyond the broad beach was the turquoise and sapphire Caribbean Sea. I smiled. This would do nicely.

My iPhone had charged enough for a data download. I picked it up and scrolled through my email. My secretary had sent a few questions, and Collin and Emily had both asked me to let them know I'd arrived safely. I did so, and scrolled through more messages, junk mostly. And then I came to one that cut off my breath: a response from Nick.

I put the iPhone down until I could breathe normally. I wiped my palms on my purple skirt, then picked the phone back up. No biggie. I was fine. The body of the email was short:

"ok"

ok. OK!! Two lowercase letters, one word. Not exactly a lot for me to go by. He could have deleted my email without reading it. He could have read it and not answered. He could have read it and answered by saying something rude (was "ok" rude?). Or, he could have read it and answered with something positive, like "I'll see you when you return" or "Good luck." My brain started speeding around its familiar Nick-paths, a NASCAR wannabe around a trailer park. This was not good.

I drained my rum punch and ate my dinner of pineapple garnish. I looked in the mini-fridge. Jackpot. A whole pitcher of rum punch was waiting for me inside. Unfortunately, there wasn't any fruit. Fruit juice was healthy enough, though. Rum punch would make a perfect island substitute for Bloody Marys. I poured myself a glass.

Nick. The incredibly cold jerk. I fought with myself not to answer him. I drank the rum punch. Fought with myself some more. Drank some more. And then I made up my mind. I was getting out of there. I grabbed my purse, phone, and room key and stomped up to the bar I'd seen during check-in.

The bar was a covered hilltop patio overlooking the beach and the ocean. I hiked up the stone steps and found a good crowd around the mahogany bar and at round tables scattered around the tiled floor. A few people danced, close and sultry, to a reggae band who sounded pretty good. They were playing a song about ninety-six degrees in the shade. The female singer growled the chorus— "Real hot, in the sha-yyy-ade." I sat down at the bar and turned to watch them when I got my Bloody Mary from the blond-dreadlocked bartender. After one sip, I realized it was all wrong and ordered a rum punch.

"You throwing out a perfectly good drink? What wrong with you, girl?" The voice pronounced girl as "gyal." I did a double take, then realized it was the singer.

"I changed my mind," I said.

"Unless you got some dread disease, you can give that thing to me," she said. Kyan give dat ting.

I pushed the glass to her, fighting back my willies over sharing cooties with a stranger. I didn't want to appear rude. "I took a sip," I warned her.

She pulled the straw out of the drink and tossed it toward the trash can behind the bar. She missed. "Thanks. Singing thirsty work." She stuck out her hand. "I Ava."

I took her hand and shook. "Katie."

"My people dem just up and leave before we through our last set. Trouble."

I tried to follow, but her singsong accent threw me. I missed half of what she said. She took pity on me.

"Lah, you don't understand me." She slugged down some Bloody Mary. "I said my bandmates just left me and we hadn't even done our last set. We're going to be in trouble with the owner." She spoke in the Queen's perfect English this time, enunciating each word perfectly.

"Oh, wow, yes, I understand now."

"Sorry. I talk Local when I'm performing, or when I'm talking to other locals. But I can Yank just fine, when I need to."

"Yank?"

"Talk like a Yankee. It's like speaking two languages. Talking Local greases the wheel and impresses the tourists. It's part of being bahn yah."

"What's bahn yah mean?"

"In Yank, it means 'born here.' You may live on St. Marcos for forty years, but you are only truly local if you bahn yah. Which I was. Now, I owe you a drink," she said, signaling the bartender, "and I always pay back my debts to my friends."

Chapter Six

I woke up on my chaise lounge the next morning, fully clothed in my maxi dress from the day before. Same song, different verse. But I was even more disgusted with myself than usual. I was here to look into the deaths of my parents and straighten myself out, which was supposed to include cutting down on the drinking. And thinking about something other than Nick. It seemed that all I had done was bring my baggage with me into this world, and that I was set to make the present into more of the past. Way to go, me.

In a moment of gut-dropping panic, I remembered part of the night before. The email from Nick. The rum punch. The hotel bar. Had I sent him another message? Oh, please no.

I shot upright, my heart pounding in my ears. Blue water was teasing the brown sand of the beach in front of me. In the distance, two small children played with buckets at the waterline. Overhead, the morning sun shone through palm fronds to kiss the carpet of grass in front of my patio. The serenity of my retreat comforted me. Everything would be OK.

I found my phone beside me and scrolled through the sent texts and emails on my iPhone. Nothing, thank God. I had blown it last night. Today, though, today I would begin looking into the mystery of my parents' deaths, and I would start over on the personal front. After a few hours' more sleep. I folded myself back into my chair.

"Lah, girl, we party like rock stars," a woman said. A woman almost right beside me, from the sound of it.

I sat up again, even more quickly. I recognized the husky voice. The name of the woman it belonged to was a blank to me. I searched for it. Abigail? Ariel? Eva? No. Ava. It was Ava.

I forced out a laugh. "Yeah, I guess we did. What I can remember of it."

I looked down at the chaise on the far side of the patio, and, sure enough, there was Ava. She stood up on her tiptoes and stretched her arms toward the sky, something better done in an outfit other than a yellow lycra minidress. I averted my gaze. She finished and plopped back in her chair, tugging at her eye.

"So, I guess we better get started," she said, and laid a set of false eyelashes down on the patio table and started working on the other eye. "I vote for a barrel of water and two Excedrin with a mess of eggs first, though."

I had absolutely no idea what this woman was talking about. I tried to shake the hangover cobwebs from my head. Should I worry? I'd read about pirates and crooks in the Caribbean. Maybe she was a swindler of some sort. I could, in essence, be her prisoner. It was a stretch, but it was possible. Something nudged my brain cells toward memory, then faded out.

Ava kept talking. "I know the cook in the restaurant. He hook us up." Ava reached for the phone on the patio table beside her.

I listened to her order in her island patois. She had continued her ablutions while on the phone—removing earrings, a bracelet, and a necklace—and she stood up again when she ended the call.

"Chop chop, Katie. They expecting us down at the station." She pulled off her dress in a single fluid motion, revealing flawless café au lait curves reined in somewhat by a leopard-print satin bra and panties. My hands found my own jutting hipbones, Pippi Longstocking next to her Beyoncé. She ducked into my room.

I clamped my jaw shut and focused on her words. Police station. Yes. That was it. Snatches of our conversation last night floated back to me, including me telling Ava about my quest to find out what had happened to my parents, and her call to some police officer she used to date or that wanted to date her or something. Yes. That was it. I remembered. Relief.

She poked her head back around the door as she gathered her long curly black hair into a topknot. "You mind if I use the shower first?"

"That's fine," I said.

She raised one eyebrow. "You OK?"

I jumped to my feet. "Absolutely. Let's hurry with the showers and try to finish before room service arrives."

"Yah mon," she said, and disappeared again.

I tipped my head back with my eyes closed and pinched the bridge of my nose. Just because I remembered last night, it didn't necessarily make today a good idea. I didn't even know Ava. Was this insane? I lifted my head back to its normal position.

Well, I was about to find out.

Chapter Seven

"I can't believe you're dropping everything to help me," I said.

Ava had poured her curves into a bikini top and blue-jean miniskirt, both of which belonged to me, then slipped on one of my button-front shirts and tied its sides together above her belly button. She was barefoot.

"Best offer I got for the day," she said. "I just move back on-island six months ago. I do the dancing-singing-acting-starving thing in New York, but my parents getting older and, well, I can't stay away from St. Marcos forever. It get in your blood." She picked up her phone, searched until she found what she wanted, then handed me her phone. She had pulled up a picture of herself standing between a much older white man and a dark-skinned woman who split the difference between his and Ava's age. "My parents," she explained. "So I can understand why you here. If something happened to Mom or Dad, I do the same thing."

I'd told her plenty last night, it seemed.

"They're beautiful," I said. "You're a perfect mix of them." I handed her back her phone.

And she was. Ava dripped sexy and, with latte skin and wavy black hair, could pass for almost any race. Italian, Egyptian, Mexican, or all of the above. It was a mix that worked.

She pulled a lipstick out of her teeny pocketbook and walked into the bathroom, still talking. "Yah, they great. So anyway, I home, but there not a lot of work on-island for NYU-trained stage actresses who specialize in Broadway musicals, and no other employable skills."

I raised my voice so she could hear me in the bathroom. "I can relate. I was a voice major in college before I wised up. I spent three years hearing how little money I'd make in music."

"You sing? Girl, why you not tell me that last night? We coulda put you up on stage."

"No way," I said, and laughed. "It was a long time ago."

"Don't mean nothin'. Well, anyway, I glad you here. This much better than watching *Oprah* with Mom." Ava came back into the bedroom and stood with her hands on her hips, studying me. "Fact is, I think you all right."

I liked her, even if she was my polar opposite. And I loved to listen to her, was even starting to understand her better. "Da" was "the" and "dere" was "there," for instance. This wasn't that hard at all.

I told her, "Well, again, thank you for helping me."

Ava put her foot next to mine and cocked her head. "I need some shoes. All I got is the fuck-me pumps I wore last night. My feet pretty big, so maybe if we try the smallest shoe you got?"

Her F word jarred me a little, thanks to the upbringing of my kindergarten-teacher mother, but I didn't take offense about my feet. I was four inches taller than her. "How about these?" I asked, tossing her some Reef thong sandals that were a half size smaller than I should have bought.

She slid her feet into them and struck a shoe-shopping pose. "What you think?"

"I think you look better in my stuff than I do, and we'd better get going or I'll start to hate you for it."

She laughed and stuck one arm through mine. "Yah, or I gonna hate you for making my bana look bigger than it already do," she said, slapping her own posterior with her other hand. "Come, let we go."

Ava slipped her arm out of mine. I put on my sunglasses, grabbed my purse from the desk, and stuck my feet into Betsey Johnson sandals that were blessedly too big for my new friend. Ava followed me out the door. I walked briskly down the sidewalk, energized by the gorgeous morning, to the rental car that the concierge had arranged to be dropped here for me.

"Slow down and lime a little, Katie. You moving too fast for island time," Ava called from behind me.

I opened the door to the lovely green Malibu. "Lime, I can lime. Check."

As we drove, Ava coached me on the niceties of island greetings, explaining how important blending was to my quest's success.

"Don't say hello. Say good morning, good day, and good night. Say it when you walk into a room full of people, to no one in particular. You don't have to make eye contact. Pause a long time after you say it, and give the other person a chance to say it back and make a polite inquiry after your health and family. Then, and only then, get down to your business. If you don't do this, you get nothing done."

"Yes, ma'am," I said, and I saluted.

"I'm serious. If you move fast, talk fast, and don't say the right things, a West Indian only pretend to listen, and you think things going fine when they not."

I reined in the mirth. "I know you're serious, and I appreciate the help."

"Still, let me do most of the talking."

I wasn't all that good at letting someone else speak for me, but I'd try.

We were in the middle of town at this point, and I swerved to avoid a limo that pulled out of a parking place right in front of me. As I pulled to my left, I felt a crunch under one of my tires. I tapped my horn. It was hard enough driving on the left without this. I cut my eyes to the rearview mirror and read the license plate backwards. Vanity plates. It figured. They read, "BondsEnt."

"That my future husband," Ava said, pointing back at the limo.

"Really?"

"Nah, he just rich enough to keep me."

A block later, I heard a thump, thump, thump. Flat tire.

"Shit," I said, pulling over.

"Sunday morning," Ava said, as if that explained something to me. I must have looked a question at her, because she added, "Broken glass from the partiers downtown."

"Ah," I said. Because I'm profound.

"It not a problem," Ava said, and jumped out.

I followed her onto the sidewalk. With a toss of her hair over her shoulder, she soon had a crowd of West Indian men ready to lend a hand.

"Ah, meh son, that what those big muscles for." She flattered her help along, bending over to let a young fellow get a good look at her cleavage.

"I can show you what they for, if you just let me," he replied.

"Lah, you too much for the likes of me. You must have women dem fighting over you day and night."

"You the only girl for me, Ava. You just say the word."

When the tire change was complete, she extricated herself from the throng effortlessly. We got back in the car.

"That was impressive," I said.

Ava just smiled.

We continued driving through downtown among the old Danish-style buildings. Stucco and arches in a muted rainbow of colors predominated. Nearly every other building was in some state of disrepair. Some were missing their roofs. Hurricanes past, maybe? Others had only crumbling rubble where walls used to stand. Locals loitered in small groups on the street corners. More often than I would have expected, we passed a ragtag vagrant pushing a shopping cart filled with castaway treasures. T-shirt-clad tourists dodged unseeing amongst the locals, shopping bags dangling from their hands, ice cream cones pressed to their lips.

Soon, though, we had passed through downtown. On its far edge, we came to a baby-blue two-story Danish building. Police headquarters. We pulled into the parking lot and got out.

It was time to do right by Mom and Dad.

Chapter Eight

Ava had arranged for us to meet her friend at the crack of 11:30. We entered the old house-converted-into-a-police-station fifteen minutes late, which Ava assured me was timely bordering on early. Ava, rolling in earthy and sexy, and me, holding back my normal long stride and feeling ridiculously virginal in my white sundress next to her. I took off my sunglasses and snapped them in their case in my purse.

"Good day," I announced as we walked into the station. A chorus of "good days" rang out in answer. I nearly laughed. Ava looked to see if I was mocking her, then rewarded me with an approving nod.

"Good day. We here to see Jacoby," she said to the female clerk seated at the desk behind the front counter, interrupting her from doing nearly nothing.

Ava was surrounded by helpful officers within seconds, all claiming to know Jacoby, be Jacoby, or be more man than Jacoby ever would be. They crowded the first-floor lobby, a small room that likely, one hundred years ago, was someone's front parlor. Now it housed folding chairs and a laminate coffee table covered with well-thumbed magazines and newspapers. I picked up a newspaper while Ava held court, and idly read about the acquisition of the local cell phone company by some big wheeler-dealer on the island. His name was Bonds. Gregory Bonds. I chortled at my secret funny. Ah, yes, this must be Ava's future husband, the guy with a bad driver. I put it down when I couldn't stand the reporter's fawning anymore.

When the real Jacoby came forward, I was shocked. He was a black Shrek, not the ebony island god I had pictured as a counterpart to Ava's sultry beauty. Ava let out a girlish squeal—another surprise—and threw her arms around his neck to a chorus of disappointed male murmurs, grunts, and a noise that sounded like someone sucking saliva through their teeth. Yuck. The other police officers dispersed, disappearing behind doors and up a staircase visible through a hall adjacent to the lobby.

"Katie, this here Jacoby. We school chums from the time we in kindergarten. Jacoby, Katie."

He stuck out his hand. "Darren Jacoby."

I took it. "Nice to meet you, Officer Jacoby. I'm Katie Connell."

Jacoby gestured toward one of the rooms off the lobby, and we walked over. He opened the solid wood door onto a spare conference room with thick interior concrete walls. Built to withstand Mother Nature. There was a folding-type metal table and more folding chairs identical to the ones in the lobby. Again, my mind regressed the room to its roots. A bedroom, I decided. We took seats around the table.

"So, Ava, I guess I didn't dream your booty call to me last night," he said.

If there ever was an example of hope springing eternal, this was it.

"You dream it a booty call, but I did ring you up," she answered. "Katie need some help. Her parents die on St. Marcos last year, when they here on vacation."

He tore his attention away from Ava. "I'm sorry, Ms. Connell," he said.

"Katie, please. Thank you."

He motioned for me to keep speaking.

Had Ava asked to do the talking? I decided she hadn't meant it and took over. "The police told my brother and me that our parents died in a car wreck. No offense at all to the St. Marcos police, but, given the circumstances as they were explained to us, it felt all wrong. Unlike them. I was hoping I could talk to the officer who worked on the case, and maybe see the file. Iron out my doubts, come to grips with it," I explained.

His eyes narrowed. "Do you know the officer's name?" he asked.

"I don't," I said. "I'm sorry." Collin would. I should have asked him.

"Their name Connell?" he asked.

"Yes. Frank and Heather Connell."

Without another word, he pushed his chair back. One of the feet had lost its pad, and it made a scraping noise that reminded me of Shreveport, and Nick. Jacoby left the room.

"That was abrupt," I said to Ava.

"They tend to close ranks, especially if you not bahn yah," Ava said. "That's why I told you last night you need me with you, and we need to work with Jacoby, at least as much as we can."

A thought occurred to me. "I hope he wasn't the officer on the case. If he was, I just all but accused him of messing up."

Ava sat there with a Mona Lisa smile on her lips. The seconds ticked forward around the wall clock behind her. One minute passed, then another, and then another. Ava pulled out her phone and started playing with it. I jerked my hand away from my mouth, realizing too late that I'd ripped the cuticle from my index finger. A drop of blood welled up.

Then Jacoby was back, his bristles filling the room. He held a folder under one arm and a small piece of paper in his other hand.

"I talked to my boss, the assistant chief. Tutein. He said to give you this." He talked in Yank, instead of his earlier Local. He handed me the scrap of paper with fringe along one side that spoke to its notebook origins.

I read the words written in pencil: Walker, 32 King's Cross. "Is this the name of the officer?" I asked.

"No, the officer that worked the case drowned eleven months ago," Darren said, his voice black water in a dead calm. He didn't offer any more details. I didn't ask.

"I'm sorry to hear that. What about the file? Could I see that?"

He glared at me. "It was just a traffic incident." He rubbed the back of his neck with one hand. "We have an accident report. I made you a copy. Maybe the coroner has more."

He held out the file, then flipped it open. One page. I took it out gingerly, my eyes tracing the names Frank Connell and Heather Connell. I scanned the rest until I got to the name of the responding police officer. Typed neatly, it said Michael Jacoby. Signed in a cramped forward slant, it said George Tutein. Jacoby. But not this Jacoby, because this Jacoby—Darren—was very much alive.

"Walker is a private investigator, the only one on St. Marcos. Tutein says Walker knows everybody he needs to know on the island, and he works for a couple of the biggest businesses here. Maybe he can help you." Jacoby started backing away. "But your parents died in a car wreck. There just doesn't seem like there's much for you to find."

"So there's nobody here I can talk to?" An angry fire started in my core and spread.

"Just Michael. And he's dead." He looked at Ava. "Good seeing you." He turned on his heel and was gone.

My cheeks and ears flamed. Everything about this rang my alarm bells. I opened my mouth but Ava held her finger up to her lips. I shut it and clenched my teeth. She motioned with her head toward the exit, then started toward it, calling out to all within earshot, "A pleasant good afternoon to you."

A wall of humid heat met me at the door, but I busted through it, fueled by my frustration. Two officers stepped past us and into the building, and then we were alone. I squinted and dug for my sunglasses.

Mindful of their friendship, I dialed my temper down. "Ava, I know he's your friend, but doesn't it feel like he stiff-armed me? I know I'm not local, but that felt all wrong."

Ava's eyes darted left and right. "Shush, Katie. Things different here than in the states."

I opened the car door and clicked the locks open. We got in.

"Let me see that report," Ava said.

I handed it to her. There wasn't much to see. One car accident, off a cliff and into the rocks below. Driver and passenger deceased. My parents.

Without lifting her eyes from the paper, Ava asked, "What make you so sure their deaths not an accident?"

"I'm not *sure*. I'm a big believer in intuition, and it's just a feeling I have, from little things that don't make sense. Like how my mom always wore my grandmother's wedding ring, but the police never found it. Not on her, and not in her stuff at the hotel. I thought that was odd. Plus, I talked to my parents that night. They'd been to dinner, and they were on their way back to the Peacock Flower. They called me while they were driving. They sounded great. And then they were dead." Shit. My eyes started leaking.

"OK, OK. It says here your dad was pretty drunk." Her speech had become more formal. More Yank.

"Yes, that's the other thing that bothers me. My father was a recovered alcoholic. He didn't sound drunk when I was on the phone with them. And I can't picture my mother just standing by letting him drink." Mom had wrangled kindergartners for twenty years, a job she liked to say made wrangling my father a cakewalk. She was two parts tender and two parts steely resolve. Only the surprise gift of Collin had derailed her plans to become a lawyer.

"Maybe she didn't know?" Ava suggested.

"Maybe. I don't know. Anything's possible." I made a confession. "That's what my brother thinks. Collin. He's a police officer. When my parents first died, he called and talked to an officer here. Collin said he was nice, he was helpful, and that he said they see it all the time on St. Marcos, tourists driving drunk and getting into bad situations. Collin thought maybe Dad had relapsed and was hiding it—the drinking—from my mom."

Ava put her hand on my forearm. "I hate to say it, Katie, but tourists and drunk drivers are the same thing to us."

That didn't help my leaky eyes. "But your friend acted so weird. Don't you think so?"

She looked at me, and her eyes were soft and sad. "The officer on this case that died? Michael Jacoby? He was Darren's brother. His kid brother."

"I'm sorry. Oh my God, I'm so sorry. I'm making everything about me. I—"

A sharp rap on the window behind my head cut me short. I yelped and jumped in my seat, banging my head into the roof. Ava gasped, too.

I turned to see Darren Jacoby's broad face framed in my window. I started to roll it down but the buttons didn't respond. Only then did I realize that we were sitting in a hot car without the windows down or air conditioner on. I inserted the keys and cranked the engine, then rolled the window down.

Ava leaned across me, pure Local again. "Jacoby, you scare us good."

He didn't smile. "I wanted to tell her," he looked directly at me, "to tell you, that I sorry about your parents. I know it hard to lose someone you love. I know it make you ask questions. But my brother a good cop, and I trust him. If he say they die in a car accident, that what happened." He had switched back to Local speech again.

"I'm sorry about your brother," I said.

He inclined his head, eyes down, then met mine again. "Good day, Ms. Connell."

I rolled the window up again as he walked away. I was more confused now than I'd been before I came to the station. It would be best to let it go, to trust

Collin's judgment, to look for peace instead of trouble. I knew that. I normally trusted Collin completely, too. But he'd had girl trouble right before Mom and Dad died. His fiancée had dumped him for a woman, and he was just not himself then, distracted with his own stuff. If I had doubts, then I owed it to my parents to do this. I had let them down for a year, letting everything else be more important than my intuition, than them, and as long as a shred of doubt remained in me, I had to keep going.

I backed out of my parking spot and put the car in drive.

Chapter Nine

Fifteen minutes later, Ava and I sat in front of the desk of a Mr. Paul Walker at 32 King's Cross Street. His office was a long narrow room with walls and floors of red brick. Probably an alley or breezeway once upon a time. It was squeezed in between a thrift store and an abandoned record store that still had dust-covered albums on display and an air of shame about it, of failure. I wondered if there were any treasures hidden in its depths. Probably not.

Walker had gone to the back of his space to a mini-refrigerator, from which he fetched two bottles of water. He used the sleeve of his shirt to wipe down the bottles and tops as he came back across the uneven floor between us. The walls squeezed in behind him, squirting him forward, or so my eyes told me. It was a house of mirrors at a low-rent carnival in here.

"So tell me about the case, Ms. Connell," Walker said as he handed the waters across the desk to us, then sat.

I'd only worked closely with one other investigator before: Nick. What a contrast Walker was to him. Walker's belly looked about five months pregnant under his Cruzan Rum t-shirt. Sweat was beaded on his forehead. His whole office smelled in need of a shower. If I'd have had a handkerchief with me, I would have held it to my face—after I cleaned my water bottle. I set the bottle down on the floor beside me.

"My parents were on St. Marcos for a week last year. They came here for their fortieth anniversary. They had a great time, and they called me every day." A twinge of guilt shot through me as I remembered the irritation I'd felt at seeing their number on my phone. People I loved interrupting a life I didn't, and I was irritated with *them*. "They did all the normal tourist things. They took a catamaran out to one of the cays. They hiked in the rainforest. They went to a secluded beach to snorkel. It was like they recaptured their youth here. They even called me one day and said they'd walked up on two people having sex on the beach, literally. My mom giggled like a teenage girl when she told me about it, some big bushy-haired blond man and a tiny black woman, she told me. But she loved it. She loved everything about the trip."

Get to the point, Katie. Funny how eloquent I could be about other people's problems, but how awkward about my own. I finished the rest of my story without diving off into irrelevant detail.

Walker's eyes lasered my face while I talked. When I finished, he remained silent, slowly tapping his pen against his lips.

"Mr. Walker? Do you have any questions?" I asked.

"Oh. Sorry. You remind me of someone I used to know," he said. His comment crawled across my skin like a scorpion. "Yes, just a few questions to help me get started. Before your parents died, where did they have dinner?"

I remembered this. They had loved the restaurant and returned to it for their last dinner. "Fortuna's. Do you know of it?"

"Yes, it's a very popular place."

My eyes strayed to the framed NYPD ten-year service award on the wall over his left shoulder. Beside it hung the obligatory island fishing picture, Walker and an equally large black man and even larger blond man standing on the stern deck of a boat named *Big Kahuna*, the three of them together hefting a huge marlin.

Ava spoke for the first time since we'd all exchanged greetings at the beginning of the meeting. "Baptiste's Bluff not exactly on the way from the restaurant to the hotel."

Walker ignored her and continued speaking to me. "Did they go anywhere else that you know of that last night?"

"Not that I know of."

"The casino? A moonlight stroll on the beach, perhaps?"

"I'm sorry, I just don't know. I have the accident report from the police, though. And they said the coroner might have a report, too." I held out the police file, and he took it, opened it, and set it in front of him.

"OK, I'll get that from the coroner."

"Also," I hesitated, looked at Ava, then plowed ahead. "The officer that investigated their deaths died shortly after them. You can see on the report that a different officer signed it than the one who investigated. I don't know if that means anything, but—"

Walker cut me off. "I'll look into it. All right." He glanced down at the opened file and the police report on his desk. "I think I have everything I need from you. There's a five-hundred-dollar retainer, to get started."

I needed to do this, but was just writing this man a check and trusting him to look into it enough? Would spending the insurance money I hadn't needed make me feel less guilty? I wanted to call Nick and ask his advice. I wanted to run out the front door. I wanted a rum punch. I wanted Mom and Dad back. I swallowed hard and pulled out my checkbook.

As I wrote him a check, he continued to talk. "My case load is very heavy right now. I know I can't get to this for a few weeks. It's not an emergency, after all, as your parents are already dead."

Another skin-crawling moment. He was right, though. Crass, but right. I set the check on the desk with my business card on top of it and used my fingertips to push them across to him. They dug a trail of clean through the dust on his desk.

"Well, thank you, Ms. Connell. I'll be in touch," he said, grabbing the check before my fingertips left it.

As Ava and I stood up to depart, he said, "Oh, one last thing. It's better for me if I talk to the potential witnesses fresh. It interferes with my investigation when my client tries to do it first herself. So, if you please, let me do what you have hired me to do, and you enjoy the rest of your stay on our lovely island."

"Fine," I said.

And we left, as fast as I could get out of there.

Chapter Ten

Ava and I traipsed down the sidewalk, silent as an old married couple instead of two women who had known each other for fifteen hours. I still walked ahead of her, but I was slowing down. From life, though, not from limin'.

When we reached the car, Ava put both her palms flat on the roof. "Tell me you hungry and ready for a cocktail." She brought one forearm in front of her face and looked at an imaginary watch. "Yep, definitely time for a late lunch."

"I need to see Baptiste's Bluff," I said. "I just need to see it. I don't think I can turn this over to Walker and let it go without seeing it for myself."

Ava struck a stage pose, putting her bent arms in the air, all ten fingers pointing to the sky, and gestured from her shoulder in a rhythmic emphasis. "Well, of course you need to see it." She dropped her dramatic stance and leaned toward me. "And I take you, but you gonna have a flying fish sandwich in one hand and a Red Stripe in the other when we get there." She pointed to a street ahead and to the left. "Drive, and go that way."

After we got back into the hot Malibu, we drove out of town along the winding north shore, blue on our right, green on our left. We rolled the windows down and let our hair blow. I needed a hurricane to blow my storm system out and into the sea air, but a strong coastal breeze would do for now. We passed a marina. The smell of diesel and dead fish were overwhelming for a moment, and I exhaled through my nose. I pulled some of the hair out of my mouth that the wind had blown in and took a sip from the water bottle I'd brought from Walker's office. The same bottle I had given a punishing rubdown with a Sani-Wipe from my purse once we'd gotten into the car.

After ten minutes of driving, Ava pointed to a hut on the beach.

"Pull over there," she said.

The hut turned out to be a small take-out restaurant, with a bar and some beach stools. There was no name on it that I could see. Ava slipped off her/my shoes and got out of the car, so I followed suit. We crossed the sand to the nameless hut and were greeted by a couple of dogs.

"Coconut retrievers," Ava said. She commanded them to get back in a deeper voice than I'd heard her use before, and the dogs obliged, tails wagging.

Ava hailed up the proprietor like an old friend and gave him our order. He stuck out his palm, so I pulled out a twenty. His eyes twinkled, and he held out his other palm. I pulled out a second twenty. He nodded, and I placed one twenty in each. He put the money under the counter in a basket and turned back to his fryers, sucking his cheeks into the space where his teeth used to be. No change. Paradise wasn't cheap.

Ava hopped onto one of the barstools and faced the sea. I joined her. What a way to grab lunch. I could get used to this. I tucked my feet up onto the support bar around the stool's legs and put my elbows on my knees, face in my palms.

"Lunch always so expensive on this island?" I asked.

"Yah mon. If you not bahn yah."

I was indignant. "So he would have charged you less than what he charged me?"

She snorted. "He? No, he a thief. But usually there a local discount."

Oh well. It wasn't surprising. I rolled my head, enjoying a few neck cracks. The water was calling to me. "Do you mind if I put my toes in while we wait?" I asked Ava.

"Go ahead. I stay here and call you when our food come out."

The sand was warm, almost hot. My feet sank in heel first, slowing me down. As I got closer to the waterline, the sand grew firmer and cooler. I didn't hesitate. I plunged into the water, ankle deep, then knee deep. I pulled the hem of my white sundress up several inches. The water surged against my knees, then rose over them and wetted my thighs. Then it rushed out past my legs again and I felt the breeze move in to dry me off. I could see my toes on the white sandy ocean floor, and I wiggled them. The water came back, lifting me up as it rose. A school of small silver fish darted around me, half on one side of me and half on the other, only inches below the surface.

"Katie," Ava called. "Food ready."

I could have stood there for hours. But I walked out of the water, splashing it up with my toes on my last few steps. Imagining my mother, wondering if she'd done the same, if she'd done it right here on this beach. If the old man in the hut looking out at me now had seen her, and from a distance thought I looked familiar to him. Since my teens, people had claimed we could pass for twins. Mom would roll her eyes and say, "From a hundred yards to a myopic septuagenarian." She was wrong, though. She was far too young to die.

I rejoined Ava, and we carried our greasy wax-paper-wrapped sandwiches and johnnycakes back to the car. Johnnycake is deep-fried bread, the Caribbean equivalent of biscuits to Southerners or sopapillas to Mexicans. Just what my cellulite needed. Except that really, it was lack of exercise in the last five years since I'd quit karate, not too many calories, that was my problem. Ava also had two icy Red Stripes between her fingers.

"How much further?" I asked.

"Ten minutes," she said.

We drove another mile along the water, then turned straight inland and upward. I hated leaving the serenity of the shoreline. The last eight minutes of our drive were on rutted dirt roads that shot off into dense bushes every few hundred yards.

"Not a place to explore by yourself," Ava said, pointing at one of the side roads. "Too isolated."

"It's gorgeous up here, though," I said. In fact, I was shocked at how gorgeous it was. Different from the water, obviously, but different in a good way, a way that was perfect. The trees were taller and met above the road, creating a roof above us and dampening the noise of the surf against sand and rocks only a mile away. I saw a bright flash of feathers in one of the trees.

"Is that a macaw?"

"Yah mon. They live up here."

I didn't know if I could ever be as blasé about this flora and fauna as Ava sounded. I soaked it in: orchids more beautiful than hothouse flowers trailing vines of hot pink, pink and orange flamboyants standing tall and proud, reminding me of the mimosa trees back home.

"Turn in here," Ava said, and I made a sharp right, back in the general direction of the water, but hundreds of feet above it now.

We drove a quarter of a mile, then broke out of the trees. The change in our surroundings was sudden, a ripping away of the quietude of the forest. My mood shifted with it. Who was I kidding? My emotions were raw, and my moods were moving up and down the scales faster than Sarah Brightman in *Phantom of the Opera.*

"You can park anywhere," she said.

I pulled to a stop and parked, then shut off the engine and held my breath.

Coming to the place where my parents died was like walking into the painted churches of the Navidad Valley. Our family visited them on a short road trip to La Grange when I was in middle school. In those old wooden churches, I knew I was in the presence of something holy and powerful, and that under their roofs, hardship and blessings walked hand in hand, just as they did here where the rainforest met the cliffs. Where life met death.

Ava was already outside, barefoot again, and walking up a rise. I trailed behind her. I wanted to take it all in. I wanted to feel my parents again, and I wanted them to know I had come here, that they had mattered to me. That if I accomplished nothing else on this trip, I would at least say goodbye.

"I love you, Mom and Dad," I whispered.

Ava crested the hill and in three steps had disappeared. I sped up. As I came over the ridge, I gasped and stepped backward from the sudden vertigo. The ground sloped away for thirty yards, then simply vanished. Beyond was nothing but sky, until it merged with the Caribbean Sea in the distance.

"They not the first to drive off this bluff," Ava said, and she was solemn.

"Oh my God," I said, because I couldn't think of any other words. I sank to the grass. I perched myself on a hummock and tried to gather my thoughts. Why? Why had they come here?

"This place kind of our Lover's Lane, in a rugged and inaccessible way. Lotta girls I know lost their virginity out here. It also been the site of a few lover's leaps. It always had this romantic allure people can't resist."

I mulled over her words. Was it possible my parents had sought this spot out? A last tryst on their anniversary getaway? I pictured the two of them, holding hands, heads touching. I hoped so. Something in me didn't believe it, but God, I hoped so.

"Goodbye, Mom and Dad," I whispered. I closed my eyes again, counted from a hundred backwards, tried to think of nothing, and offered my heart to the sky.

Chapter Eleven

We drove away from Baptiste's Bluff and back into the rainforest half an hour later. My equilibrium was on the mend, enough that the beauty of the flowers swept me in again. They seemed now like tributes to my parents. Memorial arrangements. The rainforest didn't just do my eyes good, it made me feel closer to Mom and Dad. I hated driving away.

"You know, my friend give a guided tour of the rainforest. He shuttle his group right from the Peacock Flower. You should go with him tomorrow. I'ma call and tell him you're coming."

"Hiking? I'm not a hiker. I'm a great driver, though. Is there a driving tour?"

"Nope. He a botanist, and you just hush now and go with him. It change your life."

This whole trip already felt life-changing, and I'd only arrived twenty-four hours ago.

I succumbed to a fit of honesty. "That's why I'm here, you know. To change my life. Or I'm supposed to be, anyway, as much as I can in a week. My brother pretty much insisted. He thinks I drink too much. I'm trying to look past symptoms to the source. It's not the alcohol. It's my parents. My bad choices. Pining after the wrong guy. Yadda yadda." I trailed off, embarrassed about the words I couldn't stuff back into the place from whence they came.

My confession didn't faze Ava. "Most everybody running from something when they come here. Most of the time they got to figure out whether they running from the right thing, or the wrong thing follow them here."

Her statement was deep. I was through with deep for the day, so I stayed quiet.

Ava didn't. "Didn't you say your father an alcoholic? I think I read that it a genetic trait," she said.

"Yeah. Maybe." Except I wasn't an alcoholic.

"Lotta people that move here become alcoholics," she said. "It a tough environment to quit drinking in."

"I've kinda noticed that." At least she hadn't focused on my pining away for the wrong guy, but I was ready to be done with the topic of Katie's problems altogether. We were almost back to town. "Where am I taking you?" I asked.

"Take me to my place so I can change. I have a date later, but I looking for company until then."

"You're not singing tonight?" I asked.

"Not officially."

Whatever that meant.

We pulled up to Ava's house and she beckoned me inside. It was small, but clean. Cute, with mostly wicker furniture and fluffy white cushions. I puttered around looking at her photographs until she came out of her bedroom in a shiny turquoise baby-doll-type dress with a keyhole neckline. She wore high-heeled white thongs that echoed the keyhole in the leatherwork across the top of her foot.

"Is this who I think it is?" I asked, pointing at a picture of a younger Ava with a gorgeous and recognizable actor.

"Yeah, I went to school with him at NYU. Don't tell anyone I said so, but he gay. All the really good-looking ones gay." She put a tube of lip gloss into her white handbag. "Ready?"

"Depends on what I need to be ready for, but, in general, I am ready to depart."

"You sound like a lawyer."

"Actually, I *am* a lawyer."

"Oh, that explain a lot," she said in a tone of voice that implied I had a lot to explain for.

"Yeah, yeah, yeah. But what am I supposed to be ready for?"

"To sing."

I busted out laughing. "That's random. And no, I'm not ready for that."

"Fine. Then let we go to the casino. They have a free food bar and free drinks."

Nothing to argue with there, so I didn't.

After a stop at my hotel that took far longer than it should have when I got caught up in answering work emails, we arrived at the Porcus Marinus Casino.

The casino was on the south shore, adjacent to a touristy resort of the same name and across the street from a flat white sand beach. The full moon was reflected on the surface of the undulating water. On our side of the road was a giant bunker-like building and the biggest parking lot on the entire island. We walked up the steps to the bunker and passed under a huge banner over the door that announced, "Karaoke Night."

"Karaoke night?" I asked Ava, my eyes narrowed.

"It fate," she said.

We stepped inside, and I immediately coughed. A cigarette haze hovered up against the high ceilings of the casino. For the first time since I'd arrived on St. Marcos, I got a sense of permanent midnight. No windows. Plenty of noise, though, the white noise of the jangling bells of slot machines and the roars erupting as if on regular cues from the craps tables.

And another noise. In the background, I could just make out the voice of a DJ giving the crowd a hard sell on karaoke. "Who'll be next? What about you, pretty lady? Or you, sir, over there in the shirt you stole off Jimmy Buffett?"

Ava gave me a little push between the shoulder blades in the direction of the stage. The place was packed, and it wasn't even nine o'clock yet. We weaved through bleary West Indians and a few stumbling tourists. Most of them looked like they'd have done better spending their money on a decent meal or some fresh clothes.

An eerie and unwelcome recognition hit me. The Porcus Marinus was no different from the brief glimpse I'd gotten of the inside of the Eldorado casino in Shreveport. I shook it off. It was different. A world away, different. Nothing to be ashamed of, different. I pushed my chin higher in the air.

When we reached the stage, Ava didn't break stride. She swept past me to the DJ. "Miss Ava," he said into his mike. A few people in the crowd clapped and hooted. "What'll it be tonight, sexy lady?"

"Hit me with some No Doubt, some Fugees, and," she turned to me, "what else?"

"I'm from Texas. Give me Dixie Chicks and Miranda Lambert."

The DJ said, "Miranda what?"

"Never mind. Dixie Chicks."

"They those three blonde girls?" he asked.

I was sure they'd love that description, but they'd fared better than Miranda, anyway. "Yes."

"Yah, I got them."

Ava threw her pocketbook into the DJ booth like it was a frisbee. I walked over and set mine on his counter. "Is this OK?" I asked him.

He had already loaded No Doubt's "Underneath It All" track and was grooving his head in time to the music coming through the speakers and the headphone he wore over the ear closest to me. He didn't look my way. His eyes were glued to Ava.

"What the hell," I said, and made my way to a table in front of the stage to watch her.

"Hunh UH," she said into the microphone. "You get that bana to the stage, girl." Her accent had thickened.

Now the small crowd cheered louder.

"Great," I said to myself. "I'm the continental foil. The buffoon tourist."

"I not getting any younger up here," Ava said, one hand on cocked hip. Hyeah.

I sighed and walked to the stage in the white sundress I'd been wearing since I first got dressed that morning, climbed the three steps of doom, and joined her in front of the black backdrop. I was all right angles and sharp corners next to her vavavoom and curves. If you're going to go out, go out in style, I thought, and I put my chin back up.

Now the crowd joined Ava as she whooped and clapped for me. She handed me the microphone and pointed at the monitor. "Sing," she commanded.

So I sang. Then she sang, then we sang together, and it was astonishing. My twangy voice, able to reach the highest notes but too thin alone, interlaced and thickened when combined with her deeper, more soulful voice. I harmonized with her, backed her, then she returned the favor. I relaxed and imagined that my edges had rounded, at least a bit. This was fun.

We left the stage twenty minutes later to a standing ovation, which counted even though it was only ten drunk men and one little blue-haired lady who'd gotten lost on her way back to the slot machines from the bathroom.

"Now who brave enough to follow that?" the DJ asked. The crowd yelled back at him, "Not me, no way, no sir." He put a playlist on, shot us two thumbs up, and went on a break.

I collapsed into my chair. "Champagne," I told the waitress who had followed us to our table.

"Me, too," Ava said.

She scribbled our order and strolled off, giving me the best demonstration of slowing down to lime a little that I'd seen yet.

"We rock, Katie Connell," Ava said. "And damn, you're even taller on stage."

I hadn't sung except in the car and shower in years. I felt electrified. Alive in a way practicing law didn't make me, that was for sure. "We kick ass," I said, then giggled. Kick ass. Like I ever said that.

"Yah mon," Ava said.

Our waitress sauntered back toward us, bearing two drinks on a tray. As she passed a small round-topped table on the other side of the karaoke area, a woman reached out and grabbed her free arm. Her voice cut through the crowd's noise.

"Where is my drink? I ordered it five minutes ago,"

"I bring it shortly," the waitress said, and removed her arm from the woman's grasp.

"I want my drink immediately. This is ridiculous. Where's your supervisor?" the woman demanded, her accent identifying her as a resident of New York or thereabouts.

The waitress nodded, smiled, and said, "Oh, yes, ma'am, it will be right out."

She resumed walking toward us, even slower this time. When she reached us, Ava said to her, "Wah, someone think she special."

"For true," the waitress agreed. "She 'bout to get real t'irsty."

She placed our drinks on the table and left. "What I tell you?" Ava said to me.

"I'm limin', I'm limin'," I said.

We drank our champagne from plastic cups with leaping blue dolphins on the side. I took a sip and the bubbles tickled my nose. I giggled again. I never drank this stuff. I never giggled. "Salud," I said, raising my glass. Ava and I bounced our cups off each other's, splashing champagne on our arms. More giggles.

"Is this chair taken?" a deep voice asked. One of our fans, maybe? His broad shoulders blocked out the sun, yowza. Except there was no sun in the casino. It blocked out the light from the cheesy light fixtures. The backlighting around the voice's head hid his face.

Ava recognized the voice, though. "Jacoby, sit down, meh son." She patted the padded Naugahyde seat next to her. Small island.

Darren Jacoby, still in his police uniform, sat down facing Ava, and the two locals traded cheek kisses. He had looked pretty good for a moment, in the dark.

"Hi, Ms. Connell," he said over his shoulder.

He really didn't seem to want to call me Katie. Oh, well. "Hello, Officer Jacoby."

"I can't stay long," he said to Ava. "I'm on duty. My shift end at ten. Just making the rounds when I see you. What you doing?"

"We went to the private investigator you recommended," I said to his profile.

He looked back at me, expressionless. "Well, I hope that turn out well for you. When you go back to the states?"

He was so not subtle. "Five days," I said.

"Be careful, then." He turned all his attention back to Ava. "Do you want to hang out later? I got *Love and Basketball* on DVD."

Oh, jeez, even less subtle. He might as well rent a billboard.

"Oh, Jacoby, I can't. I have a date."

His jaw bulged and anger flashed in his eyes so fast I almost didn't catch it. "Always somebody, ain't it, Ava?" The jaw relaxed. The big shoulders shrank. "Well, another time."

"Of course," she said.

"I'll just be going, then."

He and Ava cheek-kissed again, he turned and bowed his head at me, and he ambled away, a double for a grizzly bear from the back. He didn't like me much, but I still hurt for him.

Ava made a sad face. "He that way forever. He don't give up easy." She pulled out her phone and said, "I better check on my date." A few clicks later, she said, "Guy booked into a room here, up on the hill. A suite. Ooo la la."

"Will I get to meet him?" I asked.

"No. He very private about us." She pointed to the third finger of her left hand and mouthed the word "married." "He not even contact me himself. It like I having a thing with his assistant, Eduardo."

"I'm sorry," I said, because I didn't know what else to say. It sounded pretty smarmy and awful to me.

"Oh, it's no problem," Ava said, and shooed the imaginary problem away with her hand. "He's a senator. People know him. It's a small island."

So I'd noticed.

I thought of how I felt when Nick ignored me in public. And I wasn't even "having a thing" with him. Jacoby wasn't with Ava, either, but that didn't seem to keep him from having big emotions about her date. "But doesn't it hurt your feelings?"

Ava pursed her lips. "I don't love him, Katie. He nice, and he trying to get a pilot here for a TV show, starring yours truly. We get what we want from each other. I like rich better than powerful, anyway, and he not rich." She took another sip of champagne.

I tucked my hair behind my ear. Pilot for a TV show? Her senator Guy had to be my drinking buddy from my flight in. I decided not to mention it, since he'd hit on me relentlessly. Hey, if their arrangement didn't bother Ava, I wasn't going to let it bother me. Maybe I'd be happier if I was as dispassionate as she was. Maybe. But probably not.

"So, who's the wrong guy, anyway?" she said.

"What?" I asked, thinking for a moment we were still talking about Guy with a capital G.

"The one you not supposed to pine for."

Ah, him. I signaled the waitress for more champagne. Then, carefully, I picked my way through the story, trying not to set off any landmines that would blow up my fragile Nick-peace.

Ava said, "You better off without him. I'ma take care of you, and find you a man to keep your mind occupied this week."

"No men, Ava."

"Huh. So you gonna pine? Looks like you not running from him too hard."

"No pining. I'm running. Really."

Ava didn't look convinced. "If you say so, Katie. If you say so."

Chapter Twelve

The disturbing alarm ringtone on my iPhone blared in my ear at 6:30 a.m. "Damn it, Ava," I said.

I shut it off and got dressed. Ava had insisted I do this rainforest hike, and I'd eventually caved. She called her friend Rashidi to sign me up, and he made room for me. Apparently he had quite a waiting list, but would do anything for Ava. How just like everybody else of him.

When I got to the rally point in front of the resort, it took only one glance at Rashidi to understand why he stayed overbooked. He was exotic, with a lean, dark physique. He wore neatly-tied dreadlocks that hung all the way to his waist. Maybe Ava ought to give him a second look. He made Guy seem a trifle effeminate.

Rashidi walked through the tittering mass of mostly female hikers, checking us for appropriate clothing, footwear, sunscreen, bug spray, hats, and hydration. He sent a few women back to their rooms and the hotel gift shop for supplies, and one or two he delicately queried about their constitutions and health.

"The rainforest on St. Marcos one of the most beautiful places in the world, but it rugged, ladies, and it harsh." His Calypso accent was thick, much thicker than Ava's, with his "th" sounding like "t" and all the g's and d's dropped from the end of his words, but he was understandable. "There may be some of you would enjoy it more with a drivin' tour." Me! Would it be wrong to raise my hand? I thought.

"These hills steep. The sun rough. There be centipedes as long as me foot." Someone laughed. "I not jokin' you, ladies and gentlemen. You will see beautiful trees, blossoms and vines, but they can reach out with their thorns and stickers and tear your soft skin. They grow thick together, so at times I be using this," he patted the machete strung across his hip, "to clear a path for us to get through. You ain't gonna make me sad if you decide this hike not for you. I can only carry one of you out if you get hurt or fall to our tropical heat, so leave now if you gonna be leavin'."

One portly woman with tightly curled gray hair, who was already sweating profusely and sporting beet-red cheeks, opted out. The rest of us fell in line whispering and shuffle-footing as Rashidi continued his commentary. When he finished, we filed onto the shuttle bus for the ride to the rainforest. As he walked up the center aisle of the shuttle, he stopped at me.

"You Ava's red-haired Katie?" he asked.

"Guilty," I said.

He sucked his teeth, a sound I'd heard a few times in the last two days. "Chuptzing," Ava had called it, when I asked her last night. A derisive noise. Hopefully intended for Ava, not me.

I smiled hopefully, and he grinned and said, "That girl a problem. Welcome, Katie."

We drove to the west end of the island along oceanside roads and then cut up into the hills. The driver parked the shuttle in front of a restored two-story plantation home that was now a museum. Its whitewashed boards stood in stark contrast to the green of the forest surrounding it. A vegetable garden beside the house gave way to a stand of banana trees, the bunches of fruit bowing them over. Rashidi said they were called babyfingers because the bananas were short and stubby.

The group hike started from the parking lot and we crossed the road to pick up the trail into the forest. The scenery was gorgeous. Even the drive yesterday hadn't done justice to the beauty I experienced once we started walking. On foot, I could hear the macaws calling to each other. I smelled the cloying perfume of the wild orchids. I saw the bright green iguanas that my eyes hadn't picked out from my vantage point in the driver's seat.

We hiked up a steep, winding path, and I wished I owned a pair of hiking boots. The trees were tall, their leaves clustered in a canopy over our heads. The bush on the ground was sparse on the cleared path, but thick up to its edge. As best as I could understand it, "bush" referred to whatever grew near the ground: bushes, ferns with giant leaves, weeds, flowers, small trees, and grasses. Rashidi described it all, and I tried to soak it in. Guinea grass and bright red hibiscus. Ginger Thomas flowers and grape-sized gnip fruits. Elephant ears and royal palms. I concentrated on the challenge of breathing in through my nose and out through my mouth, and keeping my mind clear of he-who-I-was-not-to-pine-for. I swiped a long brown seedpod off the lower limb of a vibrant orange flamboyant. The pod looked like a sword, and I swished it in the air a few times, then felt kind of silly.

The incline winded me, and I scowled at the memories and effects of my recent debauched lifestyle. What the hell was I doing to myself? I had to stop this. The burning in my lungs began to feel good; it burned out the bush in me. Maybe it could clear a path for me to find my way.

We had hiked for nearly two hours when Rashidi gave us a hydration break and announced that we were nearing the turnaround point, which would be a special treat: a modern ruin. As we leaned on smooth kapok trees and sucked on our Lululemon water bottles, Rashidi explained that a bad man, a thief, had built a beautiful mansion in paradise ten years before, named her Annalise, and then left her forsaken and half-complete. No one had ever finished her and the rainforest had moved fast to claim her. Wild horses roamed her halls, colonies of bats filled her eaves, and who knows what lived below her in the depths of her cisterns. We would eat our lunch there, then turn back for the hike down.

When the forest parted to reveal Annalise, we all drew in a breath. She was amazing: tall, austere, and a bit frightening. Our group tensed with anticipation. It was like the first day of the annual Parade of Homes, where people stood in lines for the chance to tour the crème de la crème of Dallas real estate, except way better. We were visiting a mysterious mansion with a romantic history in a tropical rainforest. Ooh là là.

Graceful flamboyant trees, fragrant white-flowered frangipanis, and grand pillars marked the entrance to her gateless drive. On each side of the overgrown road, Rashidi pointed out papaya stalks, soursop, and mahogany trees. The fragrance was pungent, the air drunk with fermenting mangos and ripening guava, all subtly undercut by the aroma of bay leaves. It was a surreal orchard, its orphaned fruit unpicked, the air heavy and still, bees and insects the only thing stirring besides our band of turistas. Overhead, the branches met in the middle of the road and were covered in the trailing pink flowers I'd admired the day before, which Rashidi called pink trumpet vines. The sun shone through the canopy in narrow beams and lit our dim path.

A young woman in historic slave garb was standing on the front steps, peering at us from under the hand that shaded her eyes, her gingham skirt whipping in the breeze. She looked familiar. As we came closer, she turned and walked back inside. I turned to ask Rashidi if we were going to tour the inside of the house, but he was talking to a skeletally thin New Yorker who wanted details on the mileage and elevation gain of our hike for her Garmin.

We climbed up Annalise's ten uneven front steps and entered through the opening that should have had imposing double doors. We came first into a great room with thirty-five-foot ceilings, and my skin prickled, each hair standing to salute Annalise. We gazed up in wonder at her intricate tongue-in-groove cypress ceiling and mahogany beams, her stone fireplace that was so improbable here in the tropics.

We explored her three stories, room after room unfolding as we discussed what each was to have been. Balcony floors with no railings jutted from two sides of the house. A giant concrete pool behind the house hovered partway out of the ground, like a crash-landed spaceship. How could someone put in so much work, build something so magnificent, create such hope, and leave her to rot?

Gradually, ughs replaced the oohs as we discovered that we had to step over horse manure and bat guano in every room, and an old mattress with God knows what ground into it in the basement. Dead worms by the thousands crunched under our feet. Rashidi called them gungalos. One woman put her hand on a wall and ended up with dung between her fingers and gunked into her ostentatious diamond ring, which, for some inexplicable reason, she'd worn on a rainforest hike. Annalise was not for the faint of heart, and I longed for a broom. What she could have been was so clear; what she might still be was staggering. I could see it. I could feel it.

And *zing*—something hit me hard, just coursed through my head and lungs. A cold, hard, lonely place filled with crap. It was like looking in the mirror. No, it was more than that. It was like someone had whispered it in my ear. It felt personal to me that she was abandoned. Even her name resonated inside me: Annalise. Unbelievably, I had a connection on my iPhone, and I Googled the origin of the name—Hebrew for grace, favor. For some reason, reading those words hurt me. Annalise and I could both use some grace. An overpowering urge to make things right by myself and by this house rose up in me. I didn't see the irrationality of it; I saw the possibility of mutual redemption. Swept along by a powerful urge, I saved the realtor's name and number from the faded sign by the door into my contacts. It didn't hurt to type it in, I told myself.

Rashidi's voice broke through my reverie. "Ms. Katie, are you comin' with us? It gets dark up here at night, you know."

I laughed and started after the group that had left without me noticing, excitement bubbling up in me from the inside and spilling over in that forgotten sound of true joy. I had energy now and a spring in my step. The group was chattering as we hiked out, but I didn't hear a word. My washing-machine mind was churning again, but instead of Nick, this time it was Annalise spinning through it. It was as if she was calling out to me that we were the same, that we could save each other, and my mind was answering with a cautious maybe, a tentative "we'll see." I stopped to look back each time she came into view, farther and farther in the distance.

She was defiantly beautiful and strong, soaring over a sea of green treetops, and behind her, the ocean, which looked like the sky. A view of the world turned upside down. I shivered.

Rashidi dropped back a half-dozen paces from the group and spoke softly to me. "So, you like the house? I see you talkin' to her spirit."

Did this man take me for a crazy person? Or had my lips moved? If I was talking to her, and I was not sure that I had been, I wasn't about to confirm my insanity to a stranger. "Talking to her spirit? What, you mean the spirit of the pooping horse?" I quipped.

"You make like I crazy, but what that make you? You the one hear the house talkin' to you," he said matter-of-factly. "What she say?"

Instead of answering him, I asked, "Why do you say she's got a spirit? What do you mean, like a ghost?"

Rashidi's speech became more colloquial, his accent thickened, and his eyes sparkled. "Nah, she ain't got no ghost, she the spirit. She a beautiful woman, abandoned by a man. How does most beautiful women dem act when they scorned? She lonely, and she full of spite." He grinned. "She lookin' for a new lover. But most folk too scared of her to take her on. When she don't like someone, she a mean one. She been known to drop a bad man when he come for no good, hit him with a rock from nowhere, or send centipedes to bite him.

When she do like somebody, well, some people say she talk to them. Like she talk to you, Katie."

This made sense to me in a way I could not explain. It wasn't as if I was ever going to have to see Rashidi again, so what the heck, I would tell him what I had heard.

"She said we are soul mates." I turned and smiled straight on at him. "In so many words."

He didn't bat an eye. "Yah, I thought so. Annalise talk to me sometimes, but today I feel her vibrations, and she talkin' to you. Powerful thing. You gonna go back and talk to her again?"

"Ummmm, maybe," I said.

"Let me know if you need a hand. Good to have someone with you what knows the way aroun'."

"I might take you up on that."

He caught up with the group, exhorting them to "Breathe in the scent of the flowers, ladies, glory in the beauty of the forest, because we almost back to civilization, and you may never come this way again."

But I knew I would.

Chapter Thirteen

The next morning, I luxuriated in my 1000-thread-count sheets, savoring the decadence of getting up late and eating a room-service breakfast in bed. Not to mention tucking in early and waking up without a headache begging for an emergency glass of water with Alka-Seltzer Plus. My tummy was getting full, but I didn't let that stop me. I cut another bite of Eggs Benedict and speared it from the top with my fork, dragging the layers of goodness through creamy hollandaise before I placed it in my mouth and let the flavors sink into my tongue. I chewed slowly, reverently. If I'd been a dog, I would have rolled in it. When I was done with it, my plate looked sparkly clean.

I'd saved the parfait dish of mango and papaya for dessert. It reminded me of the trees I'd seen the day before. As I scooped fruit into my mouth, I took stock of my trip so far. While I'd struck out with the police, I'd hired Walker to look into my parents' death. I hadn't had a drink in more than twenty-four hours. I was holding my Nick pining to a minimum. I'd had fun and made friends. Truly, by anyone's account, I was pulling myself together. Collin would be pleased.

Probably it would be best, then, if I didn't call and tell him I was bewitched by a big jumbie house named Annalise, right?

I picked up my phone and dialed.

"Island Realtors, Doug speaking, may I help you." He made a statement rather than asked a question. The fast voice and heavy New Jersey accent surprised me.

I introduced myself, then got right to it. "I saw a property with your company's For Sale sign. I want to take a look at it," I explained.

"OK. Which property interests you here on our fair island?"

"It's one I saw on a rainforest hike. It's called Estate Annalise."

"Well, certainly a spectacular place," he said in the same tone he would have used if I'd just told him that little green men from Mars were taking over St. Marcos. "Will your husband be joining us?"

"It's just me," I said. Asshole, I didn't say.

"Have you considered any other properties? We have some lovely condos on the east end of the island. Very popular with the continentals. It's a real community out there."

This man rubbed my fur in the wrong direction. He also was steering me, without saying it directly, to the white end of the island, something I'd learned from Ava's commentary as we drove across the island to Baptiste's Bluff. All roads to Annalise went through the listing agent, though, so I tamped down my irritation.

"Annalise is the only property I want to see. When are you available for a showing?"

"I'm rather flexible today," he said. The hunger of an island realtor in off-season was lurking below the surface of his comment.

"Great, I'd love to go as soon as possible."

Since I'd "met" Annalise the day before, I couldn't quit thinking about her. I woke up again and again during the night, my circadian rhythm thrown off tempo by the unforgettable house, the tropical Wuthering Heights. In one of my middle-of-the-night wakeups I had a vivid dream that was more like a memory. It was my own Heathcliff in Annalise. He seemed right at home as he cooked pasta in a finished kitchen that was a far sight from the current dung-filled shell. The woman I had seen on the front steps of Annalise sat on a stool at a breakfast bar, as if waiting for Nick to serve her. I was frustrated. What was Nick doing at Annalise in my dreams? I didn't want the house tainted with thoughts of him.

But Nick was nowhere in my thoughts today. Just Annalise. I promised myself I was simply going to take another look at her. A harmless excursion. Something to fill my empty vacation day. I was delusional like that sometimes.

Doug the realtor picked me up at the Peacock Flower at one o'clock, greeting me like a long-lost best friend. His brown hair was still wet from a shower, and he had a speck of shaving cream on his check. This man lived alone. I climbed into his dented Range Rover, adjusted my floppy straw hat and brand-new Sloop Jones short tank dress, and pulled the shoulder strap across my body, pausing before I buckled. What in the name of God was that noise coming from the stereo speakers? Kenny G? I shuddered delicately and decided it would be too rude to ask him to turn it off. I would soldier on.

Doug pointed us toward the rainforest and started to talk about his relocation to the island from "Jersey." "Are you considering a permanent move here,
Katie?"

"I haven't decided," I said.

Doug kept talking. My resistance to him grew. I should have called Rashidi
and asked him to meet us out there. I tried to tune Doug's voice out, but when
I did it made me more aware of Kenny G. I knew my aversion to Doug and
Kenny was absurd. My mother's teachings haunted me. I dug deep for my
Southern charm and put it on a cheerful autopilot, muttering "uh huh" and
"you don't say" whenever he took a breath. But seriously, this could drive me
back to rum punch. No wonder he didn't have anyone around to tell him to
wipe the shaving cream from his face.

We took a different route to Annalise than the ones I'd driven with Ava and
in Rashidi's tour shuttle, and it was eye-opening. At the base of the rainforest,
we passed through a low-rent area where families lived in one-room masonry
homes, which Doug explained were made of cement-filled cinder blocks
covered in stucco. Sometimes stone, in other places, but not here. Curtains
hung over the doors and window openings. The houses stood side by side next
to run-down bars. I looked at the name above the door on one of the bars as we
passed: the Christmas Bar. Were they only open one day a year? It didn't appear
so. Patrons were lounging in the doorway and it was late August. And one
o'clock in the afternoon.

   Past the neighborhood was a sleepy little cement factory, fully operational,
it appeared. As we left it behind us, the road inclined steeply into the mountains. The twists and turns were harrowing. The thick trees crowded in from
both sides of the road, their leafy branches reaching for us and pushing us
toward the middle. On hairpin turns, I couldn't see if another vehicle was
careening dead-center down as we climbed dead-center up. My heart beat with
hummingbird's wings every time we rounded a blind left-hand curve. I closed
my eyes and prayed silently.

   We slowed to a near halt as we came upon a dumpy-looking restaurant, a
dilapidated shack under a palm-frond-roofed patio. The chairs and tables were
flimsy white plastic. Several filthy dogs lounged among them. On the other side

of the patio, the roof extended further to the elevated bathrooms, which made them almost a focal point for the diners. Nice.

"That's the Pig Bar," Doug explained. "Great food, and they serve a local drink with exotic herbs called Mamawanna. Supposedly, if she drink it, it make mamawanna. You know?" He winked.

Yuck.

"Do you want to stop and check it out?" he asked.

"No, thank you." I was itchy to get to Annalise. Still, I was curious, and asked, "Do they serve pork, or what?"

"Huh? Oh, the name? No, the owner named the bar after the giant beer-drinking pigs that live next to it. For two bucks, you can put a non-alcoholic beer into the mouth of a smelly, slobbery three-hundred-pound swine. Quite a spectacle."

"Why non-alcoholic?" I asked.

"They used to give them Budweisers, but the pigs were dying of liver disease."

Ah. I suspected this was more an economic than an animal rights decision, based on the stories Rashidi had told yesterday of dog- and cock-fighting on-island, recreational events he urged us to avoid. The whole Pig Bar thing was odd, yet curiously appealing. I filed it in my list of places to check out later as we turned onto another road.

"We're almost there," Doug said. He dodged, as best he could, potholes the size of the Rover. The craters made it even harder to stay on the correct side of the road.

But the stressful drive was worth it. To our left, Annalise burst into view. She was not quite as isolated as she had appeared yesterday when we hiked to her from the other direction. There were a handful of houses within a mile of her, respectable homes.

Then, just yards before her driveway, we passed a cluster of ramshackle huts. Dogs and kids ran between the dwellings. I saw a few adults, all with long dreadlocks, the women wearing theirs wrapped in low figure eights on the backs of their heads. Oh my.

Doug caught my expression and grinned. "Rasta village. They're squatters. The owner of the property doesn't seem to mind. They're the closest neighbors to Estate Annalise."

"Interesting," I said. And then I laughed aloud.

Doug shot me a look.

"They add to the charm," I told him.

He raised his eyebrows, but said nothing. He pulled into the driveway leading to the house and parked the Rover, and I shot out of the car, a runner from her starting blocks. There was a charge in the air, as if Annalise was thrumming with excitement, too. I checked for a connection, and my iPhone again found a signal. Annalise perched atop a high hill, and when I did a 360-degree inspection, I spotted a cell tower. Yet another comforting sign of civilization in this remote location.

I texted Collin and Emily. "Abt to spend my inheritance on a house here & never come back."

Collin replied, "Be sure it has a guest room for me & my lady friends."

Emily responded, "Liar. You'd miss me too much."

I laughed. If they knew I was really with a realtor looking at a house, they'd flip. More so if they could actually see *this* house. I snapped a quick picture from an angle that included the dilapidated Island Realty sign and included it with my next text.

"I can get this one for a steal."

"Just don't be calling me for cheap labor," wrote Collin.

"Very funny. Call me later. I want to hear abt the spa, beach, & men," Emily said.

One quick text to Nick? To break the ice between us, perhaps? No, no, no. I would not falter. Maybe before I would have included him, but not anymore.

Doug gave me my second grand tour, but Rashidi's had been much better. I picked Doug's brain as we walked the grounds.

"What would it cost to finish a place like this out?" I asked.

"Depends on whether you go Fifth Avenue or Harlem. Whatever you do, take your estimate and double it. It's hard to get anything done here, even worse if you're not local."

This jived with Ava's Island Success101 speech.

We continued our tour. I think Doug expected me to pack it in when the walk-through was over. No such luck for him. I clambered through the house and grounds with Doug in my wake three times over the next hour and a half. Doug glanced at his watch and checked his phone.

"Do you mind if I step to the driveway to make a call?" he asked.

"No problem," I said. In fact, I preferred it.

I wandered around to the backyard, where the butt of the concrete pool jutted out of the earth and ten feet into space. I decided to rough out what it would take to finish Annalise's build-out. Searching my purse for scratch paper, I pulled out the envelope from my last expense reimbursement check. That would do. I straddled the slanted concrete pool coping with the envelope in front of me on its grainy surface. I scribbled cramped notes in pencil on the work needed to make Annalise livable. The pencil traced the bumps of all the pebbles under the paper, making my writing wavery and old lady-ish.

The notes turned into a work list. My thoughts ran toward flooring and wall colors, although I did my best to step back further to the necessities of plumbing, electricity, and Sheetrock. My parents had built a house fifteen years ago, and they had talked enough about it around me that some of it stuck. Then, beside each item on the work list, I summed up rough cost estimates. I multiplied by two, then crossed it out and replaced it with a multiple of three.

It was a lot of work, but doable. For someone. Maybe even for me. One advantage of my workaholic life in Dallas—partner in a successful law practice, no kids—was my big, fat stash of cash. Add to that the life insurance I received when my parents died, and, well, I was in good shape. One and a half million dollars' worth of good shape. If money were the only issue, I could do this. But did I want to? Could I leave Dallas and everyone there behind and start over here, at Annalise?

Thump.

A perfect mango rolled to a stop at my toes, which were bare in the Reef sandals I'd stolen back from Ava. I leaned over and snatched it up. The backyard was treeless. I looked around. No humans. No animals. No other mangoes on the ground.

What the hell? "If that was you, Annalise, do it again."

Thump. Mango number two.

The second mango came from the direction of the house, but up high. I whipped around and saw her standing on the partial balcony outside the master suite. Her. The woman I had seen yesterday and in my dream of the house last night. She was crouching, one knee down and an elbow on the other knee, her skirt loose and puddling the ground around her. She held a mango in her right hand.

I whispered, "Holy Mother of God. You're real. Or I'm delusional. Or both."

I heard Doug on the phone, his voice growing louder. I glanced in his direction. When I returned my eyes to the balcony, the woman was gone.

"I am delusional," I said.

Thump. Mango number three.

This one seemed to drop straight down from thin air at waist height. I couldn't help it. I laughed. The air quickened in a light way, a joyous way. Was I making the jumbie happy? It seemed so. But I wasn't going to buy this house to please a spirit.

"I can't do this, Annalise. This isn't my real life. It's not logical. I like you and all, but you're kind of pricey for a delusion."

Except that my real life wasn't all that great. I worked in a profession that didn't thrill me. I desperately needed to sever my emotional tether to Nick, and I craved an escape from the lingering humiliation I'd carried with me since Shreveport. My parents weren't in Dallas anymore. In fact, I felt closer to them here than I had in the last year. And I hadn't had so much as a sip of alcohol since I stepped foot on this piece of property. What was keeping me in my old life, then? I couldn't come up with one damn thing other than the comfort and familiarity of habit. My life as an old fuzzy house slipper. How appealing.

Maybe I couldn't buy this property to please a spirit, but I could buy it to please Katie Connell. Katie Connell couldn't have Nick, her parents, or Bloody Marys. So maybe she could have this house. This beautiful house in this beautiful place that Katie really, really wanted.

Because I did. I really, really wanted it.

Chapter Fourteen

"I saw you talking to yourself. They say that's the way to be sure someone smart will always answer," Doug said, right behind me.

"Oh, you caught me," I said. I dropped the two mangoes I was holding and picked up my pencil and envelope. "I've made a list, and I have some ideas to talk to you about."

I peppered Doug with more questions about finish-out, the island housing market, and the accessibility of groceries and drugstores from Annalise's remote location. After he answered my volley of questions, he remarked, "Without construction experience, or, let's face it, a man around the place, this could be too much. Plus, you're isolated up here. I don't mean to scare you, but this part of the island sees some rough types, players in the island drug trade. I could show you other places, beautiful finished houses in safer neighborhoods. If you haven't been out to the condos on the East End yet, I think you'll be surprised at how much you'd like them."

This man was not listening to me. I hate it when that happens.

"Thank you, Doug, I sure do appreciate that," I said, my Texas accent and phrasing growing more pronounced as my irritation grew. "But I've made up my mind. How do I go about making an offer on Annalise?"

He looked stunned. I locked my eyes on his and pulled the brim of my hat further over my face. He raised his eyebrows—skepticism or submission?—and motioned me back to the Rover.

"Let's go back to my office and put an offer together."

Ah, he was getting smarter.

On the way back to town, Doug turned into a historian.

"You know why town is called Taino?" He didn't wait for my answer. "It's named after the original inhabitants of St. Marcos. Most people just call it Town and spell it with a capital T, though. They put a lot of stock in local, in bahn yah."

The information was interesting, but I wondered what his point was. If he had a point. I threw in some "uh huhs" again.

"You'll see a lot of locals with Taino traits: dark skin, wiry hair, short, and thick through the middle, but stocky, not fat. Most of the locals are of African descent, though. There's a large community of Dominicans, too, and a fair number of Middle Easterners. Caucasian is a minority."

I thought about it. Taino was its own version of the island soup, kallaloo, that I'd had instead of salad at lunch. Everything thrown in the pot and cooked up together. I liked the soup. I liked the island.

"I'd noticed," I said.

In the rainforest, "t'ings" were different from Taino, though. Not only was it ten degrees cooler than down in Town, but it was also no kallaloo. The rainforest of St. Marcos was a black West Indian world. A fact about which Doug was becoming more and more direct.

"The only community on St. Marcos where outsiders are truly accepted, especially white outsiders, is the East End. It's the way things are here. I need you to understand this before I write an offer for you. My conscience and all," he said, putting his hand on the center of his chest.

I damned him with the ultimate in Texas condescension. "Bless your heart, Doug. I appreciate your concern. And I'll be fine."

"All right, then. I'm done trying to talk you out of it." He pursed his lips. "One last thing. Do you want to see the nearest grocery store?"

Now that sounded like a smart thing to do. "Absolutely."

Doug took me to a medium-sized grocery called Courtyard. Sure enough, we were the only two people in the place with light pigment. It was astounding to me—humbling, really—that this was the first time in my life I had knowingly experienced minority status. I was a gecko who couldn't camouflage to match the background.

My minority status wasn't the only thing to get used to in the Courtyard grocery store. While the store was large, it wasn't up to stateside standards of cleanliness, nor was it well stocked. The produce section displayed mostly exotic fruits and vegetables that I didn't know how to cook, and the items that were familiar to me were scarce, limp, and close to rotting. I picked up an item marked "cassava" and another with a label that said "breadfruit." Completely foreign.

The cassava fell from my hand. I set the breadfruit down. As I knelt to try to pick the cassava up, I bumped into a small woman I hadn't seen. Actually, I bumped into her walker. She squawked.

"Oh, ma'am, I'm so sorry," I cried. I stood up quickly and put my hand on her back. "I am such a klutz. I dropped a . . . vegetable . . . and I didn't see you, and, well, I'm sorry."

"She's fine," a voice behind me said, in a "no thanks to you" sort of way.

A big hand extended the errant cassava in front of me, and when I turned to face him, it was Jacoby.

I took it from him. "Thank you, Officer Jacoby. I am so sorry."

"Mind yourself around the elders. My grandmother is fragile."

So warm, so friendly. Not. "Yes, of course." I remembered my manners. "A pleasant good afternoon to you, ma'am, and to you, Jacoby."

The ancient wisp of a woman said, "Good afternoon, dear."

Jacoby said nothing.

I walked away, smarting. It didn't appear I was growing on Jacoby.

"Did you run into friends?" Doug asked, rejoining me with two bottles of ginger beer.

"Not hardly." I motioned toward the exit. "I'm ready whenever you are."

I tried to resist looking back at Jacoby as we walked out, but I couldn't stop myself from stealing a quick glance. I shouldn't have. Out of uniform and in baggy black jeans, he was even more imposing. He glared at me, the very picture of malevolence. Note to self: Ask Ava what Jacoby has against me.

When we got back into the Rover, Doug handed me a bottle of the ginger beer. "A local soft drink," he said. "One of the local favorites. It's like root beer with a ginger bite."

I took it from him and sipped it. The spice was almost peppery. "Thank you," I said.

Doug asked, "So, if you were to buy this place, would you get a mortgage or what?"

I cleared my throat. "No. Just cash."

"Oh, wow, well, that changes things. The owner—a bank that foreclosed on the property—highly prefers cash. This will really help you."

I didn't say anything. The bad juju from my Jacoby encounter had messed with my head. You should go back to the resort and sleep on this overnight, I told myself.

Doug said, "Last time I'm going to ask. Wouldn't you prefer to sleep on this, think it over, and get back to me tomorrow? Annalise will still be there. I'd hate to see you get in over your head."

What was he thinking? Sleeping on it was a terrible idea.

"I'm a decisive person, Doug. I'm making an offer."

So I did, and I couldn't even blame it on rum punch. I didn't take time for reasoned deliberation. I acted exactly opposite from the way I would counsel my clients. I didn't seek advice from my new island friends or my loved ones back home. I didn't do any research or consult any experts. I ignored the implications on my life in Texas. Something about my voodoo-like connection to Annalise offered salvation. Maybe it was crazy, but I believed.

It was an impulsive decision, but hell, there was no way they would accept my lowball offer anyway.

Chapter Fifteen

I decided the offer on Annalise should be my little secret. It helped me keep it out of my mind, since at least I wasn't talking about it to anyone. What I didn't hide was that I was going to try to remain alcohol-free for the rest of the trip. It seemed right, as if the time had come. Just like the time had been right to make the offer on Annalise.

"It won't hurt me to dry out for a few days with you," Ava said. "But the universe hate a vacuum." She switched to Continental and spoke like she had a clothespin on her nose. "We must replace deprivation with indulgence."

"Chocolate?" I suggested.

Back to Local. "If I going to suffer, I going to lose weight. I got something better in mind."

And so we sampled the resort's spa treatments and "body and mind experiences." I embraced Ava's indulgence philosophy and tried every decadent pampering the spa had to offer.

I loved the spa from the moment we stepped through the door. Soft steel-pan music seeped out of hidden speakers and a delicious coconut scent tickled my nose. We changed in a locker room reminiscent of my suite's bathroom, then entered a waiting area where we sipped cucumber water in front of a burbling stone fountain.

I totally got into the treatments, the indulgences on the "body" side of their brochure. If I were naturally the self-indulgent type, I would have someone wash my hair in a garden courtyard while I got a foot massage every day, but my parents had raised me to be too frugal for that. I was worried that my credit card bill would send me into a grand mal seizure, as it was. But as for the "mind," let's just say I wouldn't be joining a Bikram yoga studio anytime soon. All the clearing of the mind stuff just gave me more time to stress out. I said as much to Ava after we walked out of my one and only meditation session.

"It help if you don't bring your phone in with you," she said. "He not going to call."

"What? Who?" I asked.

She rolled her eyes.

Ava was right. About not bringing the phone, and that Nick wasn't going to call. But Doug might. I snuck another peek at my phone. He had promised to contact me as soon as he heard something. I had promised myself I would patiently wait for him to contact me. I was the epitome of lime. Yeah, right. But I was trying.

After a very full day, we had run out of spa services to sample, so we hit one of the resort's beaches. And it was there that I finally discovered my personal key to turning off the bedeviling voice in my head: beach walking. My brain rested when my feet were moving, and when I went beyond cell range. The sound of the waves soothed me. The water on my toes was a mother's kiss, the warm sun on my skin her hug. When we had hiked the length of the two beaches adjacent to the spa, we ventured outward. I swear, we tramped every beach on the island over the next two days. White sand. Brown sand. Lava rock. Water-smoothed pebbles. Miniature mountains of gray boulders. My sedentary and sunless lifestyle was turned on its head. I'd never had a problem with my weight, but lately I'd noticed that all of me was sagging more than it used to. Now my butt was perking up as my head cleared. Bonus.

I spent most of my time with Ava, but not all of it. On one of the days, I sweated through a nerve-wracking lunch alone on the boardwalk downtown, surrounded by enthusiastic drinkers of fruity rum concoctions. I couldn't even enjoy myself. I was practically chanting "Thou shall not drink" to keep a mango banana daiquiri at bay. The leathery couple at the next table pretended not to be scared of me. It definitely was easier when Ava was there to abstain alongside me. And to remind me to put my phone down. Why hadn't I heard from Doug?

By my last day on St. Marcos, the aching desire for just one rum punch— and the shakes that I tried to pretend weren't happening—was tapering off. Thank God. A shakeless me could talk to my creepy investigator, Walker. I decided to barge in unannounced after breakfast, even though that was practically the middle of the night on St. Marcos. He'd told me that I couldn't expect results yet, but I needed to look him in the eye one more time before I left so he'd know I was serious about the work I'd hired him to do.

When I got to his office door, I stopped for a moment, gripped by a momentary uncertainty. I surveyed his street front. No shingle hung announcing his place of business. Just the number, 32. Through the window, I saw the back of his head. I heard his voice through the glass pane in the door. He was talking to someone, but I couldn't tell if he was on the phone or if there was someone in there with him in the back of his office, not visible to me on the street. I leaned close to the glass so I could hear better.

"I said it's not a problem that I can't handle. I think you just need to let me worry about my part of the business, and you worry about yours. Have I let you down before?" he was saying, and not quietly.

I froze, ears straining. I was totally wigged out. I put my hand on the doorknob.

"That's what I thought. Now, if you can just keep your pants zipped, maybe we won't have any more problems like her." He swung around in his chair and looked out through the door at me. Now I could see his headset. Telephone.

Damn. He'd seen me eavesdropping. I held steady, then turned the knob and walked in.

"Gotta go," he said. He reached down and pressed a button on his phone.

"You're back," he said.

I stepped fully into the dark office that was much brighter in the afternoon sun. "I am. I leave the island tomorrow, and I just wanted to stop by one more time, in case you'd had time to give any more thought to my case. And to make sure you had my card." I stood close to his desk and held one out.

He gestured at his desk. Today there were mounds of paper where days before there had been only dust. "No. I've only had time to give thought to the cases that are in line before yours." He lifted one hand in a stop gesture of refusal. "I have your card and your number, though, and I'll call you when I get to it."

I put the card back in my purse. "That's fine. I also realized I forgot to tell you something. Maybe it's nothing, but the police couldn't find a ring that my mother always wore. It was a small gold band, with the name Hannah engraved in it. When you talk to the hotel staff, I don't know, I thought maybe you could ask about it? If you found the ring, it would help me resolve things in my mind. About how they died."

And then he grinned at me, without any smile in his eyes, like a crocodile's smile. "Duly noted."

I took a step back, and then another. "As long as I know my case is on your list and you'll get to it as soon as you can, that's all I need to know, then," I said, and reached behind me, missing the doorknob, groping for it, fumbling, and then grabbing it tight. I twisted and pushed. "Thank you for your help."

I burst out of the dark space. I could see he was still watching me, so I turned back to him and waved. Idiot, I thought. You're acting like a brainless beauty queen in a parade. I put my hand back down.

Thinking of Ava's categories of people on the island, I put him in the "running from" category, and I imagined it was from something no good. That man gave me the creeps. If there were another investigator on St. Marcos, I'd forfeit my retainer with Walker with no regrets and hire someone new. But according to Jacoby, there wasn't anyone else. I shook off the sensation of those amphibian eyes following me and got back in my car.

That afternoon, I lay draped over a lounge chair on my patio, attempting a siesta. I was on the final day of a spa vacation. It was practically obligatory to try things like afternoon naps, but my type A personality not only wouldn't nap, it refused even to fake it. I decided solitaire on my phone would suffice as a nap replacement.

The phone rang and brought my game to a halt. My heart shot up into my throat when I saw the number on caller ID, like it was a target I had hit with a sledgehammer in one of those high-striker carnival games, the ones where muscle-bound high school jocks tried to ring the bell at the top of a pole. Ding ding, I was a winner! It was Doug. Finally. This was it. My life was about to change forever. I answered.

"Katie, you're not going to believe this. I can't believe it, and I'm so sorry. I'm the listing agent, after all, and I didn't even know." His voice sounded more angry than sorry.

Nothing he'd said so far sounded like the words I wanted to hear. I wondered if I hung up the phone whether he would call back with different words. I hovered my index finger over End, but I didn't press it.

"The bank accepted a different offer. It didn't even come through me. If they think they're going to get out of paying my commission just by making an end run and selling this house to somebody's second cousin, they're crazy. By the time I got your offer in front of Ms. Nesbitt, she'd already said yes to someone else."

"Who's Ms. Nesbitt?" I asked, for something to say.

"The Bank of St. Marcos officer handling the property. The one I had better not learn is getting some kind of kickback on this deal. But I digress." He paused for me to speak, but I didn't.

"Katie? Are you there?" he asked.

I sat on the patio of my posh suite in silence, aware of every cell in my body crying out in loss. I was losing, again, losing something else. Something important. Not just a house, or a spirit. I was losing myself.

This time I didn't pull back when my finger sought the End key.

Chapter Sixteen

The return to Dallas was jarring. The concrete. The traffic. The gritty air. So many people. A secret part of me had started to believe I could escape to the islands, disappear into the ripple left behind by my parents, and leave my old life in the states behind. It wasn't a wildly original dream, but the difference between me and everyone else that had dreamed it was that, for me, it was a realistic one. I was *so close* to grabbing that brass ring, so close.

Oh, who was I kidding? Every beach bum that ever stowed away in a bottle of Captain Morgan's thought they were the only one. I was a mere ditto.

I slunk into my condo on Sunday night. The phone rang and kept ringing. I didn't have to check caller ID to know who was calling. I sent Collin and Emily a carefully worded message about my wildly successful trip. So I exaggerated a little. I needed some re-entry space.

I didn't get any at work. I'd hardly had time to boot up my computer, much less fetch coffee from the break room, when Gino showed up at my door. Nine o'clock sharp.

"Thank God you're back, Katie. You're in trial tomorrow," Gino said. He hadn't bothered with "Hello, how was your trip."

So much for a quiet Monday easing back into things at the firm. "You're kidding, right?" I asked.

Gino dropped into the chair in front of my desk. "Nope. We got a call Friday morning. A big shot defendant dumped his law firm just a few days before his trial. He insists he has to have you as his lawyer. He agreed to pay double your rate when I told him you weren't available."

He dropped a bulging redweld accordion file in front of me and its contents gushed out all over my pristine desk. An 8x10 photo surfed the top of the overflow. I stared into the eyes of Zane McMillan in a mug shot. The same Zane McMillan who'd led the Dallas Mavericks to their second NBA title the year before and topped the league in scoring. A big shot, indeed. Another sports "hero" who didn't play by the rules the rest of the world followed.

"Zane McZillion?" I said. "Why would he ask for me? I've never even met him." I peeled the mug shot off the top of the stack and rifled through the documents. "What did he do, or supposedly do?" I envisioned a civil suit filed by an angry photographer who'd gotten too close to the mercurial basketball star. Last season, Zane had wreaked havoc on some paparazzo's camera equipment to the tune of several thousand dollars in damages.

"He's accused of raping a woman he met in the VIP lounge at Good Sportz. Haven't you heard about it? It was tabloid fodder all summer."

Somehow I'd missed it, but then, something had kept me a smidge distract-ed. "Whoa, a rape trial? Surely you can find someone better suited to this case. What about Shannon? If Mr. McMillan insists on me, maybe I could be her second chair?"

Shannon was the firm's token criminal law expert, and a fine attorney. Whenever one of our rich clients' progeny ran afoul of the law, Shannon came to the rescue. Usually this meant drug possession or a DUI, not rape, but still, she knew her stuff. I, on other hand, didn't have a shred of criminal law experience.

"Shannon's out recovering from liposuction, but she said you can call her if you have any questions. You've handled sexual harassment cases. This is almost the same thing."

I searched for signs of dementia in Gino. "They're nothing alike. Nothing at all," I argued.

He waved his hand back and forth dismissively. "You're great in court. You'll do fine."

I was not so sure. "Why did he dump his lawyers at the last minute? That's a bad sign." Surely this fact alone would sway Gino from the insanity of me trying this case tomorrow.

"They wanted him to testify. He didn't want to."

"That's pretty weak. Did you talk to them?"

"They didn't return my calls, but I asked Zane for an explanation, and he gave me one that satisfied me." Gino stopped there, but I raised my puny eyebrows until they quivered with exertion, so he went further. "He thinks only bad PR can come of his testimony, and bad PR could threaten his big Nike endorsement deal. That's good enough for me. His case is a slam dunk without his testimony, anyway.

He waited for me to laugh at his basketball humor. I was not in the mood to oblige him.

I played my trump card. "I can't take this case. I'm philosophically opposed to criminal defense work. My dad was the chief of police, for crying out loud. My brother's a police officer. This goes against everything I am."

And Gino played his. "You really can't afford scruples right now."

I burst into flames, loudly. "Excuse me? I brought in a million-dollar fee for the firm last month."

"And that's all you did for the last year. You know how much it costs to run a law firm like Hailey & Hart. Do you have anything lined up, now that Burnside is over?"

A cold dread doused my flames. I mentally ticked through a list of several small matters I was working on, but the truth was, Gino was right. I had nothing substantial. "No," I admitted. "But I'll get out and find new work."

"Partners have to pull their share of the load. This is a double-fees case. End of discussion."

Yes, it was. I tried a new tack. "Can we at least try to get the court date pushed back?"

"I filed for a continuance Friday. We lost. It's in the file." Gino stopped the argument. "Emily and Nick prepped all Friday and through the weekend. They'll get you ready."

I swallowed hard. Nick. Gino was making me work with Nick. "Did you tell him you were giving me this case?" I asked, hoping Gino hadn't heard the squeak in my voice when I said "me."

"Yes." Gino glanced at his watch. "Sorry, but I've got to get to another meeting."

"Can I have a second chair?" I flailed like a drowner.

He edged toward the door. "I wish we had someone who could, but it's summer. Everyone's out. We just don't have the manpower.. You don't need one, though. You, Emily, and Nick are a great team. Katie, don't worry about this case. There's an eyewitness who saw and heard it all and is on Team

McMillan." He stopped just outside my office for a moment. "Oh, and I almost forgot. Your client will be here to meet with you in twenty minutes."

And then he was gone, leaving me short-circuited from emotional overload. Tomorrow. I wouldn't even finish meeting with the client and reviewing the file in time to call Shannon with questions until tonight. This had malpractice written all over it.

Chapter Seventeen

My new client arrived before I'd finished reading the first document in the file. Lovely. I went to meet him in the reception area. Tan on beige on drab brown accented by more tan met my eyes. After a week on St. Marcos, the expensively understated scheme seemed dreary. McMillan, dressed in black from head to toe, didn't exactly blend into the décor. He leaned over our entry desk, chatting up the receptionist. Tina, all of twenty-three years old, simpered and gushed, putty in his very large hands.

I hated to interrupt such a special moment. "Mr. McMillan?"

Zane stood up, and up, and up, and up. He was the tallest person I'd ever seen, but he wasn't just tall. He was enormous. His file claimed he was 6'9" and 270 pounds. I believed it. And all muscle and bone, encased in baggy black jeans riding low on his behind to showcase his black Calvin Klein underwear. Nice.

He pulled a cellophane-wrapped item from his pocket and tossed it onto Tina's desk. "I always leave a package of McZillions when I meet a pretty lady."

Please God, not condoms. My eyes darted around the lobby. No other clients. Only Tina to worry about, and the sexual harassment lawsuit McMillan could bring on our firm. I moved closer, ready to snatch them from her hands.

She beamed and ripped the package open, then out came something that didn't appear to bear any relation to contraception. I exhaled. Long shoelaces dangled from her fingers, sparkling in the light of her smile. He thumped his chest twice with his fist and shot her a peace sign. Finally, he acknowledged my greeting.

"Yo, McZillion here. Are you taking me to my lawyer? Whoa, no, you are my lawyer. You look like your picture," he said. He looked me over, head to toe. "Fine, damn fine."

I tried not to let my distaste show. Yet. "I'm Katie Connell, your attorney. Nice to meet you." I grasped and shook his hand. It swallowed mine whole. "Right this way."

I escorted Zane to my office through the quiet main hallway of the firm. Or at least it was normally quiet. News of Zane's arrival had zipped through the instant message boards at warp speed from the tips of Tina's typing fingers, and every single human in the firm had invented a reason to be standing in the hallway. Zane strutted by them like an oversized rooster, and held his hand out to slap high fives as he went past. The fleshy sounds of slap, slap, slap followed me. Finally, we reached the celebrity-worship-free zone of my office.

Zane dwarfed the same chair that Gino had sat in a half hour before. He leaned back, legs askew, and said, "What now, lawyer lady?"

I had intended to prep him for the do's and don'ts of trial, explain my rapidly-percolating action plan, and run some strategy by him. But I had a question for him first.

"Mr. McMillan," I said.

He interrupted in a voice that I assumed was "street," but I wasn't down with the 'hood, so who knew. "You can call me Zane or McZ if you want. Nobody calls me Mr. McMillan."

I was tempted to call him Vanilla Ice. "Zane. My partner Gino Hart said that you asked to work specifically with me. Have we met? Or do I have someone to thank for the referral?"

"Honey, if we'd met, you'd remember me. I always give my women something to remember me by."

I held up my hand in the "stop" position and just managed to stop it from continuing on to the "gag me" one, too.

"Sorry, just playing with you." Witchu. Oh, brother. "No, we don't know each other. But you come highly recommended."

"By whom?"

"Shit, I can't remember. By lots of people. I told them what I was looking for, and they said you was it."

No one to punish. Great. The pain was all mine.

I spent two hours with "McZ," an exercise for which I deserved combat pay. After I was able to pry him out of my office by pleading my very real and urgent need to prep for his trial, I hooked up with Emily. We crammed for the rest of the day like it was a final in a class we'd never attended. She had done a brilliant job putting together our exhibits and trial notebooks, though, and she confessed she'd called Shannon more than once for help. Emily should have gone to law school; she was wicked smart. It was just my good luck that she hadn't. My blood pressure went down ten points due to her efforts alone, and I read every word she had put together for me on Zane's case. I drafted my opening statement. I typed out witness questions and listed our exhibits.

All of this was good, but none of it substituted for hearing what Nick had to say after working the case for three days. And Nick was nowhere to be found. It was after five. Where was he? The trial started at 9:30 in the morning.

I looked out my office window. No beach. No ocean. No canopy of branches and vines. Levolor blinds sliced the views of traffic gridlocked on I-35. On the wall beside the window, the big hand moved steadily toward the six on the clock, the clock my parents had given me to hang in my office when I'd first graduated from law school. My heart hung low in my chest. I was already back into the thick of a job I hated, on this case of all cases, without having made meaningful progress on the investigation into their deaths. How easily my life here pulled me away from what was important.

Like Collin's birthday. I dialed his number. "Am I still your birthday date, or have you thrown me over for some sweet young thing?" I asked when he answered.

"I would never," he said.

"That's exactly what you did last year," I retorted. And he had, in the wake of his humiliation at the hands of his former fiancée. She'd been a cellist in the Dallas symphony. He'd chased anything in a skirt that looked fast and easy since then.

"Who, me? Well, this year I am all yours, sis. Tell me about your trip."

"I'll have to save it for dinner Thursday night. I got stuck defending that basketball player, Zane McMillan, in a rape trial. I need to get back to work," I told him.

"What?" Collin barked. "Your dog has fleas, Katie. I'm warning you."

"It seems OK," I told him. "We've got a witness. The girl's own roommate has sided with our guy. I just hate taking a criminal defense case, because it feels disloyal to you and Dad."

"It doesn't exactly light me up with happy, either." No one would ever fault Collin's honesty. "Listen to me. I didn't work this one, but I'm tight with the guys that did. They're confident. They're beyond confident. They're giddy this one's going to trial. Fleas," he said again, drawing the word out this time. "Be careful."

"That's it? Fleas? Can you tell me anything else, or give me the name of someone to talk to?"

"You know I couldn't, even if I knew the details, which I don't. I've said too much already."

We ended the call. Great. I hung up and closed my eyes. I'd renew my efforts to talk Zane into a plea bargain. To ward off my mounting stress, I tried to use one of the visualization techniques I learned at the Peacock Flower Spa. Picture yourself in a peaceful, happy place, they taught us. I pictured myself barefoot and walking on the beach beside the flying fish hut. That didn't work. Maybe I should have paid more attention to the instructor. I tried again. I pictured myself strolling through Annalise's orchard. Standing in the backyard with a mango at my feet. A pungent odor filled my nostrils. Ah. Heaven was the scent of fermenting mangoes. I concentrated on breathing through my nose so I wouldn't lose the smell.

"Good. You're still here." Nick's voice. The scent of mangoes wafted away. I opened my eyes slowly.

The sight of his face was a gulp of fresh air after too long in a stale room. My traitorous heart fell for him all over again, just that easily. God, who was I kidding that I could forget about him? I loved to look at him. I loved him, dammit, and it was just awful. I held onto that breath of air as long as I could. Keep it normal, Katie, keep it light.

"Yep, I'm still here, and very eager to talk to you," I said. "About the case, I mean."

Nick stood in front of my desk holding a redweld folder. "Did you have time to review the file today?"

"Every word of it. It seems straightforward. The state will claim that Zane gave the alleged victim, a Miss Tabitha Brown, a ride home from Good Sportz, and that when she said goodbye outside her apartment, he forced his way in behind her, and then tied her to her bed with his shoelaces and raped her."

"Right," he said. He propped his redweld on my desk and held it with both hands.

"But we've got her roommate, Sherry something-or-other, who's going to provide some colorful testimony about Tabitha dragging Zane into the house, climbing all over him, and telling him to tie her up and give it to her rough," I said.

"Talmadge. Sherry Talmadge. Right again," he said.

"Here's a question for you. Do you know if there were any problems with the search of Zane's house? Zane's making a big deal about how the police took things they shouldn't have. I think he's watched too much CSI. I don't know if it was a good search or not, but if the whole theory of our defense is that Ms. Brown had sex with him voluntarily, I can't see how this matters anyway."

"I haven't seen anything about problems with the search. Sounds like a lawyer question to me."

"Yeah, I guess so. I'll have to research it tonight. So, what don't I know, and what else are you working on?"

"I'm trying to track down and verify all the information in the file we got from his old law firm, and I'm making good headway. I don't want any surprises in court."

"Agreed."

"What is your plan, then, tomorrow?" I asked.

He lifted a hand and straightened the lapel on his shirt. Nick didn't dress up unless we were in trial. He wore khakis and an orange golf-type shirt today, with the words "Aransas Pilots Association" on the left breast. "That depends. Do you want me there to help you pick the jury?"

Nick had a sociology degree with a minor in psychology from Texas A&M University in Corpus Christi. Lots of firms paid jury consultants big bucks, but Nick had filled this role very well for us in the last year. What he couldn't intuit from observing the potential jurors, he could find by working his investigative magic online. Nick's advice to me in the Burnside case had resulted in the selection of a pivotal juror, someone I hadn't thought we should keep, but who ultimately became the jury foreman in our multimillion-dollar verdict.

And even if he was terrible at it, I'd still want him there.

"Absolutely," I said.

"OK. I'll come for jury selection. You can text me anytime if you have questions or need me to chase something down for you."

I thought, "Actually, Nick, I've done that before and it didn't go so well for me."

But I said, "That sounds good to me." If nothing else, I'd get to spend the morning with him.

He picked his file back up and turned to go.

"Nick," I said.

He stopped in my doorway, his body facing me, one hand on the frame. "Yes?"

"Are you OK—I mean, I assume you're OK—that Gino has us working together on this? After what you said in Shreveport. I just don't . . ." I got tangled in my words and couldn't finish.

"I'm fine," he said.

I tried again. "I didn't ask for the case. I didn't want the case."

"I said it's fine. It is. It's fine."

We stared at each other for a moment, and then he turned and left my office. Maybe it would all be fine. Maybe this case would bridge the gulf between us. Maybe this was the start of something wonderful. A tiny match touched the wick of the candle in my heart. Maybe.

Chapter Eighteen

I arrived at the courthouse during the morning rush and looked up at the utilitarian hunk of gray concrete that punched a bleak hole in the sky. I remembered when the city built it, and how my father had grumbled about it.

"The old red courthouse was just fine. I can't find my way around in that new place," he'd said on the way into the kitchen, where Mom was cooking dinner. He'd tried to swipe a piece of chicken-fried steak. She'd swatted his hand and smiled.

She took us to see Dad testify in the new building once when Collin and I were in high school, but I don't remember much of it. The earth rotated around me in those days. Going to court had irritated me, had interrupted my all-important social life. The courthouse seemed like a prison, with inmates allowed to roam free in its crowded halls. It must have been a big case, for her to pull us out of school. Collin always said that was the day he decided he would follow in Dad's footsteps. As I walked into the building, I wished I could remember more about it.

Even more desperate souls roamed the halls today than on that first visit years ago. Their odors mixed into a smell at once indefinable and yet absolutely recognizable to me as court. Stress. I touched my purse-sized Lysol antibacterial spray and Clorox wipes for reassurance. I studied the blank faces streaming past me. How many people had passed through this building on their way to a life sentence? How many had walked out free? The building stood impervious to all the drama. Cold, distant, aloof.

I took the elevator up to the fifth floor, to the courtroom of Judge Hutchison, who would preside over our trial. I'd met him at a party once, and he had a reputation for being unpredictable. Hopefully he would be unpredictable in a way that was good for us. He had assigned us three days on his docket, and he dang well expected us to use that and nothing more. Three days of purgatory for me. It was a tight schedule, but I was glad for it.

This courtroom looked almost exactly like the one I remembered from my visit as a teenager. The monochrome room had wooden benches for the spectators, a paneled jury box, and a large area for wooden benches. Dad had sat in a paneled witness box to the left of the judge, just like the configuration in this courtroom. The décor was stark. No paintings hung on the walls. The two tacky pre-fab counsel tables loaded with high-tech equipment gave the courtroom an unintended flea-market ambience.

The only thing in there that looked really good was Nick. He was wearing a navy suit with a blue shirt—standard trial attire for men—and a navy tie with angular shapes in yellow, white, and black. It looked like a geometry quiz question. He'd tamed his unruly dark hair, but I knew it wouldn't take long for it to reassert its independence.

Focus, you idiot, I told myself, and I pretended to review notes from my file.

Opposing counsel arrived and set up at their table. Since this was my first and hopefully last criminal trial, they were new faces to me, prosecutors for the state. The older prosecutor walked over and introduced himself, a young woman right behind him.

He leaned in and made sincere and meaningful eye contact. "Mack Duncan," he said, putting my hand into a vise lock as he pumped it. I winced. He'd have to loosen his killer grip before he ran for public office. He handed me a business card with his free hand. How ambidextrous of him.

"Junie. Junie Timms," second chair said, shaking my hand without inflicting violence.

I'd seen a lot of Macks in my day. He couldn't hide his small-town Texas roots, nor did he try to. His accent would work well with the jury, as would his graying blond hair cut with military precision. Junie looked fresh out of law school. Her ginormous emerald-cut diamond engagement ring dominated both my first impression and all of her attention. The sucker shined like a disco ball, so it wasn't surprising she couldn't tear her eyes away from it. I wondered how much longer until she turned in her resignation.

"Nice to meet you both," I said.

"I knew your father, and I'm sorry for your loss. We worked together many times. He was a great man," Mack told me.

My eyes burned. "Thank you very much," I said.

Junie turned to Mack, confused. "Did I know him?" she asked.

His jaw bulged, but he answered her with no trace of irritation. "Chief of police for Dallas for ten years, Frank Connell."

Junie's jaw dropped. "Oh," she said. She looked over at McMillan.

I straightened my posture.

"Honestly, I was surprised to see his daughter had taken this case," Mack added. He paused to give me time to say something stupid or angry, but I just thought it instead. "Almost as surprised as I am that McMillan hasn't taken a deal. The plea bargain offer stands. Five years for sexual assault. He could be out in less than two years, if he's a good boy."

I held up my hand to stop him. I had called Zane last night, and he gave me emphatic instructions on plea offers. "Mr. McMillan is unwilling to enter any plea bargain agreement that results in a felony on his record or jail time. Your offer to him includes both. Unless you've got something better, his response of no still stands as well."

"He's making a big mistake," Junie piped in.

Now there was no mistaking the irritation on Mack's face, but he reined it in, as before. "This offer is withdrawn, then. Any further plea discussions will start from a clean slate."

"Understood. Thank you. Now, if you'll excuse me, I need to resume preparation for voir dire."

I lied. I wasn't preparing for jury selection. I was trying not to throw up. I went to the bathroom and splashed cold water on my face. I told myself, "You didn't create this mess, you just have to get through it. Double fees. Focus on the double fees."

When I returned, the bailiff was leading in the potential jurors. They soon overflowed the spectator benches. This was the type of case people try to get picked for. Normally, the excuses to get out of jury duty are numerous and weak. Everyone has sick kids and nonrefundable airfare on jury selection day. Ah, the power of celebrity.

Nick sat on one side of me, Emily on his far side. Zane sat on the other side of me. His large body lounged uncomfortably close. He was also dressed up for court, but, despite my instructions yesterday to tone it down, he had chosen a shiny black suit with fat white pinstripes, a white shirt starched to pop, and a sparkly red tie that looked like he'd dunked it in a vat of glitter glue. He had arrived with a black bowler perched over his shaved head. It now sat in front of him on the table, but only because I'd made him take it off. His black oxfords, size seventeen, were squared off at the toe box. Maybe this was his conservative outfit.

No matter what he wore, the result would have been the same. Every eye in the room locked onto the effervescent grin on Zane's face. He just didn't get it. I'd already had to stop him from signing autographs for the court staff.

Nick whispered in my ear, his breath rustling my hair, "He's not impressing the juror candidates. Can you do anything?"

I resisted the urge to lean into Nick's breath. Instead, I passed Zane a note: "No smiling. Look serious."

He flashed the grin at me, crumpled my note in a ball, and did a pretend jump shot from his seat to deposit it in the trash can at the end of the row of counsel tables. He raised his arms triumphantly and mouthed, "Three pointer."

Lord help me not kill this man before the jury reaches a verdict.

Judge Hutchison entered the courtroom, and we all rose until the bailiff asked us to take our seats. The judge preferred things to move crisply, and within minutes he had delivered his opening speech to the jury pool. Voir dire had begun.

Once again, Nick and I had to lean close to speak. I felt my breath mix with his. Heaven. "Strike number four. I don't like the way he's looking at Zane," Nick said.

"I think we should keep number eleven. He sounds like he has an open mind," I said.

Nick was as professional as always, sharp and on top of his game, but one thing was markedly different from the Burnside trial. He was distant. He might be sitting next to me, but he stayed ten million miles apart in all the ways that counted. His physical nearness was torturing me, intoxicating me. I wanted it to end, I wanted it to last forever. The "last forever" part won out, and I worked as slowly as I dared, debating issues with him far longer than necessary. I couldn't stop myself. It hurt so good.

As we neared the end of voir dire, I tried to think of excuses to get him to stay and help with the trial. But I couldn't. I had Emily, and he wasn't a paralegal. I knew it, and he knew it. My stomach ached. I barely even registered when we got the jury we wanted. Yay us. Woo hoo. Nick would leave now.

The judge dismissed us all for lunch. "Do you want to grab a bite with us before you take off, Nick?" I asked.

"No, I've got to get going," he said. He was packing his notepad and pen into his briefcase as he spoke, and he didn't meet my gaze. My hopeful, pleading gaze. My limpid, longing gaze. I had put myself together that morning, too, hoping to impress him. A classic black Worth pant suit that Emily told me made my butt look good. Black slingbacks instead of traditional pumps. My long wavy hair in a loose French twist with the perfect number of tendrils escaping around my face. All for naught.

He stood up and walked away.

It sounds so simple, doesn't it? To get up and walk away? Innocuous, impersonal. And so final. I was nothing to him. Nothing more than a lawyer at the firm that paid him. And he was so close to everything to me.

"Honey, are you all right?" Emily asked. She put her hand on my forearm. "You're pale as a bedsheet."

"Migraine," I lied.

"I'll get your Immitrex and the emergency bag of Lay's," she said, leaning over to dig in my briefcase for pills and potato chips. Her bangs knocked the edge of the table as she bent over, but her head missed it by two inches.

"Thank you," I whispered. *Thank you for letting me lie to you and pretending you believe me.*

The afternoon might have gone fine except that the post-Nick migraine I'd lied to Emily about slammed into me like an eighteen-wheeler for real, right when we started opening statements. Unfortunately, my migraine drug makes me into a drooling zombie with no control of my lips. Not good when you're making your big impression on the twelve people who will decide your client's fate. So I held off from taking my big white pill as long as I could, only swallowing it toward the end of Mack's predictable yet well-delivered opening statement. I took my turn after him, fighting not to let the jury see my pain, willing my tense shar-pei face to smooth out into a golden retriever calm. I had rehearsed my opening statement late into the previous night, so I was able to deliver it from memory, even if I couldn't dial up as much passion and conviction as I'd hoped. When the deadening side effects of my meds hit with full force about the time I finished speaking, I slumped back into my seat. My heavy head felt like it pulled my body into a sideways list.

Luckily, the state put on its case first. All I had to do was lodge the right objections and cross-examine the witness. Two more hours and the judge would send us home. I could do this.

Mack first called to the stand the officer who had responded to dispatch after Tabitha's call to 911. I could barely follow the questioning through my brain fog, but thankfully Emily was no stranger to the impact of my Immitrex. Whenever Mack did something particularly offensive to the rules of evidence, she knocked her knee into mine and whispered the appropriate objection under her breath, sending me leaping to my feet and slurring, "Hearsay. I object, Your Honor." Judge Hutchison cocked a bushy eyebrow the first time this happened, but he didn't remark on my odd behavior. Still, I didn't win many objections. Emily and I continued our Abbott and Costello act through the rest of the afternoon and the state's witnesses.

As soon as the judge dismissed us for the day, I made my goodbyes and got the hell out of there. I didn't want to imagine what the two prosecutors were thinking about me. I was too sick to care and too sick to drive. I took a taxi home and left my car parked in the downtown garage.

At my condo, I managed to stay upright long enough to prepare for the next day, then I took another migraine pill and flopped onto my bed, hoping to sleep it off. No such luck. The pain kept me awake. If I didn't take my meds early enough in the migraine cycle, then nothing could stop the train. And the train was here, blowing its whistle so close to my head that my eardrums collapsed inward and my brain was threatening to explode.

Finally, about two a.m., the migraine broke and I fell asleep. Almost as soon as I'd drifted off, I jerked awake with the after-image of the young black woman from Annalise seared into my cerebral cortex, beckoning me from the front door of the house, standing between my parents. Shit.

"Leave me alone. Torture the jerk that bought the house out from under me."

I stared at the ceiling until I dozed again. It felt like only moments until I jerked awake a second time, now with visions of Nick taking over my dreams.

But it wasn't just any dream. These were my spontaneous combustion dreams. The kind that are great if you're a teenage boy, but aren't so great if you're a thirty-five-year-old woman rejected by the object of your desire. Over and over, I woke up sweating and thrashing, orgasms ripping through me.

"Stop it," I cried. I turned on the lights. I leaned against the headboard.

At six thirty, my alarm woke me. I was still sitting upright in bed, and I was a wreck, a literal freakin' sleep-deprived wreck. I forced myself into an icy-cold shower and let the needles of water pierce my consciousness. I had a criminal defendant counting on me, never mind that he was an asshole that I couldn't stand and who I suspected was guilty of something horrible, maybe even the rape in question. I had no backup, there was no second chair attorney waiting in the wings. I had to get into a taxi, wobble into that courthouse, and zealously represent him. Period.

I needed a power outfit. I jumped out of the water and into my black Salvatore Ferragamo pumps. I zipped up a black Ellen Tahiri dress and topped it with a white jacket, conservatively mirroring Zane's obnoxious look from yesterday. I ran from my lobby to the waiting taxi I had scheduled the night before, and we sped to the courthouse.

I could do this. I had to do this.

Chapter Nineteen

I dumped my briefcase onto the counsel table with five minutes to spare. Emily looked at me with round blue eyes and raised eyebrows. Her long blonde hair was defying gravity, as usual, in a way that said, "I got up an hour early to sculpt this perfection." Her nails were bright red, freshly painted. She wore a white blouse with tuxedo pleats under her version of Nick's navy suit from the day before. She was bold and confident, everything that I was not today.

"I'll be fine," I said before she could ask.

"You look rode hard and put up wet," she said.

"That's enough, Miss Rodeo Amarillo," I replied, but without rancor. My friend did not lie. A great outfit couldn't hide the truth from her.

Zane was engaged in deep conversation with a woman in the first row of the spectator's gallery. I studied him critically. He was dressed slightly less offensively today, except for his bright purple tie. He had a matching purple fedora with a zebra-striped hatband sitting in front of him. I grabbed it and stuck it under the table while his eyes were still glued to the breasts in row one.

The state continued with their witnesses, building the blocks to their case, with Mack still taking the lead and Junie still gazing in awe at her engagement ring. Emily continued propping me up, although I was better than the day before. No egregious malpractice, at least, and that was a miracle.

We broke for lunch halfway through our allotted time in front of the judge. I remained seated in my chair. A herd of wildebeests stampeded through my brain until a voice interrupted my trance.

"How do you think we're doing, counselor?" Zane asked.

I thought I saw a flash of something in his mouth. Had he been eating chocolate? It looked as if he had something on his teeth. Whatever it was, hopefully it would come off when he ate lunch.

"Um, everything is fine. No surprises. Just like we expected," I said. Which was true. It wasn't my whole truth, but he didn't need that.

Emily was standing on the other side of Zane. She drew his attention away from me and said, "It's going great, Mr. McMillan. Katie is one of the best trial attorneys in the city. Is everything OK, from your perspective ?"

I was giving Emily a raise when we got back to the office. Just then Zane checked her out, his elevator eyes taking long stops on every floor. I'd get her a spot bonus, too.

"Nah, I'm good if you guys are good," Zane said. "Just checking. I'm paying for no surprises," he said. But he was mumbling, and his voice sounded different. It was an odd statement from an odd man.

As Emily and I walked off to find ourselves some food, she said, "If Zane doesn't quit staring at your ass when you stand up, the jurors are going to find him guilty just on general principles of common decency."

Ugh. I just wanted this trial to end so I could crawl in a hole and sleep for a week. Or a month. Or a year.

After lunch, Mack put on the police officer who would testify about the bag of McZillion shoelaces they'd confiscated in the search of Zane's condo. These shoelaces were the source of Zane's angst from the day before. I'd researched the legality of the warrant and the resulting search, but I hadn't had enough time or experience to reach a solid conclusion. Frankly, I had no idea what the right play was here—challenge or not? This was something Zane's previous firm should have handled weeks ago, months ago, if it was to be done at all. Trial was the wrong place to go on the defensive on this issue, in my opinion, in front of a jury that already didn't like Zane, if it had any sense. Shannon had agreed with me when I ran it by her. However, if I didn't raise the objection, I'd risk upsetting my client and lose the right to appeal on the issue.

Mack offered the search warrant into evidence. It was now or never, decision time. I could feel Emily and Zane watching me. I pictured myself objecting. In my mind's eye, I saw the jury react, looking at Zane like he was a guilty dog barking. Besides, who the hell else carried around $150 custom-made Nike shoelaces with "McZillion" stitched in real gold thread? We weren't arguing that the shoelaces belonged to someone else or that he hadn't tied her up with them, anyway. Our only issue was whether she'd wanted him to.

I thought of my father, and of all the hard-working officers I'd known in my life. This was ridiculous. I passed the witness without cross-examining him, and without objecting to the evidence. Zane needed to watch less crime drama and have sex with fewer strange women. He was just pissed the cops snagged three thousand dollars' worth of his booty favors. He stared daggers at me from the other end of the table, and I pretended not to notice.

The state finished the day and their entire case with Tabitha. When she stepped up to the witness box, I did a double take. The woman—all of twenty-five, maybe—had freckled pale skin and long wavy red hair. A younger version of my mother. Hell, a younger version of me, except with better breasts. The photos in the file hadn't done the resemblance justice. Apparently McMillan had a type, in sexual partners and lawyers in rape trials.

I shot a glance at Zane. The daggers were gone. He grinned back at me, exposing a silver grill with "McZ" written in embedded rhinestones. *Oh my God.* I didn't grin back.

"Take that off right now," I ordered him, trying to whisper. "You look like you're mocking her. Take it off before the jury sees you."

Zane flashed a wide smile at the jury. I watched in horror as the two women nearest us in the front row cringed in disgust. He pulled the grill out of his mouth and set it on the table, then leaned back and crossed his arms over his chest. The prosecutor continued his direct exam of Tabitha, unaware of the distracting show my smarmy jerk of a client was putting on for the jury.

I eyed the grill. No way was I touching that spit-covered metal monstrosity with my bare hands. I grabbed my Clorox Wipes handipack out of my purse, snatched a few out, and used them as a barrier between my skin and Zane's saliva. I put the grill in the outside pocket of my leather briefcase, then shoved it away from me. I could dry-clean the case later.

I would have to worry about Zane's behavior later, too. Right now, my job was to make them forget about him and his vile grill while I handled the cross-examination of Tabitha Brown in such a way that the jurors didn't think I was a big insensitive meanie.

This was a challenging prospect, since I had some hard questions to ask her. But I could pass as her older sister, so I'd try to act like one. I channeled my inner loving-while-proving-she's-a-liar big sister and got to my feet.

"Ms. Brown, just a few questions. Before we begin, do you need anything? More water? A tissue?" Tabitha's tears from her direct testimony still lingered in her lashes.

"No ma'am, thank you." Her voice was soft, high. Young. Innocent-sounding. She had dressed the part, too, in a Peter Pan-collared navy dress nipped in at her narrow waist with a thin belt in matching fabric. Sunday school teachers, eat your heart out.

I asked her, "Had you met my client, Zane McMillan, before the night in question?"

"No, ma'am, I had not."

"And you met him at Good Sportz?"

"Yes, ma'am."

"How did you meet him?"

"How?"

"Yes, how did you come to meet him? Did he walk up to you and introduce himself, or did you have mutual friends that introduced you?"

Some of the story that Zane had told me had come out during the state's direct examination of Tabitha. All of it had come out in her deposition, which I had read in preparing for trial. Unfortunately, it was my job as defense counsel to make sure the jury heard all of it from the defense's perspective. Which made me a shitheel.

"I, uh . . ."

"I apologize if this gets embarrassing for you, Ms. Brown. I certainly don't mean to make you uncomfortable, but I'm going to have to ask you a direct question since you can't think of an answer for me. So, did you have a note delivered to him with your phone number on it, asking him to text you if he wanted to 'see some great tits'?"

Her voice got softer. "I may have."

"Is that a yes?"

"Yes. Yes, ma'am."

"Did Mr. McMillan text you?"

"Yes, ma'am."

"Did you text him a picture of your bare breasts that you took yourself right there in the club?"

I could barely hear her as she answered. "Yes, ma'am."

"I'm sorry, Ms. Brown, but could you speak just a little bit louder, so the jury can hear your answers?"

She tried. "Yes, ma'am."

"Thank you. Did Mr. McMillan then ask you to meet him in the VIP room?"

"Yes, ma'am."

"And when you got there, did he ask you to perform oral sex on him in a private room?"

She started to cry again. "Yes, ma'am."

"I'm sorry to make you remember this, Ms. Brown. It can't be easy talking about what you did."

Mack jumped to his feet. "Objection, Your Honor. That's not a question."

"Sustained," Judge Hutchison replied. "Remove that from the record," he instructed the court reporter.

I continued, not caring about the objection. The jury had heard me. "So you went into a private room and performed oral sex on a man you'd only just met because you'd texted him a photo of your bare breasts?"

"Yes, but I—" Tabitha said.

"Hold on, Ms. Brown. I only asked a yes or no question."

"But—"

I cut her off. "Did Mr. McMillan ask you to leave Good Sportz with him for the purpose of having sex at your apartment?"

"Yes, but when I got in the car I sobered up, and I changed my mind."

The jury had already heard all about her drug and alcohol use on direct. Now I objected. "Objection, as to everything but 'yes' as nonresponsive, Your Honor."

Judge Hutchison was agreeable today. "Sustained. Remove that from the record, please."

I knew the young woman wouldn't give me the answer I wanted to my next question, but I asked anyway. The jury needed to see me do it.

"Ms. Brown, Mr. McMillan couldn't have sexually assaulted you because you consented to have sex with him at your apartment, isn't that correct?"

"No," she protested, "I—"

I interrupted her as I walked briskly toward my seat. "No further questions at this time, Your Honor."

Mack asked Tabitha a few more questions, then the judge excused her.

My cross-exam of Tabitha lasted ten minutes. Ten minutes in which I felt like the world's biggest sleaze, except for maybe my client. Zane deserved a good defense, or at least that was what they taught us in legal ethics class in law school, but I just wished I didn't have to be the one providing it and putting all this tawdry garbage out into the universe.

"We'll reconvene at 9:30 tomorrow. Court is adjourned for today." The judge banged his gavel and left the courtroom.

I had managed to complete the whole day without turning into a gargoyle or collapsing into a snoring heap. I had survived Zane's antics. Hell, I'd made it through two whole days. Two days on emotional empty defending a case I was clueless about for the world's most obnoxious client. I was whipped.

My goodbyes were even shorter than the day before. I bolted out of that courthouse and into my Accord, and drove away with my air conditioner cranking full blast. The August heat could wither stronger women than me in an instant, and I was far less than strong right now. I jerked out the bobby pins that had held my hair in its severe knot, snatched a kleenex from the console, and scrubbed my lipstick off. The urge to call my mother was so strong that I had my phone out before it even hit me that speed dial wouldn't reach her where she was now.

"Son of a bitch," I screamed, and pounded the steering wheel. More softly, I repeated it. "Son of a bitch."

When I got home, I threw my contaminated briefcase down on the coffee table. Thank God I only had one more day, that I was home now, that I could hide from the eyes of everyone in that courtroom until tomorrow morning.

I looked at the freezer. I knew what was in it. I wanted what was in it.

I redirected my thoughts. A good cry might help. Or a hot shower. I should try one of those. Or both.

Or neither. I opened the freezer and got out the icy-cold bottle of Ketel One. I pulled a can of V-8 out of the pantry. I retrieved a Waterford crystal tumbler and stir stick, thinking maybe my uptown drinking accessories would make me feel less low-class about this. I mixed my concoction, then used antique silver tongs to drop the ice cubes in gently, one at a time so they wouldn't splash. I took one teensy sip. I'd pace myself, just have one to settle my nerves.

I sat down on one of my barstools, the kind with the twirly seats. Hands on the black granite countertop, I twisted one way, then the other. I should make myself something to eat, I thought, but I didn't want to. I could watch TV or read a book, distract my mind from recycling the last two days, before I dove back into prep for day three. I took another sip. And another.

Tomorrow I'd put on our case, which included a few experts to rebut the state's conclusion that sex between Tabitha and Zane was nonconsensual. We'd finish with our death blow, testimony from the roommate Sherry. Sherry's testimony would plant reasonable doubt in the jurors' minds, no matter what I did. I would under no circumstances ever permit Zane, his roving eyes, and his enormous ego on the stand, so I didn't have to worry about preparing for that.

Maybe just one more drink. I could do tomorrow in my sleep. Or with a wicked hangover.

I gave in and poured.

Chapter Twenty

The next morning, I sprinted to the courts building from my parking spot on the street. I knew I'd get a ticket and that the city would probably tow my car away, but that was the least of my worries. I was late for court. I'd slept through my alarm and only woke up when one of my condo building's security officers knocked on my door, courtesy of a call to them from the best friend and paralegal in the world. Thank God for Emily. I just prayed she hadn't called Gino first.

Today I ran through the halls, dodging people, repeating, "Excuse me," over and over. I hated people that did this. I hated me for doing it. I hated me.

I glanced at my watch as I hit the courtroom doors. It was 9:55. Trial was to have started with our case—our witnesses—at 9:30.

I took a deep breath to quell my nausea. And then I was inside. A hot mess in heels, clippety clopping far too loudly as I race-walked to the bench to present myself to the honorable and righteously pissed Judge Hutchison. He glared at me, his black eyes ringed with bright white in his coal-black face. Mack joined us. He was glowing.

I looked down and saw a flash of white lace bra. I pulled at the neckline of my navy coatdress until I was decent again, then spoke.

"Your Honor, I'm so sorry. I've been quite ill. I will be able to continue, but I had a very difficult night, and I just didn't wake up this morning. I live alone, so there was no one around who knew I was sick, to check on me and make sure I woke up. I am incredibly grateful to my paralegal for contacting me. I beg your forgiveness, the state's, and the jury's, for wasting everyone's time. I have practiced for years in the Dallas courts, sir, and this has never happened before. It will never happen again." I prayed that a giant B for Boozer hadn't appeared on my forehead.

Judge Hutchison leaned back in his chair. "I don't know what to say, Ms. Connell, except that it will absolutely not ever happen again, or it will be the last time you argue before me. If you are as sick as you say, you'd better not get me ill, too. Please return to your table." He looked at me again. "You really do look awful."

"Yes, Your Honor. Thank you, Your Honor."

Mack looked disappointed that the judge hadn't spilled any of my blood, but he didn't protest. Maybe he thought it was better for the state that the judge let a "sick" defense attorney proceed. I couldn't disagree.

I took a seat as close as I could get to Emily, whose hairsprayed cosmetological creation kept me at bay. She didn't look at me. Zane, however, leaned around her and winked. I noticed his attire for the day. Finally, he'd taken my advice. If I hadn't known he was nine inches taller than Nick, I'd think he had borrowed his navy suit. It was like Zane and I had planned a matchy-matchy day.

He burst my short-lived bubble. "Rough night, counselor? Got the wine flu, or did you lose sleep knocking boots with some cowboy?"

I was too sick to punch him and the trial wasn't over, so I gave him a wan smile. Later, I promised myself. Later. I reached into my briefcase to get my notes for my direct examinations of the witnesses this morning and my hand found something solid with sharp edges. I realized I'd fondled a handful of Zane's grill, and jerked back like it had jolted me with electricity.

Never again, I promised myself. No more criminal trials, ever.

"Are you ready, Ms. Connell?" Judge Hutchison asked.

No, Your Honor, but I have no choice in the matter. "Yes, Your Honor."

"Call your first witness," he said.

I wished I could stay seated, but the judge would never permit it, so I stood, careful not to jostle my brains. I needed all the cells I had left fully functioning. While the court reporter swore my first witness in, I drained a bottle of water and then concentrated on holding it down. I'd never brought a hangover to trial before. It would have devastated my mother.

"Shame on you, Katie," she used to say when I chose badly, like when I bent the legs of Collins' favorite GI Joe in the wrong direction until they broke.

Actually, I was pretty much ashamed on her behalf. "Shame on me, Katie," I thought, then pushed it aside. Any more of that would border on self-pity.

The first two witnesses went fine, better than I deserved. They were our experts on the crime scene evidence. We weren't contesting that the evidence existed—that it was his semen and shoelaces, that the shoelaces had abraded Tabitha's wrists and ankles, and that her body had been covered with bruises. We were simply arguing that it wasn't rape. The only important point I needed to establish with them was that nothing about the scene or her injuries precluded a conclusion that Tabitha had consented to sex with Zane. The longer I knew him, though, the less I believed in the possibility of anyone consenting to having sex with him.

In a truly shocking turn of events, Junie cross-examined the experts. What was Mack up to? She did a competent job, but they both held up quite well. Score one for defense, times two.

I began to think everything would turn out OK despite me. I hadn't tossed my cookies, and I'd still have time to put Sherry Talmadge on before lunch. That meant we could deliver closing arguments immediately after the jury got back from lunch. If so, we could send the case to them before the end of the day. That would make the jury happy with me and meet the judge's deadline of three days.

And then I could relax for a nanosecond and figure out what the hell had happened in my life since Bloody-Mary-thirty last evening.

I cleared my throat. "Your Honor, the defense calls Sherry Talmadge."

A short, pregnant Caucasian woman made her way from the back row of the courtroom to the stand. This was my first time to lay eyes on Ms. Talmadge. She was cute bordering on pretty, or on used-to-be-pretty. Her straight brown hair clung to her head. The dark bags under her eyes over sallow skin told us all about her lifestyle, bun in the oven or not. I reached up and touched my own face. I shuddered.

I shook it off. It was show time. As I stood to start my direct, I looked around the courtroom for Nick. It was our last day of trial, and I hadn't checked in with him last night. He wasn't here. Our possibly-last trial together was almost over.

I took Ms. Talmadge through the easy parts of her testimony first—her name, her address, her occupation—while I got a feel for her rhythm and tempo. She fiddled with the cuff of her long-sleeved mauve maternity dress. She stuttered some and looked down more than I would have wanted, but testifying in trial was scary, and lots of people did far worse than she. Once we had established her presence for the events in question, I got to the point of her testimony.

I opened it wide for her. "Ms. Talmadge, please tell me what you observed and heard happen on the night in question, from the time Ms. Brown and Mr. McMillan got to your apartment, until Mr. McMillan left."

Sherry drew a deep breath and blew it out forcefully, and took her time with both. When she spoke, she spoke rapidly, looking at Mack and Junie instead of the jury or me. "Tabitha came home and tried to lock Zane out but he pushed his way in after her and dragged her to the bedroom and shut the door and then she screamed at me to call the police because he was raping her and he threatened to kill me if I did." She stopped speaking and looked down.

It took me a moment to realize what I had just heard, which wasn't what I had expected to hear. It didn't take Zane nearly as long as me. He jumped to his feet, taller by seven inches and heavier by a hundred pounds of muscle than anyone else present. His jacket fell open, exposing the shirt I hadn't seen earlier. It read, "Ladies, wait your turn."

"Bitch," he screamed. "What the fuck do you mean, you lying fucking bitch?"

Everyone gasped.

Chapter Twenty-one

Judge Hutchison's gavel crashed down three times. "Bailiffs! Get him under control. Mr. McMillan, one more word, and you are out of here."

Two bailiffs weaved toward Zane, hands on their guns.

But Sherry now jumped to her feet with surprising agility, given the seventh-month state of her belly. "You think you can pay me to lie and then dump me like garbage when I'm carrying your baby? I told you last week I was done lying for you. You raped her. I was there. And you are going to pay for what you did to both of us."

This couldn't be happening, yet it so very much was. The drama was electrifying the bored jurors. They'd have something worth talking about over the water cooler for the rest of their lives. I'd have something to ensure years of financial security for my therapist. But what the jury didn't seem to comprehend yet was that this was not theater. There was no director to yell cut.

"But I gave you more money, you greedy slut," Zane screamed.

"Yeah, because you're stupid as shit," she screamed back. "And guess what? Last week when we met in your car? I taped you on my iPhone, asshole. How about I give your confession to the cops, huh?" She held her phone aloft, her victor's trophy.

Zane lunged around the table and charged at Sherry. The bailiffs moved faster now, and they made it in time to get between the two. The courtroom went off like a bomb, everyone talking at once.

My brains rattled in my head. I shouted over the melee to be heard. "Your Honor, objection. Please strike the witness's testimony as non-responsive."

"Sustained," the judge shouted back. "Jurors, disregard Ms. Talmadge's testimony, and please go to the jury room, at once," he ordered. "Gallery, please exit the courtroom."

The jurors stood, looking around at each other, but they didn't budge. The spectators didn't even bother standing up, not a one of them willing to give up their prime seats to the drama unfolding before them.

"I said OUT," Judge Hutchison screamed, "or I'll hold you all in contempt."

The crowd had drawn courage from each other in their defiance, and no one moved a muscle. If the judge stuck to his threat, the jail cells would fill to capacity tonight.

The bailiffs pulled on Zane by the arms to no avail as he and Sherry screamed and flipped each other off. They needed to get both of them out of here, but they looked unsure of what to do next. Zane was huge, and he was livid. The judge sat still and quiet. I knew he had a panic button under his desk. Dad had told us about their installation years ago, after a defendant had assaulted a judge in a murder trial. I prayed the judge had already pushed it.

Without pausing to think, I came from behind the counsel table and approached Zane. I stabbed my finger into his chest three times, turning his attention away from Sherry for a moment, hoping it would give someone time to neutralize or remove her. "You knew she was lying, that she had decided to quit lying, and you didn't tell me?" I asked.

He smirked. "Yeah, well, I had it covered." When he continued talking, his voice rang through the courtroom as if he was hooked into surround sound. "I didn't need to worry about nothing because I had Police Chief Daddy's little redheaded girl getting me off." Zane chose to illustrate his point by jerking his hand up and down over his crotch, despite the restraining grasp of the bailiff, whose arm moved with Zane's like a profane puppeteer. "Daddy's not here to save you now, is he? Too bad."

My reflexes were still pretty awesome, even if I was thirty-five years old and mortally hungover. Quick as a whip crack, I slapped him across the face with all my strength. Only a desire to avoid jail time kept me from giving him a judo punch to the crotch. I would have loved to end his manhood completely on behalf of womankind, but I congratulated myself on my restraint and leaped out of his reach. Sherry was cheering and screaming in appreciation. The jury and the spectators had abandoned decorum and the room buzzed and crackled. One of the bailiffs jumped between Zane and me.

"Stand down, Ms. Connell," he warned. "Let us get him out of here."

A hand grasped my shoulder. I jumped and turned around.

It was Nick.

"What the hell have you done, Katie?" he asked, his voice raised in the din. It took a lot of blood to make an olive-skinned face tomato red.

"What do you mean, what did I do? I didn't do anything," I yelled back. "I called Sherry to testify. I had no idea she would turn. You sure didn't tell me."

"I left you voicemail last night, I emailed you, I texted you. I told you as soon as I found out she'd turned state, and I absolutely told you not to call her." His words pounded my skull.

Oh, God. I stared at him. My mouth hung open, but I couldn't find any words. I'd been scrambling so fast since I woke up that morning that I'd never looked at my iPhone. And then I'd just assumed . . . Oh, God, it was my fault. Oh no, no, no. It was my fault.

"I'm so sorry," I said, to no one, to my mother who never got her chance to be a lawyer, to my father who dedicated his career to justice. To Nick. To Emily. To everyone, even myself.

What the hell had I done?

"Stay the fuck away from me," Zane was saying to a deputy, who had rushed into the courtroom from behind the judge and made it to the front of the witness bench, handcuffs in his left hand and his right hand on the stock of his holstered handgun. He was fifteen feet away from where Zane was now dangling one bailiff from each arm, Incredible Hulk-style, and ten feet from Nick and me. "Man, don't make me do something you'll regret," Zane said to him.

Nick jerked me out of the line of fire and back behind the defense table.

"Sir, I need you to put your hands behind your head and stand very still. I am going to move closer, and then you and I will exit the courtroom together." The deputy eased himself between Zane and the judge.

"Put my hands on my head? Like I done something wrong? I ain't done shit. The bitch is lying. Arrest her."

And then ten seconds of pure chaos reigned.

The doors to the courtroom burst open with concussive force, slamming into the walls on either side. Five armed officers barreled in, one screaming, "Everyone down!" I hit the floor in a crouch, hands down. Three officers assumed firing positions and pointed guns at Zane's head. Two others rushed forward. Zane released the two bailiffs, spun, and assumed a flexed-kneed stance as if he would fight the interlopers off, as if he were fighting for his very life—which he was. His life as he knew it, at least. The bailiffs were behind him now. One had handcuffs at the ready. They both reached for his arms again, and he whirled on them. The two officers didn't hesitate. They jumped onto Zane's back, tackling him before his body finished its rotation toward the sounds behind him. Zane and the two officers went down hard, but I couldn't hear the impact over the screams of the jurors and spectators. Theater had ended and reality hell had set in. The screams subsided into weeping and a cacophony of voices.

I realized I had stood back up, and that's when I saw her. Or thought I saw her anyway, the nameless woman from Annalise. I was suffering simultaneously from lovesick rejection, sleep deprivation, a hangover, extreme stress, and a punishing wallop of humiliation, so it was possible I was hallucinating. She was standing between me and the door. Her eyes looked hollow with sadness. She was saying something to me, although not loud enough that I could hear her. She motioned me toward her with her hand.

"Order, order, order!" The judge's gavel punctuated his thin voice, but the crowd ignored him. He turned on his mike and tried again. "I will have order in this courtroom right now!" He slammed down his gavel right in front of the microphone, an echoing rifle shot of sound. This time he got all of our attention. Slowly, the panicked group settled back into their seats and their voices lulled to a buzzing. I jerked my head back around toward my imaginary friend, but she wasn't there.

"Ladies and gentlemen, we've all had a bit of excitement, but the officers have it under control and we need to let them do their jobs," the judge said.

I heard a keening noise. The kind a cat makes when it's trapped up in a tree.

Hush. I thought. Just hush. Everyone hush.

I sank to my knees on the courtroom's tile floor. I put my head in my hands. And that's when I realized the sound was coming from me.

Chapter Twenty-two

After I quit mewling like a crazy cat woman in front of the whole courtroom and started acting somewhat attorney-like again, I asked the judge for a mistrial.

He actually considered it for about five seconds. Or at least he stayed completely silent for that long. He could have been devising elaborate torture rituals or plotting my death. When he said no, I knew he meant "Hell No Katie Connell And Don't Ever Darken The Doors Of My Courtroom Again." I'm empathic like that.

It didn't improve things for me when Mack and I were walking away from the bench and the prosecutor said, "Bet you wish your client had accepted that plea bargain now."

Mack almost became the second person I assaulted that day.

Not surprisingly, the jury found everyone's favorite basketball star guilty and set a land speed record doing it. They gave him twenty years. It didn't sound like enough to me, but the law constrained their choices. They would have probably sentenced him to death if they could. Luckily another jury would get a chance to add to his sentence later, because he would be charged with several new crimes, including witness tampering and going apeshit in the courtroom while scaring the bejeebers out of Judge Hutchison—better known as criminal contempt of court.

I wondered if his next attorney would try to get him a new trial by arguing inadequate representation, or if Zane would just sue me for assault. Or malpractice. Or both. Best not to think about it.

I had already used my iPhone to pull up the ignominious pictures of myself online, crumpled and weeping on the floor of the courtroom. Let's just say they didn't show off my good side. I didn't know if I could fall any further or feel any worse.

But it wasn't the verdict or the pictures that had shattered me. I'd come apart at the moment when Nick said, "What have you done, Katie?" I didn't think all the king's horses and all the king's men could ever put Katie together again. I had screwed this trial up. I had disgraced my father's name. I had made a sham of my mother's dreams of being a lawyer. Me. I had done that. And Nick had disappeared in the wake of Zane's apprehension.

At five o'clock, Emily and I slunk back to the office. I hated her humiliation by association to me. Add another gold star for Katie today. The elevator doors opened onto the seventeenth floor and the lobby of the Hailey & Hart offices. I tried to sneak past the front desk, but it didn't work.

"Party!" Tina chirped when she saw us. "Bill won a huge case today."

She handed me a party hat that said "Congratulations" on it. Oh, no. Maybe she didn't know about my trial? Maybe she hadn't seen my picture?

Tina told us, "Bob's Irish Bar is open. Everyone's gathered in the conference room to celebrate."

Bob's Irish Bar was a longstanding tradition, named in honor of the firm's founder, Bob Hailey, who was definitely not Irish and didn't even work at the firm anymore. The man had loved his Bushmills then, and he still did, I heard, well into his retirement. You would think a law firm would be concerned about the potential for liability if one of their employees had a drunken wreck driving away from the office, but you'd be wrong. Our office looked for any excuse to throw a party.

"Thanks, Tina," Emily said.

The original Bob's Irish Bar had centered around Bob's office, his Irish whiskey, and an actual bar setup he had installed beside his desk. The modern version more closely resembled progressive drinking, where revelers wandered from room to room to see what people were pouring. Today the firm had a cooler of Miller Lite in the main conference room and Cook's champagne in the ice-filled break room sink. We weren't shelling out for the good stuff this time, apparently.

Emily and I had to breach the main party areas to make it to our own offices. The PA system was pumping out "We Will Rock You" by Queen. We accepted plastic champagne glasses as we passed by the break room, victorious Amazon warriors returning from battle.

Only we weren't.

We crept past the conference room. Celebrants spilled out into the hall. At some point, people became aware of who was making the walk of shame through their midst, and I could see them start to whisper. Tina might have missed it, but my humiliation was, no doubt, the talk of the Dallas legal scene. Hell, all of Dallas. I steadied my chin. *One foot in front of the other, Katie.*

I tried not to be obvious as I searched for Nick. I saw him.

"Emily, I have to try to talk to Nick," I said.

You'd think Emily would have had enough of me by now.

"I'll meet you in your office in five minutes," she said. "Not a minute longer. I'm serious, Katie."

"I promise," I said.

I crossed the crowd like a salmon swimming upstream to get to Nick. He watched me approach, let me get ten feet away, then turned his back and left. In front of everyone.

I froze. I was Medusa with a head full of red stone snakes. Maybe I imagined it, but his Obsession cologne stayed in my senses long after he'd left, rooting me to his scent. I stood motionless as people streamed past me toward the drinks, the bathroom, another pod of revelers. Their snippets of conversations boomeranged around the room. My ears caught some of them, but only for a few seconds at a time before the sound spun back in the other direction. I could only imagine what they were saying, what I would have been saying in their shoes.

"See Katie standing over there? God, she's pathetic."

"I know. Could she be more obvious?"

"Helloooo, girlfriend, you're the laughingstock of Dallas!"

Peals of laughter, male and female. I recognized voices, but in the din, I couldn't place them. I strained to hear as the sounds receded, confusing me further.

"Please tell me we won't be like her."

"A dried-up workaholic with a desperate crush on a married private eye? Fat chance."

"No wonder she drinks so much. Oh my God, and did you hear about her trial today? She was mewing like a cat. It's on YouTube."

My brain was playing cruel tricks on my ears, but I somehow knew the words were figments of my imagination, not real. My eyes were on fire with unshed tears. Volcanic lava rushed through the veins over my entire head. I clenched my fists so tightly one of my fingernails snapped in my palm. I didn't care. I'd started a pivot toward the lobby, away from here, as far away and as fast as I could go, when Emily appeared out of nowhere and grabbed my arm.

"Stop, Katie," she said.

"Let me go," I said, pulling hard against her grip. My chest was heaving. "You saw him walk away from me?"

"No. I just saw your face, and I came right over." She gave my arm a tug. "We're out of here."

I didn't like it, but I let Emily prod me forward. She propelled me out of our offices, down the elevator, into the parking garage, and over to my car, where she insisted on driving me home. I plotted revenge on Nick and my other nameless, faceless enemies while she drove. One of them looked surprisingly like me. I wanted to dismember my foes slowly and boil their bones. My anger dulled quickly, though, and I was still as a corpse by the time we arrived at my place.

Emily had called ahead for a cab to meet her. I walked her to the curb.

"Are you going to be OK?" Emily asked.

I knew she wanted me to say yes. And actually, I kind of was. I was as low as I could ever imagine getting, but I feared that the worst thing now was that I'd live through it. Screw Nick, I thought. Screw everyone. I made one mistake. One. I can run circles around three quarters of the lawyers in town.

"Yeah. I'm over it. I am." I dug in my purse for a twenty-dollar bill. "You're a much better friend than I deserve. Let me pay for your cab."

She did.

"I'll call you in a little while," Emily said.

She hugged me hard, then left to return to the office for her own car. I wandered inside, numb, trailing my fingers over the standing marble bust as I passed it in my building lobby. The condominium association aspired to a Greco-Roman theme. Not in a papier-mâché way, but in a classy way that said, "I'm old-school elegant." Them, not me. I rode the elevator, which dinged nine times, then opened.

The hell of it all was that after this, I had to go out with Collin for his birthday. I had to drag my hungover, humiliated ruin of a self back out the door and appear in public during my moment of infamy. With Collin, who was on the side of apple pie and the American way, good not evil. Unlike me.

Time to pull it together. I spruced and spritzed without much hope for a miracle. The lines between my eyebrows get deeper when I'm upset, and I cursed Zane, Sherry, Nick, and myself as I covered up the furrows with Clinique's Airbrush Concealer. This me would have to do.

Chapter Twenty-three

Collin met me in the lobby at 6:30, looking as cool as I was overheated, his cheeks still pink from the shower. I knew he worked out at the downtown YMCA every day when he got off shift and he took exceptional care of his body. He would have made a good Marine, run-marching in combat boots and scaling obstacles. It would do me a world of good to follow his example. We got in the car and he led the conversation.

Without turning to look at me, he said, "I heard you had a bad day."

I tried to laugh. It came out as a pathetic snort. "You've turned on the news, then?"

He kept his eyes on the road. "And seen you on YouTube, too. I called Emily," he added.

I rotated my head and my neck popped once, twice. "Then you're fully informed."

Now Collin cut his eyes over to me. It was almost as if he'd patted my leg. "If it makes you feel any better, he's a bad man who deserves to be in prison. I told you a few days ago: fleas."

That he had. And God, was he right. I didn't trust myself to speak.

"But did you learn anything?" Collin asked, channeling Dad.

My voice came out high-pitched, whinier than I wanted it to sound. I wanted to suck it back in for a do-over. "Learn what? That I hate criminal law and never want to walk into a Dallas courtroom again? That it only takes fifteen seconds to disgrace your dead father's memory in front of the entire city he loved?"

"Well, yes, but no. More along the lines of elemental truths. That hell hath no fury like a lover scorned. A lover scorned is a witness turned, every single time."

"I messed up, Collin." I held in my tears, but my lower lip trembled. Traitor.

"Yep. Sounds like you had a breakdown."

"More like a nuclear meltdown."

"Agreed. But you're still alive. That's something."

The word "alive" triggered something in me. "Collin, Zane picked me because of Dad. He wanted me because of who Dad was. And because Dad was dead, he couldn't fight back against the message that it sent to the jury for me to take Zane's case."

Collin reached up to his bottom lip and pulled it with his thumb and forefinger. "That's pretty awful. I'm sorry," he said.

"If only Dad were here," I replied, and a sob caught my voice halfway through. "This never would have happened if Dad were here."

We drove in silence. The sun was high in the sky and starting to fall, burning through the smog of an ozone-advisory August day. Collin pulled up to a red light. We were landlocked in a sea of cars, two thousand miles away from St. Marcos and the ocean on its shores. I had left there only five days ago. It might as well have been forever. This trial had consumed me, and I hadn't even followed up with the investigator. The light turned green. On our right a yellow stucco two-story house caught my eye. Annalise. Maybe I could find another Annalise. There were other houses on St. Marcos. Plenty of them on the East End, according to Doug. That almost made me smile.

Collin pulled into the drive-through for Popeye's Fried Chicken.

"What are you doing?" I asked.

"I'm dying to get fried chicken grease on your white carpet and watch you squirm. That's all I want for my birthday," he said.

"Asshole," I said. I really loved my brother.

He laughed.

Fifteen minutes later, we were sitting cross-legged on my carpet scarfing dark meat spicy and downing large iced teas. Actually, we were sitting crosslegged on towels on my carpet. I wasn't about to let Collin get chicken grease on the Berber.

After I finished my chicken and was shoveling in red beans and rice, I told him about Nick. More than I had ever told him. Collin listened with every bone in his body. I came to the penultimate moment between Nick and me from today, and I got out my phone.

"I've been too scared to look at it, Col," I confessed.

He held out his hand. "I can do it for you."

I shook my head back and forth, fast. "No, I have to do this myself."

I scrolled through Nick's messages. He hadn't lied. He'd left word for me in every possible medium. I suspected I would find them on my home voicemail, too, but I spared myself for the moment from enduring his voice. Then I came to an email from an hour ago, after he'd walked away from me at the party.

To: katie.connell@haileyhart.com

From: nick.kovacs@haileyhart.com

Subject: I'm sorry

I waited for you in my office. I thought you were following me. I wanted to talk to you. To tell you I'm sorry. I was too harsh today. A shit. Again. It's as much my fault as yours. I should have gotten hold of Emily when I didn't hear back from you, but things got crazy in my life that night and I forgot.. I know I've failed you as a co-worker and as a friend. If I'd have acted like a friend, I would have done what Emily did, and I would have found you. I would have helped you. I am ashamed of myself, because somewhere inside me, I knew you needed help.

Please let someone help you.

Nick

Before I could react, before I could process, before I could show Collin the message, my phone rang. It was from the 340 area code. St. Marcos. I answered.

"Are you sitting down, Katie?" a male voice asked.

My heart quit beating for a moment, frozen up in my chest like the engine in my car when I had let it run out of oil in college. "I'm sitting." After Nick's email and this introduction, I couldn't have stood if I'd wanted to. I put my head down on my legs with my face between my knees to keep from blacking out.

"Congratulations, Katie. The other buyer's deal fell through and the bank accepted your offer on Annalise."

"Doug? This is Doug, isn't it? I thought they rejected it?" I raised my head slowly.

Doug it was. "Surprise! They never even considered it. I hadn't put an end date on it, either. So when the other deal fell apart, Ms. Nesbitt picked up your offer and faxed over an acceptance. Can you beat that?"

"No," I said, and I was barely able to speak audibly. "No, I can't beat that."

"Come on, now, show some enthusiasm. This is huge," Doug urged.

Was it my imagination, or did he sound amused? Maybe it was pity I heard instead. When my heart began to function again and my brain had received its normal supply of oxygen, I realized we were discussing the expedited closing provision I had requested in my offer.

"You should have a deed and keys—strike that. There aren't any doors, so there aren't keys, are there?" Definitely amusement that time. "Well, you should have a deed, anyway, in two weeks. That's very fast by St. Marcos standards, practically unheard of."

No matter how much I rallied, no way could I add much to this conversation. "Doug, can I call you back?" I asked.

"Sure," he said. "Congratulations!"

I thanked him and hung up. Collin stared at me.

"Give me a sec, Col."

He grunted.

I processed the news. In two weeks, I would squander three quarters of a million dollars in cash on an isolated St. Marcos rainforest money pit and the 110 acres upon which it perched, which, unless I moved down there and took up full-time management of the finish-out, would remain an overpriced horse latrine and depreciate faster than the Titanic sank. I would not only blow a large chunk of my reserves, but also torpedo my job, lose any chance I might have had with Nick (*You have no chance with Nick, you idiot*) and throw away my entire support network. I was a thirty-five-year-old, single, probably alcoholic, soon-to-be-unemployed female attorney with no construction experience, and, more portentously, I was alien to the environment. An environment that might be involved in the island drug trade, and was just down the road from where my parents mysteriously died.

Wow. Double wow. I swallowed. Collin cleared his throat, hinting.

My phone rang again. Another from the 340 area code, but a different phone number. I hesitated, thinking about not answering it.

"Go ahead, sis," Collin said. "If it's important, take it."

I took the call. "This is Katie Connell."

Now I heard crying on the other end. Soft crying. What the hell was going on?

"Who's there? This is Katie. Talk to me."

"Oh, Katie. It Ava. Last night. Last night something terrible happen."

Her accent was so thick I could barely understand her. More crying.

"Ava? Are you OK? Can you tell me what's wrong?"

"Last night, Eduardo told me to meet Guy at the suite on the hill behind the Porcus Marinus again."

"Yes?"

"I went. And someone else got there first. And Guy—Guy dead, Katie. Sitting in the chair at the desk, slumped over. Someone come up behind him and slit his throat. He dead. Guy dead."

She sobbed now, her breath in gasps, her wails wrenching me.

"Ava, oh Ava, I'm so sorry. What can I do? Is there someone with you? Can Rashidi or Jacoby come over?"

"I here with my parents. I call Jacoby when it happen, and he stall so I could get away from there. I just, I just—oh, I don't know. Everything so crazy. I need to sleep. I can't sleep. Every time I close my eyes, I see him there again, all that blood, his blood."

This made my troubles seem petty. "I'm so sorry for him, and for you."

"I call you. You the one I want to call. I hope you don't think I'm crazy. I just, well, you my friend. It didn't take me long to know that. First time I seen you, I knew you were different. So I call."

And I realized that she was my friend. Out there on the edge, maybe, but a friend all the same, and she lived on the island where I had just bought a house. And just like that, I knew that I had to leave and start over there, and it couldn't happen fast enough for me.

"I'll be there soon, Ava. I'll be there soon."

Chapter Twenty-four

My phone rang again. Dallas this time. Emily. I could be a switchboard operator for old Ma Bell at this rate.

I showed Collin the caller ID. He sighed. I wasn't giving him the best birthday of his life. I pressed Speaker to answer the call.

"Hey, girl. Just checking on you," Emily said before I even spoke.

I checked on myself for her and found that I was shockingly improved from earlier. "I'm better, Collin's his usual self, and we're having a floor picnic. I was about to send him out to pick up his birthday cake."

"Rich is at a long dinner thing. He took the car," Emily said. "But I want birthday cake." She and Rich shared a vehicle. His office was a block from their condo, so most of the time he made do on foot or by mass transit.

"I'll come get you," Collin said. Collin had a soft spot for Emily, and I knew he secretly hated that she'd married Rich Bernal long before Collin ever met her.

Serendipity. I needed to tell both of them about my rather sudden change of heart and plans as soon as possible. "Do you mind if I wait here?" I asked Collin.

"I'm just your beast of burden," he said, but he was halfway to the door, and his voice was light.

"Thanks," I said.

" I'll be back in fifteen minutes," he said. "You can tell me what the hell is going on then."

"Oh, yeah, of course," I said, as if none of it was any big deal.

As soon as he was gone, I jumped up and paced around the living room. I collapsed back onto the couch. My head was spinning at the speed of my life in Dallas, but my heart beat with longing for a St. Marcos pace. I put my head in my hands and began to laugh, finally throwing my head back and letting my mirth resound to the heavens. Holy shit. I was doing this.

Well, an announcement of this magnitude took planning. I didn't have much time left before Collin and Emily would arrive. I would not panic. I grabbed a piece of paper and a pen. I wrote:

Do Not Drink.

I underlined it twice. Bloody Marys screamed my name. Getting schnockered and forgetting about this abortion of a trial sounded awesome. But I needed my wits about me.

I wrote again.

Call Ava And Rashidi

I needed local help. Ava would for sure, and Rashidi had offered, after all, sort of. Was it OK to impose upon him? I would call them first thing tomorrow.

I wrote one more:

Do Not Call Nick.

No matter how nice—and surprising—his message was, it wasn't a proposal of marriage. I could not contact Nick. I knew if I did, if I answered that email, if I stepped through that door, I wouldn't be able to walk back out again. I had to get away from this life and how badly I'd screwed it up, how I'd humiliated myself and everyone I cared about. I was done here. I read his email five more times, then deleted it, which hurt like carving the damn thing out of my heart with a spoon, but I did it.

Fifteen minutes and many cleansing breaths later, everything started to feel right. Astounding, really. Maybe it was normal to have a freak-out in the midst of big life-changing decisions. That didn't mean this decision wasn't the best thing that could ever happen to me.

I listed the positives of moving. The people I cared about would come to visit me. Probably. When the house was done, I could be a lawyer right on St. Marcos. If I had to. I could find a new career, possibly, or maybe I could sell the house for a huge profit when it was ready. I would have a year-round tan. I wouldn't drink as much, and I wouldn't think about Nick, except occasionally. I would never see Zane McMillan again. Can someone give me an amen? I would spend less money on clothes, shoes, handbags, makeup, and jewelry.

Wait, that wasn't a positive. I scratched it off the list.

Most people would kill to be in my shoes, moving to the Caribbean on a semi-permanent sabbatical. I was a courageous risk-taking adventurer and I would have no regrets. I closed my eyes and conjured Annalise. I was so doing this.

Collin and Emily returned with a Baskin-Robbins cookies-and-cream ice cream cake and birthday candles. Emily and I stuck them in the cake, lit them, and sang while Collin blew them out. I served the cake, then broke the news while their mouths were full.

"Repeat all that slowly, sis." Collin was calm, but looking at me as if he needed to call in the white coats.

Emily didn't say anything. She just stared at me from her perch on my over-stuffed peach armchair a million miles across the living room. She looked hurt.

"I fell in love with St. Marcos, and I bought a house. Well, I didn't know I'd bought a house. I made an offer, and I didn't think they would accept it, but they did. I'm quitting my job and moving there in two weeks. I'm going to do a few renovations—" I had my fingers crossed, so this was not a lie, "then practice law on the island." This part was. I was tempted to speak loudly and draw my words out longer, since this was seeming hard for them to process, but I thought better of it. I was delivering them a game changer. "I'm excited, and I wanted to tell you guys first. After today, you've got to admit that I need a total life makeover."

They turned to each other, twin images of dismay. They didn't speak. Now did not seem the appropriate time to disclose that the house "spoke" to me. I'd left out that my realtor didn't think it was a safe place for a woman to live alone. I also omitted that I took inexplicable comfort from the house's nearness to where Mom and Dad died. And I sure hadn't told them that it would take a year and another half a million to finish the house. I felt the first reemergence of the confident and strong Katie that had been hiding from the world for the last month.

When they did start to speak, I agreed to "think about it carefully" and "not rush into anything." Not that I intended to think or slow down. I only needed them to know my decision. I was a grown-up, and I didn't need their approval. But I wanted to make them feel better about it. I would no more change their minds than they would mine. I needed to get to work, not argue with Collin and Emily about the inevitable.

"And all this happened since I got here tonight?" Collin asked.

"No. It all happened since I went to St. Marcos. But I got the call tonight telling me my dreams were coming true. All since you got here."

Emily nodded, but Collin just stared through me. I waited for more questions, but there were none. Really, there was nothing more left to say.

Chapter Twenty-five

The next day, I called my island friends.

First Ava. "Guess whose crazy red-headed friend is moving to St. Marcos in two weeks?" I asked her.

Ava shouted so loud I had to pull the phone away from my ear. "For real? You moving here for real?"

"I am. I bought Estate Annalise."

"You crazy. Anyone buy that jumbie house crazy. Good crazy, brave crazy. But then I know that about you already."

"Well, that jumbie house won't be ready for me to live in for a long time. I need a friend who'd like a roommate for a few months."

"And that friend be me, of course," she said.

"I'm going to need more help, the kind of help that requires a truck and a lot of experience on the west end of the island," I said, putting my drop line in the water.

Ava bit. "Rashidi good for that. You got his number?"

I didn't so she gave it to me. One issue solved. I called Rashidi next.

I was unsure how to begin. "This is Ava's friend Katie. How's it going?" I asked him.

He made things just right immediately. "I good, but I hear a rumor some continental lady trying to buy Annalise. That be you?"

"Not only tried, but was successful," I said.

"Wah? You buy the jumbie place? You for real?"

"I'm afraid I am. I think I'm going to need some help. Ava suggested I call you."

"No worries. Any red-haired friend of Ava a friend of mine."

I told Rashidi I needed an agent to help me buy a truck before I got back on-island. He informed me I needed a pack of dogs more.

"Locals scared of dogs. All dogs. You gonna need them to watch over Annalise once you start prettying her up and putting supplies and things there. And you gotta have dogs dem to protect you if you live up in the bush. I get you some good dogs, three or four be about right."

I hadn't anticipated a pack of guard dogs, but I could see his point. And he was the local, not me. If I remembered correctly, I liked dogs. Or maybe it was cats I liked. We'd had both when I was a kid, twenty years before. It didn't really matter, though, as Rashidi and I were talking about outside, working guard dogs. I wouldn't have to deal with slobber or dog hair or bodily functions.

"So, if I wired you the money, could I get you to pick up a truck for me? I found a used one for sale in the *St. Marcos Source* online. It looks like exactly what I need."

"Yah mon. Why don't you let me drive it 'round first, make sure it OK."

"Wow, thanks. I'm going to pay you for your help, of course."

"Now why you want to insult a man like that? We new friends." First Ava, then Rashidi. It was raining blessings.

"Fine, thank you. Then I'm at least going to feed you when I see you."

"That I let you do, for true."

He hung up, promising to check out the truck and start the hunt for the right dogs immediately.

More issues resolved. I pinched myself. It hurt. This was actually going to happen.

I continued making my mega-list, because that was just the way I rolled. I had only four big things left on it for Dallas. I needed to give my two-week notice at work, list my condo, secure the services of a moving company, and finish things gracefully with Nick.

I told Gino that same day. My decision shocked him, if his slack face was any indication. That or he had a mini stroke.

"Take a leave of absence instead. We can give you up to a year," Gino said.

That was gracious, especially given the disastrous outcome of Zane's trial and my new internet fame.

"Thank you, Gino, but I want to make a clean break," I said.

"Is this because I made you take the McMillan case? I'm sorry for that. I had no idea that witness would turn," he said, the epitome of concern and kindness.

I winced. Emily and Nick must not have told him the story behind the story, or he'd have kicked me out of the partnership. Instead, he felt responsible. Which in turn made me feel guilty. I'd been wasting a lot of time on guilty lately. I'd been causing my own trouble.

"I'm not leaving because of that. Thank you, though. None of us knew about Sherry." And now I was going to hell for lying, but no good could come of fessing up now. "It was God's way of making me earn the double fees," I said, and Gino laughed.

Wrapping up my law practice took most of my attention over the next two weeks, but there were no complications, other than warding off the morbid curiosity of the onlookers who lurked outside my office door whispering to each other. "Did Gino fire her?" "It's probably because of the McMillan case. Did you hear she had a nervous breakdown in the courtroom? I saw it on YouTube." Seriously, if YouTube's world headquarters burned to the ground, the authorities would be crazy not to take a hard look at me. But I ignored them all. Their opinions didn't matter to me anymore, and I had things left to do.

My condo building had a waiting list of potential buyers. It was on McKinney Avenue in the uptown area, close to downtown Dallas and humming with the energy burned by the upwardly mobile. It was either trés chic or way cool, depending on your demographic. I found someone eager to pay my price and close immediately. Not only that, but the couple recognized me from the TV coverage of Zane's trial. Super. And guess what? They'd even seen the YouTube video. I asked. Now they'd have stories to tell at their dinner parties about how they bought the place from the Paula Abdul of defense attorneys.

With the condo sold furnished, I had much less to ship, which was good because shipping to the Caribbean was quite pricey.

"You realize that mid-September is the peak of hurricane season?" the representative from the moving company asked me when I called. "Some people would rather store their belongings until the season is over, then ship them."

I hadn't thought about that. Wasn't that why God invented insurance, though?

"I want to ship now," I said.

No escape hatches. All in. And everything fell into place so easily that I knew it was meant to be.

Except for one thing. The finish-with-Nick thing.

After deleting the email Nick sent after the McMillan trial, I'd hidden from him at work like a yellow-bellied sapsucker. When I caught a glimpse of him, I ducked into the bathroom or reversed course as if I'd forgotten something. I wasn't yet ready to explain myself about anything. Like ignoring his olive branch. Or moving. The awkwardness between us. I wanted to wait until the day before I left to talk to him, so I wouldn't have to face him again afterwards. The last minute in the last hour of the last day, if I had my choice. Bwock bwock, said the chicken.

I rehearsed every word I was going to say to him. The gist of it? I wanted to tell him I was sorry. For Shreveport, for the McMillan trial, for everything. That I appreciated his email, and that he had nothing left to apologize for to me. I knew he was my true friend before Shreveport, and that I'd driven him away. I needed him to know that I was leaving. That I was taking his advice and accepting help. Granted, it was my kind of help from a jumbie house and friends I barely knew, but I would leave that part unsaid.

And when the conversation was over, then I would let it go, and I would have the closure I craved. After that, I didn't ever want to see him again. Unless he declared undying love for me. Which he wouldn't.

The days flew by. I didn't see Collin or Emily as much as I'd hoped. When I did, it was hard. They kept trying to talk me out of the best decision of my life.

Collin tried emotional pressure. "You can't sever your ties to our past, Katie. This is where Mom and Dad raised us. You're going to lose your connection to everything that has always mattered to you."

Emily worked the same theme, without the sledgehammer. "You can change jobs and condos here, you know. You don't have to run halfway around the world. Besides, I haven't even taught you to ride a horse properly yet."

When the emotional blackmail didn't work, Collin suggested a compromise. "Back out of this purchase for now. Wait a month and I'll come with you for a visit. We'll work this through together. It would be good for me to go to St. Marcos and face what happened to Mom and Dad, too."

Finally, Emily broke. "What about me, with my best friend so far away? I'm at least coming to help you get settled, and I won't take no for an answer."

Now this was the kind of emotional gesture I could work with. "Of course!" I said. We booked her a flight to follow me the day after I left. I could show her a good time on St. Marcos and pay her back for all she had done for me lately, for the embarrassment I'd made her a part of. St. Marcos was a long way from Amarillo, even from Dallas, and she had never been to the Caribbean.

And then, the night *after* the painful but well-meaning going away party the firm threw for me at Uncle Julio's, the party where I spent the entire evening fake-laughing at McZillion jokes and eyeing the exit, I got an email from Nick. Nick who had not come to my party.

I opened it cautiously, hoping for a miracle but expecting the boogeyman to jump out.

To: all@haileyhart.com (Hailey & Hart, All Attorneys and Staff)
From: nick.kovacs@haileyhart.com
Subject: Out of the Office
I will be out of the office from August 15 through August 29. If this is an emergency, please write "Emergency" in the subject of your email, or call me on my mobile phone.

It was a Thursday. I was flying out Saturday. And he was already gone. My Friday afternoon speech would never happen. I would never see him again. Never.

Months of fighting it had made no difference. I loved this man. I needed to get over it and move on. But how was I supposed to turn my Only One into nothing? I couldn't. Not yet, anyway.

Well, that was that, then. I drew three lines through the last item on my list, ripping a hole in the paper as I did. I was ready to go. But I would keep my same cell phone number. Just in case.

Chapter Twenty-six

Thank God for my on-time plane. I stuck my hand into the recess in the wheel well above the front driver's-side tire of a gold Chevy Silverado pickup and probed around. Dirt. Something greasy. Keys—right where Rashidi had promised to leave them. Excellent. I love it when a plan comes together.

A voice behind me pulled a smile from my lips. "Good afternoon, miss. Welcome to the islands. Can I interest you in a rainforest tour?"

I spun around to hug Rashidi. "What are you doing here?"

"I figure I stay to greet you, since I only drop the truck five minutes ago," he said sheepishly.

I put my hand on the front hood of the Silverado. Still hot. I laughed. "You were cutting it close. I can't tell you how much I appreciate it." I glanced at my watch, then unfastened it, removed it, and dropped it in my purse. I was on island time from now on. "Hey, I have an hour before I have to be at the Annalise closing. You have time for me to feed you like I promised?"

Rashidi straightened a pretend collar on his green-with-yellow-letters "University of the Virgin Islands" t-shirt. "Let we go."

I followed closely behind Rashidi's old but well cared for red Jeep as he led me to his favorite vegetarian restaurant. I had forgotten about his whole vegan lifestyle thing. Oh, well. I could always drive through Wendy's on my way to the bank, although when I'd done that on my last visit I'd had to honk the chickens out of the drive-through lane, and then sat there for twenty minutes until my food was ready.

Rashidi and I sat at a window table inside the dark soul food restaurant. Jimmy Cliff was crooning "I can see clearly now," the reggae song by Johnny Nash he'd remade and performed far better than the original. There wasn't an excess ounce of body fat on anyone besides me in the place. And I thought I was skinny. I was also the only patron without dreadlocks.

I perused the menu, lost. Protein, protein, where could I find protein? A turbaned Rasta waitress took our order. In a tone of reverence, Rashidi ordered rice noodles with Asian pesto and stir-fried vegetables with lemongrass. I settled on a red pepper and garlic hummus and roasted Mediterranean eggplant, and hoped for the best.

"The food here manna from the gods. And it close to the university. That good. I teaching a class in an hour," Rashidi said.

I realized I knew next to nothing about Rashidi, other than he was kind to white tourist ladies. "What do you teach?" I asked.

"Coupla things. I'm an associate professor, not tenured, so I teach classes as part of degree programs, like botany, and I do continuing education classes, too, community stuff," he said. "This afternoon I teaching a hydroponic farming class."

I was impressed, and lost. "A what?"

"Hydroponic farming. I trying to get the local farmers to use fish to fertilize their plants. Farm the tilapia, farm the crops. It's Jah's perfect match."

"Jeez Louise, Rashidi, where'd you learn to do that?"

"I got my degree in botany from the University of Florida. I learn about the fish farming there."

"So where do the rainforest tours come in?" I asked him. He was a professor dragging the likes of me up and down the hills of the rainforest. On a haunted house tour, no less.

"Cash," he said, and his white teeth gleamed in his wide smile. "U.V.I. don't pay enough for me to eat here."

Our food arrived. Rashidi bowed his head and whispered a prayer under his breath, so I ducked mine, too. I decided to eat my eggplant first, while it was still hot. I slid my fork slowly into the gooey golden mess and lifted it to my face, trying to smell it without making my concern obvious to everyone in the building. Allspice. Nutmeg. Garlic. The aroma was shockingly good. I slipped it into my mouth and the flavors melted into my tongue.

"Oh my God," I said, or tried to, through a mouth full of eggplant. "This is amazing."

Rashidi nodded as he ate. We chewed in bliss together until we had polished the surfaces of the bowls before us. Rashidi pushed his chair back a few inches from the table like a fat man from Thanksgiving dinner. This mannerism from the lithe Rashidi tickled me.

He spoke again. "Ava not doing so good. She pretty beat up about her friend dying."

I wondered if Rashidi knew that Guy was more than a friend to Ava. I wouldn't be the one to unload that on him, just in case. "I hope I can help her," I said.

"It help just you coming. A good distraction. She talking 'bout working with you to find out what happen to your parents here," he said.

"Yes. She's already been invaluable with that."

"The cop on that case my school chum. Michael. He at the University of Florida for a year when I there, but he drop out and come home."

"Really?" I asked. "Do you know what happened to him? I was told he went out fishing alone and drowned less than a month after my parents died."

Rashidi shook his head. "Make no sense. I fish with Michael, time to time. He never go out alone, he can't swim. Loved to fish, scared of water. They found his empty boat floating a mile off the west end of the island." He shook his head again, his eyes far away.

I swallowed. "You think someone killed him?" I asked.

"Dunno. Maybe an accident and folks dem scared they'd get in trouble. Maybe he helped into the water by someone bad. Maybe I wrong and he fish alone."

My antenna quivered. I couldn't believe Michael's death was a coincidence.

The Rasta waitress brought our bill, and I handed her a twenty and a ten. It covered the bill plus tip. The food here rocked and was cheaper than the flying fish hut. Quite a find.

Rashidi changed the subject. "Ava say you a lawyer."

"Was." I looked down. "Now I'm a house remodeler."

Rashidi's eyes cut to the wall clock, and he stood abruptly. "And I a teacher almost late for class," he said. "I'll come around Annalise later today. Ava want me to bring her by."

I stood too, and we walked out together. "Thank you so much, Rashidi. I love the truck."

"No problem. Thanks for the food," he said. He put an arm around my shoulders for a side hug, and we parted ways.

I got in my snazzy new-to-me Silverado and fussed and putzed with the gizmos and gadgets on the dash. Satisfied with my changes, I drove into Town. I headed straight to the Bank of St. Marcos to meet Doug for the closing on Annalise. Doug would never be my favorite person on the island, but we chatted amiably about my move, my new property, and hurricane seasons of yore. Ms. Nesbitt only kept us waiting for half an hour before she ushered us into the bank's main conference room. I don't know why it surprised me, but Ms. Nesbitt wasn't the heavyset aging woman I had expected. Instead, she was petite, 5'1" or less, and couldn't have topped a hundred pounds. While she was well over forty, she looked younger than me. She wore a two-piece knit suit in dark green with gold buttons and a skirt that ended an inch above her knees. Her perfect legs ended in closed-toe black pumps. Very professional.

Doug kissed her on both cheeks. "Good day. How are the husband and kids, Lisa?"

It seemed all was forgiven between the two of them for the earlier almost-sale to her mystery buyer.

"Oh, good day to you, too, Doug. We all good. Thank you for asking after them." She turned her diamond-bright smile on me. "Congratulations, Ms. Connell. Welcome to our island, and to your new home."

"Thank you so much, Ms. Nesbitt. Now I just have to figure out how to finish the house so I can actually call it a home," I said.

"I set you up, Ms. Connell. The contractor for the buyer that fall through, he already know the house real good. He go up there and put a proposal together for you. He come with my highest recommendation. I give him your number. Here's his card." She handed me a white rectangle with "Junior" and a phone number written on it. Well, that would work.

"Thank you. I appreciate that very much," I said.

"He meet you there today, then?" she asked.

"Sure, that would be fine," I said. Why the heck not, after all?

Although the closing lasted two hours, Doug pronounced it speedy and a smashing success. The three of us parted jovially in the bank lobby. I got back into my truck and headed out to Annalise down Centerline Road. The Silverado rocketed over the road's notorious potholes like a flying tank. I had dreamed of a big truck with a lift kit like this since I was an elementary schooler. I was punch-drunk in love with it already.

Half an hour later, Annalise came into view. On a romantic whim, I parked on the side of the road to take a better look from this vantage point. I got out and a dilapidated car pulled up beside me, all its windows down and Puerto Rican music blaring. I felt a twinge of nervousness. Was I about to get robbed? I anticipated my defense, but relaxed when I saw a family in the car. They were doing the same thing as me—paying homage to Annalise.

"Good day, miss. She's beee-ewe-teefull, ain't she?" the woman asked me, leaning her head out of the window. Children spilled over from the back seat to the front, tugging on her hair and pointing at the imposing structure standing tall in the distance like a peak above the mountain of trees in the valley below.

"Good day to you, too. She is breathtaking," I said, and shivered.

I returned to my car and pressed on, eager to close the distance between me and my house. Half a mile from the house, I saw the gate. Stone columns without the stones around a gateless opening. My Grinch heart grew three sizes as I turned onto the driveway and made my way through the welcoming rows of guava bushes and flamboyant trees. When I pulled up beside her, I leaped out and ran straight to the front steps.

I sat down and put my cheek against a pillar, and positive energy seeped into my body from the sun-warmed concrete. I closed my eyes and listened to the birds singing. The breeze cooled my face. This was my peaceful place, where I could leave the world behind and dream any magical dreams I wanted. Nothing could bother me and my fortress of a house.

I whispered to her, "We are both going to be OK, Annalise, more than OK. I know we will."

Lost in reverie, I somehow missed the sound of footsteps.

A voice behind me said, "'Scuse me, miss?"

I jumped so high and fast that I scraped my cheek on the rough edge of the unfinished column. I turned and saw a dog and four shirtless local youth. One of the boys was riding bareback on a scruffy paint horse. Another carried some kind of long-barreled gun. The other two held machetes. If I had seen these young men in Dallas, I would have grabbed for my pepper spray. Who was I kidding? I would have grabbed for my pepper spray right then and there, if I'd had it with me. As it was, I positioned my feet shoulder-width apart, my right foot just slightly in front of my left, my knees soft, hands loose.

"Good afternoon, miss," one of the boys said. "We didn't mean to scare you. We didn't think anyone here. We from there," he pointed in the general direction of where I thought the Pig Bar was located, "and we like to come up here and do some limin', time to time. Sometimes we stay in this house."

Underneath his twig-filled dreadlocks, this was a polite kid. I willed myself to act naturally. They were my new neighbors, after all. Sort of.

I said, "Well, I bought this house. I like it a lot, too."

A chorus of "no ways" and "iries" rose up. "Irie" was, I had learned from my masseuse at the spa, a local expression that meant "that's cool" or "it's all good," as in, "Ms. Connell, how that massage make you feel? Irie?"

The boys wanted to hear what I planned to do with Annalise, which was a short conversation. I didn't have the slightest idea yet. As we wrapped up our chat, Ms. Nesbitt's Junior—or someone I really hoped was him, since it was a strange man in a truck parking beside my house—showed up. The boys waved to me and headed straight back down into brambly manjack I would have sworn was impenetrable moments before, making the sound of a rainstorm as they rattled the seedpods on the small tan-tan trees.

The man I prayed was Junior was wearing low, baggy jeans and a knit Rasta cap over long dreadlocks. He was also carrying a few extra johnnycakes around his middle. I remembered what my father used to say about men with soft hands and wondered if it applied to contractors with big guts. But maybe his workers did the heavy lifting. I shouldn't stick out my tongue at good fortune when it sent me a contractor referred by a reputable source and available to work so soon.

"Good afternoon," he said. "I'm Junior, here for Ms. Connell."

Phew, it was Junior. I hoped this, after the Wild Boys' visit, would be the last of my scares for the day.

Junior and I discussed in broad concept the work the house needed. "To-morrow, early, I bring my plumber, my 'lectrician, and some boys dem to clean." He gestured upwards and then made a broad sweeping motion. "Big clean. I put dem up on the scaffolding and they scrub down the ceilings and walls, way up high, all the way down low."

Cleaning? That sounded heavenly. We agreed he would bill me for time and materials and we shook on it. Junior got back in his brand-new dark blue Chevrolet Silverado. Well, well. It made my Silverado look like it belonged to the hired help.

I saw Rashidi coming up the drive in his Jeep as Junior left, with Ava in the front seat beside him. Estate Annalise, otherwise known as Grand Central Station. I hugged Rashidi as he got out of the Jeep, then Ava, longer and tighter, after she came around from the passenger side.

"I'm so sorry about your friend," I said in her ear.

She squeezed me and her head rubbed against mine as she nodded. Her phone rang. "Jacoby," she said. "I have to take this." She walked fifty feet away and sat against the thick trunk of a mango tree. Its heavily laden branches draped a shade of leaves and mangos three feet above her head. She kicked a rotten one away from her with her heel. She had tied her long curls back in a red scarf that doubled as a headband and a low ponytail holder, and she twisted the end of it around her finger.

"So, the house like you remember her?" Rashidi asked.

"Better," I said. "Isn't she fabulous?"

"Yah mon, she fabulous. But what Junior Nesbitt doing out here? He has-slin' you?"

Nesbitt?

"I hired him, at the highest recommendation of another Nesbitt at Bank of St. Marcos. Ms. Nesbitt, the bank officer there in charge of Annalise. Only I didn't know him as anything other than Junior from her referral."

Rashidi chuptzed. "The little woman his sister."

"Did I mess up?" It was all about who you knew. And didn't know.

"Maybe he straightened out. I got your back. There is a problem, though, a big problem," Rashidi told me.

My stomach clenched. "What is it?"

"You buying Annalise and all. This mean I gonna have to change up the grand finale of my rainforest tour. Ain't no big thing if it just another ole rich white folk house."

I stared at him blankly until I saw he was kidding me, and I laughed.

Chapter Twenty-seven

That night, I moved in with Ava, a process which consisted of me dragging two suitcases, a carry-on full of toiletries, and my laptop bag from the truck to her couch. Or, rather the floor beside her couch. My Rimowa bags in Ultra Violet and Inca Gold stood in a colorful row like soldiers guarding the entryway from the living room to the kitchen.

"Are you sure about this?" I asked again. "I could be homeless for months."

"I making room for you in there," she said, pointing vaguely toward her bedroom. I now saw there was a smaller bedroom next to it, one without a bed. And with a lot of boxes stacked haphazardly in the middle of the room. "That OK with you?"

"As long as you're OK, I'm OK," I said, and meant it. "I'll stack the boxes against the wall and get a futon tomorrow." I'd have to do it before Emily arrived in the late afternoon. Emily. I'd forgotten to tell Ava about Emily. Oops. "My friend Emily is coming tomorrow and staying on-island for a few days. I can't wait for you to meet each other. You're going to love her. Where do you think I should book her a room?"

"If you have a futon, she can take the couch. Unless she just made of money."

That she was not. So we'd sardine together. Cool.

After all that strenuous unpacking, we celebrated at Toes in the Water with burgers. We sat at a picnic table in the sand on a small ledge above the beach proper, not far from where a hammock filled with young children was swinging between two coconut palms. The tiny establishment consisted of a handful of half-filled picnic tables, a roofed patio bar and stage, and three structures in various states of sun-bleached, windswept disrepair. A faded mural of Toes in the Sand was painted on the side of one of them, and I caught a glimpse of the cook when he stuck his head out of another to take an order from the waitress. A communal washbasin inlaid with glitter and shells ran the length of the third building. If Annalise hadn't already lured me away from Dallas, this place could have. I tingled with delight at the sound of the surf kissing the beach boulders goodnight.

The sight of the ever-hopeful Jacoby was no surprise when he met us there. We'd already taken our seats when he walked in from the parking lot on the west side of the restaurant, carving a black hole in the sun behind him as he made his way over to our table. He expressed no delight at my presence, but it didn't faze him, either. He stuck out his ham-sized paw and shook my hand. Please don't hurt me, I thought. Then he sat by Ava and soaked her in as if I didn't exist. I slid my feet out of my shoes and buried my bare toes in the sand underneath our picnic table, listening to Ava. She had a lot to say.

"Everywhere I look, people still talking about Guy's murder. It all over the TV, the paper. I can't get away from it. All of it just make my blood chill. There a killer out there," she said.

Jacoby was digging his right heel into the sand with heavy thumps as she spoke. He said, "The detectives doing all they can to find the murderer. A lot of people hate that man, though. A lot of suspects."

"I know. I know. I just so grateful you kept me out of it, Jacoby." She put her hand on his arm and stroked his skin with her thumb. I could see the goose bumps in his flesh. "It could have all been so nasty, instead of sad. It supposed to be sad when someone die." Tears pooled in the corner of her eyes but didn't fall.

"Anything for you, Ava. You know that."

"Still, I don't want you to get in trouble," she said. "You took a big chance, helping me."

"No one gonna know except us. Everyone believe the call anonymous, and you make it from the hotel phone to 911, just like I tell you. You cover the phone with a cloth, disguise your voice, everything. They couldn't even tell it a woman. It gonna be all right."

"He was a good man," Ava said.

I could see she'd taken a wrong turn in the conversation as Jacoby stiffened and spoke. "He a big man, but he no good. I coulda told you 'bout all his girlfriends before, if I knew about you and he. I'm sorry he dead, but I glad you not with him anymore."

Now it was Ava who stiffened. "Just please tell me if you hear something, anything, about who did it. Promise me, Jacoby."

"Yah mon. I promise."

Just when I was getting seriously uncomfortable, a perky waitress in a threadbare khaki miniskirt and braless lavender tank top diverted our attention.

"Time for sunset shots," she said from underneath her unfortunate over-bite, setting three plastic cups in front of us. "Coconut rum, Cruzan, of course. Watch for the green flash."

I started to tell her to take mine away, but the words didn't come out. The bartender counted backwards from ten, and all the patrons held their shot cups aloft.

"Three, two, one," he shouted.

Jacoby and Ava threw back their shots. I looked around in the fading light, taking in the rolling waves as they broke over the reef twenty yards away, the curve of the shoreline as it folded into the two miles of white sand around Cape Bay, and the green of the palm tree tops extending down the beach toward the hills of the rainforest. I was at peace here. I didn't have to contend with Nick's draining presence or flip-flopping witnesses. Here, I could do moderation. I could be smart, be measured. I was in control. I downed my shot and savored the delicious and instantaneous flood of warmth through my body. As I stared westward over the horizon, the sun sank, and I saw a flash of green light.

I jumped to my feet. "I saw it!" I yelled. "I saw the green flash!"

The bartender rang a bell above his head. "Green flash, everybody. She saw it."

Ava and even Jacoby slapped me on the back. "I only seen it once, myself," Jacoby told me. "Powerful good luck."

That would make for a nice change. The waitress showed up again, barefoot like us, this time with a pitcher of margaritas.

"Green for the green flash," she explained, and handed me a cup. "On the house."

"Thanks!" I said. "This is what we drink where I'm from. That and Lone Star beer," I said. "Want some, y'all?"

Ava emptied her water in the sand, and Jacoby followed suit. They both held out their empty cups. I poured. "To the green flash," I said.

Ava said, "To the singing sensation, Ava and Katie."

"What?" I asked.

"Just drink," she said. "Then I explain."

I drank, swallowing slowly, enjoying the reunion my bloodstream was conducting with its old friend tequila, then refilled our glasses.

"OK, so here what I thinking, and don't stop me until I'm through," Ava said. "I have a synthesizer and sound system. I buy it cheap from a continental who drink himself into an island stupor. Same old story. Anyway, I do a couple of solo gigs, getting my feet wet, but solo don't do so good here. Katie, you and me, we sound goooood. More depth. More range. Plus, two hot chicks better than one. Four breasts, you know."

Jacoby acted as if she'd said something profound and I spit margarita in a jet-propelled arc that hit the guy at the next table. Oops. But he was pickled, and didn't notice.

There was no reason not to join musical forces with Ava. The point of studying music in college was the joy of making it. I thought of all the hours I'd spent in tiny soundproof rehearsal rooms with my voice professor at piano, a metronome beside me, and a music stand in front of me. Again, Katie. Round your mouth. Open your chest. I remembered the two best years of my life, of a standing bass, a snare drum, an electric keyboard, and a guitar, my lips against the microphone. It was so long ago. The only time I sang now was after three or four shots on karaoke night.

My throat tightened. The joy of making music. That was the subject of the last good conversation I'd had with Nick, back in Shreveport. I almost smiled as I recalled him talking about his high school garage band, Stingray. I had defended lead singers, a category of musician he defined as egomaniacal. By reflex, I looked for messages on my iPhone. Nope. As if. I was the one who'd deleted his last message, anyway. "Why not?" I said. "Sign me up."

"Yay! We gonna be the toast of the island!" Ava said, and hugged me.

"Was that we gonna be toasted? Because I think I am already," I said.

"Oh, hush you mouth," Ava said.

So I was to be Eliza Doolittle, and Ava my mentor. I didn't want to be another Ava, though. I could never out-Ava the real Ava. Everywhere she went, her ribald personality lit up the room and a horde of male admirers vied for her attention. I was the awkward one, the redheaded stepchild, too tall, too thin, too many angles. I needed my own shtick. I could do elegant as a foil to her sexy vamp, for instance. I knew my fine-boned features spoke of class, whether I had it or not. So I wouldn't copy Ava, but I could certainly emulate her confidence and learn about the island music scene from her.

She began instructing me right away on the art of performing for slightly disinterested audiences, starting with the nearest one—Jacoby. She grabbed my margarita-free hand and pulled me to the square concrete stage. We stood under the peaked palm-frond roof and faced the ocean, and it roared its approval. Ava blocked out where she wanted us to stand, demonstrated a few easy dance steps, and explained how she sets the equipment up in relation to the microphones.

A giant of a man with unruly blond curls and effeminate tortoiseshell glasses at another table did a double take at us. His stare wasn't admiring. He looked as if he was trying to decide whether to swat us with a flyswatter. His companion turned to look in our direction, and this time I was the one who did a double take. The investigator, Walker. He gave no indication he recognized us, just turned back to his basket of fries.

"Did you see Walker over there?" I asked Ava. "He's with some big guy who was staring at us."

Ava was singing below her breath and working on a step-ball-change-spin sequence of dance steps. "Just a second," she said, holding up her hand and working her feet.

I waited five beats, then said, "Ava."

"Yes, I with you. Now, what you say?" she asked.

"Do you see Walker over there?" I asked, and pointed over my shoulder with my thumb.

"Where?" she said, looking all around.

I turned back to where Walker and his large companion had been just moments ago. Empty.

"Oh, never mind. He's gone." I scanned the restaurant and the parking area. No sign of them. They'd certainly split fast. I'd ask Walker about it when I caught up with him, hopefully tomorrow.

Ava was unconcerned. "I giving you a songbook to study tonight, and you can sing a few with me at my gig tomorrow night," she said.

"That soon?"

"Yah mon, nobody care if you read the words. We all chill here. It be fun."

I stepped off the stage and put my head back. The sky was a blanket of stars now. I picked an extra bright one and made my wish: that things could always be as perfect as they were right now.

Chapter Twenty-eight

The next day, Ava woke me early. Too early. Wait, make that on time. Woops, I had forgotten to set my alarm. I lifted my head from the too-flat pillow on the couch. I hadn't bothered to put on a bottom sheet. I shucked off the top one and swung my bare legs to the floor, smoothing with my hands my Phantom of the Opera nightshirt, a treasure from a long-ago trip to New York City with my mother. My head barely hurt. I congratulated myself on my decreased intake the night before. I could do this moderation thing.

Ava said, "We got more to learn, island girl. I gonna teach you things best done before the sun high in the sky. To Annalise!"

I dragged myself out to the truck behind Ava. I had promised to meet the contractors by 8:30 anyway. I drove like a mad thing, and we arrived at 8:40. I parked in the driveway and pressed both palms to my cheeks. The flesh on my face tingled as if it had fallen asleep. That's what thirty minutes of violent bouncing on a St. Marcos road could do to a girl. I wondered if I could rig up some kind of a face bra so I wouldn't end up with the jowls of a Great Dane. Still, we beat the contractors. That was all right. I hadn't expected them to be on the early side of on time.

"So what are you teaching me today, Dr. Doolittle?" I asked Ava as we climbed out of the truck.

Ava reached into the truck bed.

"Close your eyes," she said.

I did, with trepidation. In my experience, surprises don't always end well.

"Tada!" Ava said. "Open your eyes. A housewarming present. You very own machete, which every good islander needs. Trust me."

"Wow," I said. I had no words. A six-inch black handle joined a two-foot wicked sharp blade, straight on one side and curved on the other. She handed it to me and I gripped the handle with both hands, holding the business end far away from me.

"Learn from the master," she said, brandishing her own machete.

She crossed the lawn through a stand of trees and headed for the manjack and tan-tan bush my neighbors had come and gone through the day before. She swished the blade through the air and made solid contact on a large manjack. She repeated the move from the opposite direction once, twice, then three times more, and the bush hit the ground. She turned to me. "Just picture the face of someone you really hate, and whack it good. I imagining it the face of whoever cut Guy."

She turned back around, ferocious, and attacked the bush. I knew she hadn't loved Guy, but she had cared about him. He was good enough to her, in his own way, a way that was good enough for Ava. Like trying to get her the TV show. I didn't like him much, but I mourned for her grief.

She wheeled back around. Her voice was tight. "I late getting there, you know, and if I been on time, ten minutes earlier, I be dead, too."

"My God. I didn't know." Out of nowhere, the words came to my lips. "I'd met him, you know. Guy. I sat next to him on a plane. He was very nice. I'm so sorry, Ava."

She nodded, then swung the machete at nothing, her body gyrating with the weight of the blade as she sliced it from one side of her to the other. Take that, air. And that. And that. I marveled at her physical strength as she exorcized her demons. Ava was definitely not the talk-out-your-problems kind of woman. But maybe her way of dealing with loss had its merits.

I hefted my own machete and went after the next bush. Whack. Whack. Whack. Ava stopped and eyed me critically, staying well clear of my blade. I rested, panting loudly. I was probably going to chop off my leg with the damn thing, and the bush looked no worse for my efforts. Ava nodded, then got back to work. I resumed whacking. We fell into a rhythm of sorts, my one chop to each of her three. Five minutes later, the small tan-tan tree—well, large bush— actually fell over. I set the machete down and beamed. I was the soon-to-be butt-kicking goddess of the St. Marcos rainforest, no doubt.

"Man, you whup that bush's ass and good, girl," Ava drawled. Five felled bushes lay behind her.

"Sure, laugh at me, but it's all about the baby steps. Woman against forest."

We walked back to the house through a stand of tamarind trees with thick trunks tangled with passion fruit vines. Rashidi had told us on our tour that the tennis-ball-sized passion fruits were pulpy and seedy, and had to be boiled and strained before you could eat them. The Peacock Flower had served sweetened passion fruit juice, and it was delicious. I plucked one and stuck it in my left shorts pocket, then added a few tamarind seedpods for good measure. I would try them both later.

When we got back to the Silverado, Ava said, "Keep that machete under the seat in your truck. Then you a for true island girl. Ready for anything."

I shoved the machete under the seat, blade side in, handle toward the passenger side. I didn't want a handful of ouch the first time I pulled it back out. I stood back up, straightening my pleated shorts. My Gap tee had long since come untucked, and I left it that way, but brushed the bugs and mud off my sweaty legs. What I wouldn't give for a hose.

Ava excused herself to the optimal cell reception of the backyard pool, to call the manager of the club where she was singing that night. I heard the sound of heavy wheels turning fast on the gravel road. I pulled my iPhone from my shorts pocket and checked the time. It was 10:30. I frowned. I exited the garage, all set to meet Junior and discuss his tardiness, but saw Rashidi's red Jeep instead.

He pulled to a stop, leaned across the interior, and opened his passenger's side door. Out jumped a large black dog. Then a yellow one. And a brown one. They just kept coming and coming. Rashidi hadn't just brought the troops, he'd brought an entire cavalry. He was saying something, but I couldn't hear him over the dogs.

The pack of yelping mutts milled around me. I hadn't owned a dog since I was a child, and now I was counting five heads and five tails.

"My God, Rashidi, did you rob a pet store?" I said. "Why so many? I thought we said three or four?" I crouched down and rubbed the ears of a large yellow lab.

"A friend of mine moving back to the states, and his dogs need a home. I didn't want to break them up, and they good dogs. But if they're too much, we can find other homes for a few of them."

Break up a family? "No, no. They should stay together. I can handle them." *I think.*

Rashidi introduced me to each of them, describing their histories and dispositions with familiarity. The alpha male of the group was Cowboy, a freakishly large yellow lab. The lead female was Sheila, a rottweiler mix who didn't trust men and was skittish around everyone, but Rashidi promised she was sweet on the inside. There was a crotchety old dog named Jake, an awkward cocker spaniel/Dalmatian hybrid. Cockermatian, Rashidi called it. There were also two young females: Karma, a golden retriever, and Laila, a boxer named after Muhammad Ali's boxing daughter.

"You sure you all right with them?" he asked.

"I'm sure. They'll be great," I said. They were. Great, and really slobbery. This would take some getting used to. Kind of like bugs in leg sweat and carpets of gungalos. But I had asked for this.

"Good. Because I got one more surprise for you."

This was my day for surprises. Rashidi turned back to his Jeep and opened the driver's door. He untied something, then made a huffing sound and snapped his fingers. He stood back and I saw that he was holding a leash. He gave it a tug.

A gorgeous black and tan German shepherd sprang out of the Jeep. He was a puppy, but a big puppy, with alert ears and ginormous paws. He held his head and tail high and trotted toward me in that singularly shepherd prance, a miniature show horse.

"This here Poco Oso. We going to make him your personal guard dog. A woman traveling about alone on the island need a big dog with her. He nine months old. A beaut', isn't he?"

I was on the ground by then, my hands deep in Poco Oso's fur. "Oh, Rashidi, he's perfect. I love him. Thank you. Thank you for all of them." Oso was sniffing my hair and neck, and I let him take his time imprinting on my scent.

"Good, so where you go, he go. Get him used to his job. The rest the dogs dem stay here."

"You're awesome, Rashidi." I meant it.

"So put in a good word for me with Ava now and then," he said, his voice softer than before.

"Oh, Lord, Rashidi, not you, too?" I asked.

He shrugged and chuptzed himself.

Ava appeared from around the back of the house. "Good God, where all these wild animals come from?" She waded into their midst and rubbed one head after another. "Ah, I know you guys. These here were John Beillue's dogs."

A line of trucks came barreling up my driveway, as many as there were dogs. Lord have mercy, where would they all park? Junior was in the first truck, his snazzy midnight-blue Silverado again. A short wiry local man exited the passenger side. Junior bounded out to greet me.

"Ms. Katie, good morning, good morning, and a pleasant good day to you." Junior's smile stretched from ear to ear.

Mine didn't. I couldn't even choke out a fake good morning. "I've been out here for two hours waiting for you, Junior."

"Oh, yeah, I sorry. I call to tell you we late, but no answer."

I held up my iPhone. "No messages, no missed calls, and I'm in cell range. Maybe you should check the number you dialed. Or text me. It's important to me that we can count on each other." I put on my witness cross-exam face. "Next time, either be here when you tell me, or let me know. Then we'll be fine."

I trusted him less the further his grin spread across his face. "Yah mon, for true, we be fine." He stuck out his hand and I shook it briefly. "I get the cleaning crew started while this mon look at the 'lectrixity and the plumber see to his business."

Not great, but good enough.

Ava broke in. "We haven't been introduced."

"Sorry," I said. "Ava, this is Junior. Junior, this is Ava."

"Very nice to meet you," Junior said. His eyes gleamed, of course, as he took Ava in.

"Pleasure," Ava said politely.

It was time for me to leave if I was going to track down Walker before I picked up Emily.

"I'll see you later, then, Junior," I said. Farewells rang out from all sides.

Ava and I walked to my truck, Rashidi behind us, Oso behind him. Rashidi leaned in the passenger side once Ava and I were seated.

"Don't forget your guard dog," he said.

Ava opened her door and Oso climbed in. He snuggled down between Ava and me on the bench seat and Rashidi handed Ava his leash. I stroked Oso's luxurious fur, loving how soft he was.

"Good boy, Oso," I said.

"I stay out here just to keep an eye on t'ings for another hour or so. I see you ladies later." Rashidi saluted and backed away.

Oso had already put his head down on the seat. We drove out slowly, honking the rest of the dogs out of the way. I made a right turn out of the dirt driveway onto the gravel road, and we passed the ramshackle wooden shanties in the village of Rasta squatters a few yards down the lane from Annalise. All the times I'd passed it before, the old patriarch and at least a few of his kids or grandkids and their pets were milling about. Today, it was quiet. A woman's flowered housedress still hung on the line. Plastic Coca-Cola bottles and Cheerios boxes littered the ground and the stink of garbage still hung in the air. But no people, no animals.

Ava teased, "White lady move into the mansion down the street, and old Rasta man say, 'There go the neighborhood.'"

"That was pretty funny, Ava."

"Yah mon," she said. "I funny."

Actually, for across-the-street neighbors, I would rather have a shanty village of peaceful Rastas than empty shacks. It was definitely something to keep an eye on.

Chapter Twenty-nine

When we pulled up in front of Ava's nondescript white masonry house, I decided I'd have just enough time to shower before I went to see the investigator if I could get her to pick up the futon. I pulled out a fistful of bills.

"Ava, could you get someone to run you out to buy a futon? I smell awful, and I only have time to shower if I don't go to K-Mart."

"No problem, mon," she said, taking the money and getting out of the car.

I ran into the house and made a sharp right into the shower. She had decorated her blue bathroom with swirls and twirls of seashells glued right to the wall in a Nautilus pattern. The room was so small that I had to stand partway in the shower to blow-dry my hair. I donned a yellow linen sundress. I wanted to feel put together when I saw Walker, and this appointment had me out of sorts. I'd left three voicemail for him the week after the McMillan trial, none of which he'd returned. Then, of course, I'd seen him last night, only to have him pretend he didn't see me.

"Jacoby on his way to get me," Ava said as I left.

"Thanks," I yelled as I ran out the door.

I cruised past the farmer's market downtown, where for half a block, islanders displayed their wares in wooden bins under thatch-roofed huts. Big green breadfruit. Ovals of avocados. Bunches of tiny babyfinger bananas and their larger cousins, the starchy plantains. I couldn't wait to do my shopping there. A round-bellied black woman sat in a rocker on the sidewalk, legs splayed, fanning herself with a paper plate as a handful of customers milled around between the bins.

I found a parking place on King's Cross street about a half block from Walker's office. As I pulled into the spot, a paw reached out and pushed on my thigh. Oso used my leg as leverage for his stretch, raising his hindquarters until he was in the perfect downward dog position. I guess I'd learned something in the Peacock Flower's yoga class, after all.

I wasn't used to carting a half-grown dog around town. What was I supposed to do with my new pal? I couldn't leave him in the truck on our first day together. He'd feel abandoned. I clipped the leash to his collar and tugged.

"Let's go, Oso," I said.

Oso pulled back against the leash. OK, so he needed some training. No time like the present to start. I tugged again. He shook his head back and forth and chuffed. I looked at the clock on the dashboard. Emily would arrive in one hour. I had to hurry.

I approached Oso through the passenger's side door and scooped the sixty-five-pound dog into my arms. Whoa, some puppy. I hefted his front legs over one shoulder to take some of his weight, then I slung his leash and my purse strap over the other shoulder. I'd just put him down when we got to Walker's place. I shut the door with my hip and started down the street, then caught a glimpse of myself in a window. I was a red-haired version of a 1950s movie star, and Oso was the giant beaver stole over my outfit. Pretty ridiculous. I couldn't do this again or I'd have escaped my crazy cat lady reputation in Dallas only to become the crazy dog lady on St. Marcos.

Walker's office was only four doors down from my primo parking space, which was good, because I don't think I could have dragged Oso any further. I didn't have to go even that far, though, because Walker was leaving his office and locking his door behind him as I approached. I'd passed a law firm and a surf shop before Walked turned and saw me. He grunted.

"Mr. Walker, good afternoon," I said. Oso squirmed.

"I'm on my way out," he said.

"I can see that. Would you mind if I just walked with you for a moment?" I looked at the dog. "Oso, be still."

"Actually, yes, I do mind. I'm not ready to discuss your case with you, and I don't hold private client conferences in public."

We were the only two people within one hundred yards in either direction, but I decided not to debate the relative public-versus-private aspects of conversing with me here. Oso decided he wanted down right that second, and he made it happen. *Okay, then.* I caught the end of his leash and wound it around my hand twice.

"When will you be ready to update me, Mr. Walker?" At this point, I just wanted a report, and to be done with him. Then I could regroup.

Oso lunged toward Walker and growled, nearly pulling my shoulder out of socket. I didn't mind at all. Rashidi might be right about this dog escort business. Oso's instincts were spot on. I didn't like Walker much, either.

"Mind your dog," he said, stepping back.

"Oh, he won't hurt a fly," I cooed, hoping I was wrong. "As to you updating me, since I've moved to St. Marcos, I'm available tomorrow. Or the next day. Any day. You name it."

He didn't remark upon or react to the news of my relocation. What great manners. "Wednesday. Wednesday at ten," he said.

"Perfect. Oso and I will meet you here Wednesday at ten." Walker was already backing away again when I remembered that I had another question to ask him. "Oh, Mr. Walker? Who was that man you were sitting with at Toes in the Water last night? The guy staring at my friend Ava and me?"

Now Walker was turned away from me and striding in the opposite direction from me and my truck. "I wasn't at Toes in the Water," he said, not even slowing down.

Chapter Thirty

I pulled into the airport parking lot with no time to spare. I circled the lot three times before I saw a couple on the way to their car with twins pulling Minnie and Mickey Mouse suitcases. One was crying and the other kept dropping her suitcase, and their progress was agonizingly slow. When they were finally loaded into their car, I pulled into their spot, although I had to stare down a driver in a silver Lexus to get it. Apparently, she didn't believe in waiting her turn.

The St. Marcos airport is small by stateside standards, but its runways are big enough to land some of the largest planes in the world, or so our captain had told us on my last flight in. Like most of the buildings on the island, it was stucco, and it was painted a festive salmon pink. There was a large private hangar on the far left, then a hangar for small Caribbean airlines. The ticket counters were in the middle of the airport, and customers queued up there under a porch-like roof. On the right side of the ticket counter was the door to Customs and Immigration, and beyond that was the hangar for the commercial flights to the states. The baggage claim area occupied the far right-hand side of the structure.

The smell of jet fuel lingered in the air and taxi drivers milled around the entrance to the bag carousels, offering their services and a rum punch to every traveler that passed. Piped in steelpan music played in the background, loud enough to hear over the rumble of the crowd deplaning to the left of baggage claim.

Oso and I met Emily at the deplaning passenger door. She had to be hot in her Wrangler jeans and white long-sleeved western shirt. And cowboy boots, of course, high-heeled cowboy boots, brown with turquoise inlays and stitching up the sides. Emily might dress for the Dallas legal scene at work, but when she didn't have to play the part she reverted to her Amarillo roots. Her tall blonde hair was drooping and the strap of one of her cherry-red carry-on bags had pinned a large section of it down on her left shoulder, but she had a million-dollar smile on.

"Katie!" she hollered, which made me smile back.

"God bless you for packing in carry-ons," I said. I hugged her, then picked up one of her bags. "You saved us an hour." Plenty of people would be standing shoulder to shoulder in high humidity waiting for bags that only had to move thirty feet from the plane to the conveyor belt.

Emily hardly heard me. She was crouched down on the ground loving up Oso. In addition to the horses and cows on their small ranch, Emily's family had raised some kind of hunting dogs. She kept pictures of them in her cubicle at work. Retrievers? Pointers? Spaniels? I didn't know. Dogs for sure, though.

"I visit Rich's family in Colombia every Christmas," she said. "I figured quasi third world is the same everywhere." She stood up. "Can I take your dog?"

I handed her the leash. "Be my guest. He hasn't had any training yet, so you'll get a shoulder workout. His name is Oso."

I picked up her other bag. Now I was balanced.

"He's perfect. I'll have him trained before you know it. Won't I, Oso? Because you're a good, good boy, aren't you?" she said.

Oso wagged his tail and fell in on her left as we walked to the car. I loaded her bags into the back of the truck, then pushed the clicker to unlock the doors.

"I hate to break it to you, Katie, but there's not a thing wrong with Oso's training." Emily laughed and opened the door to my truck. "Up, Oso." The dog jumped in obediently. "But don't worry, I'll have you trained by the time I leave instead."

"Ha ha," I said. But what was the saying about no bad dogs, only bad owners?

I exited the parking lot and decided to take the long way back to Ava's. It was lunchtime, and I wanted to give Emily a taste of island culture. I turned right, toward the road that cut across the west side of the island. We'd swing near Annalise and cut back through the rainforest to drive along the beaches of the north shore.

Emily chatted as I drove. "You're so damn tan, after only two days. Wait, no, your freckles have just gotten closer together," she said.

"I can't even disagree with you on that. I'm a freakin' snow leopard. But it looks good from a distance. You, though, Ms. Rodeo Barbie, you will have a killer sunburn when you go home. Two words: sun screen."

"Who, me?" She slung her hair over her shoulder with a dip of her head, then batted her eyes. Her personality was a positive force that was already pushing out most of the poison left over from my Walker encounter.

"Was Rich OK with you coming?" I asked.

"Rich Shmich," she said, rolling her eyes. "I love the man, but this isn't the trip for him. He needs testosterone around or he doesn't know what to do with his machismo self."

Just then, my heart leapt into my throat as a tree branch ripped the driver's side mirror off my truck. Emily screamed.

Crap! In order to avoid head-on collisions, I tended to drive as close to the left—and the bush—as I could. Sometimes this worked out better than others, roughly in proportion to when I was paying attention to what I was doing. This time, I'd gotten close enough to do about $350 worth of damage.

"Nice driving," Emily deadpanned.

"Woopsie," I said.

"How did you get used to driving on the wrong side of the road?" She craned her neck to see around the next curve.

"I'm not yet," I confessed.

Emily gripped the armrest like it was a life preserver as we whipped through the trees. "Are we there yet? I'm too young to die."

"Almost, but let's stop for lunch first."

"Is there a Dairy Queen around or something?"

"Or something," I replied.

I pulled to a stop at the Pig Bar.

"This place serves food, and you eat it?" Emily's mouth hung open and her upper lip curled down tightly as she took in the ramshackle grass-roofed hut.

I led her in. Now wasn't the time to tell her I'd never tried the food here before.

By the time we left, though, Emily had wrapped Nancy, the proprietress and head cook, in a big bear hug and proclaimed herself a devoted fan. This had been Emily's first johnnycake and Caribbean fry chicken, so I understood her enthusiasm. She had ordered a second johnnycake, and then a third for the road.

"Really?" I asked her, laughing.

"I know. If I don't work it off, I'll be the size of Goldie before I leave." Goldie was her favorite horse, and not a small one at that.

Oso sat inert by her side, hoping for a scrap of leftovers, but Emily didn't leave a crumb.

We arrived at Ava's twenty minutes later, and Ava and Emily hit it off, as I knew they would. Neither was the jealous friend type. They wouldn't be besties without me, but I bridged the divide between vampy Ava and wholesome Emily.

Ava offered us a bowl of fresh mangoes. "From Jacoby," she said.

"I'd love one," Emily said.

Ava pounded a mango against the table with its skin on to soften the fruit inside. When she had it pulped to her liking, she tore a hole in one end and sucked out the liquefied fruit. Ava made mango sucking sexy, like soft porn. Ava pounded another and offered it to Emily.

Emily stared at it. "Lord have mercy," she said.

"Here, Emily," I said. I took the pulverized mango from Ava, went into the narrow yellow galley kitchen, and tossed it at the garbage can. It knocked the hinged chrome top inward and fell to the bottom with a thunk. Oso sat on the Saltillo kitchen tile with his head cocked, studying me. "Dogs don't like mangoes, boy." I grabbed another mango, washed it and my hands, peeled and cored the fruit, then sliced it into hunks. I pulled a plate decorated with a spray of peonies from a mismatched set in Ava's whitewashed cabinets and slid the slippery pieces of fruit onto it, then brought it back to Emily.

"Thank God," she said.

"What?" Ava asked, but the gleam in her eye was knocking her halo askew.

I unloaded Emily into the living room that I had stayed in the night before, then went into the extra bedroom and saw the new futon with its black wooden frame. It was unfolded into its bed position, sans sheets. Details. I would put some on it later, if Ava had any more. Other than the futon and a wall of boxes, the room was empty. A orange and yellow metal sunburst three feet across adorned one wall, the sole decoration in the space.

Ava brought out a lighted tabletop mirror and her large bag of makeup. She started painting on her performance face at the round green Formica-topped dining room table.

"Hey, I want you up there with me tonight, so get your slut face on, too," she instructed me.

"You'll get used to her," I said to Emily. "Either that or you'll be scarred for life, but either way you'll never forget her."

Just then, Ava yelled at her fat black cat. "No, Elvis! Don't eat the lizard."

"Lizards make cats sick, but Elvis loves them," I explained to Emily.

"They make him hack up white goo on my sofa cushions and go loopy, and I hate them," Ava said.

Emily pointed at Ava. "I love her," she said to me. "Capital L Love her." She put her hands on her hips and cocked her right one. "I just can't believe you're singing for money, Katie, since you've given it away for free at every open mike in Dallas for years."

"Hoo, that a good one," Ava said. "But I ain't paying her tonight. This here a tryout."

"Har de har har, tryout," I said.

But truly? I was nervous. I had barely glanced through the playbook Ava had given me when we got home from Toes in the Water the night before. Sure, I could read music like a pro, but I hadn't done it in years. I had a newly ripped cuticle to show for my fears. I found a band-aid under the sink in Ava's bathroom and hid the damage.

Chapter Thirty-one

After securing Oso in my bedroom so he would leave Elvis in peace, the three of us struck out for The Lighthouse on the boardwalk in Town, where Ava was booked that night. The Lighthouse was a restaurant and bar with a small stage. The open-air eating area faced a courtyard where anyone could stop for some chat or a dance. The bar was cattycorner to the restaurant. The music varied during the week, but the owners brought in a steelpan band on Sundays, so brunch there was a real treat.

Emily and I chilled with ceviche and Red Stripes while Ava set up and then warmed up the crowd. A Caribbean beer seemed like the choice a controlled drinker would make early in the evening. About ten minutes into her set, Ava motioned me up to join her. Butterflies attacked my stomach, but I lifted my chin and marched to my spot.

Ava wore a fire-engine red tube dress, a good contrast to my zebra-print wrap sundress. Her hair was down, curls gone wild. Mine was scooped into a clip from which it spilled in a waterfall. Ava had matched her nails and lips to her dress; I went for earthier tones that wouldn't clash with my hair.

"We look like Lil Mama and," she studied me, "that *Gilligan's Island* chick, Tina Louise."

Tina Louise. She was elegant, right? "Who's Lil Mama?" I asked.

Ava handed me the open songbook. "Never mind. You ready?"

I took it from her. "Not hardly, but I'll do it anyway." I gulped air like I had gills.

Ava hit Play on the background music for the next song. The first notes of a Macy Gray number played, and my mind went blank of the words. I read them quickly from the page. I could do this. I'd been singing in front of people since high school, just usually with an entire choir or at least a jazz ensemble to back me.

I came in on the right beat and the right note. A good start. I leaned into the music with Ava, and within seconds I was singing for the pure joy of it, and time flew by. Songs ended, people clapped, and then we'd do it again. The bartender sent free drinks between every song. I opted for a dry white wine, since I was taking it slow and it wasn't late yet. Moderation in all things, I reminded myself, and I declined every other offer of a drink. This new lifestyle really worked for me.

Before it seemed possible, it was time for the break between sets. Emily came to the stage to meet us as we came off. She was having a blast, basking in the reflected glory of our modest success. She cornered me, and the glint in her eyes concerned me.

"The good-looking guy over there, see him?" she asked.

"No," I said.

"Don't be difficult."

"I'll try."

"He wants to meet you."

"Out of the question."

"Don't be a butthead. Come on."

"Absolutely not."

Emily pouted, then punched. "So, is your spontaneous combustion enough for you? Do you still have that to keep you company at night?"

Never tell Emily anything you want to forget later.

"None of your business, Miss Nosey Posey."

And, yes, if I was completely truthful, Nick still visited me in my dreams. Not that I owed anyone the truth. I didn't answer her.

She pressed on. "Katie, it's time for you to meet a flesh and blood man. And do a little mattress dancin'."

"Don't even go there. I have zero interest. Besides, tourists are looking to get laid and leave. It's a well-known fact, Emily. I am hereby establishing a strict no-tourist rule."

I knew immediately from the smug look on her face that I was in trouble. "So if he wasn't a tourist you'd meet him?"

I wasn't going to get out of this. Emily was dogged. "A short, supervised conversation with him before we go back on, and nothing more. If he's not a tourist."

"He's not a tourist! He lives here. He's a chef." She chortled.

"Gloating does not become you," I sniffed, but she didn't hear me. She was off to fetch Chef Boyardee.

I glanced at my watch. Only five blessedly short minutes until I could end the conversation and go back onstage. I busied myself reading Ava's next set list and marking the songs in my notebook. If I was going to read the words, at least I wouldn't be frantically flipping pages.

Emily and the chef returned. At least he wasn't in a cooking smock and pants, I thought, and patted my cheeks which were surprisingly numb. In fact, he was dressed normally in a moss-green crewneck shirt and matching plaid shorts. Topsiders and a brown belt. He was attractive, if you were into chiseled features, blue eyes, and short blond hair. Emily introduced him as Bart Lassiter, and he was a nice guy, if you were into charming, successful men who went out of their way to flatter you. He was head chef at Fortuna's. The last place my parents went, before . . . before they didn't get to go anywhere else.

"Born and raised in Missouri. A flyover state. It took this long to save enough money to fly out of there. I got here less than two years ago," he explained.

"Texas," I said. "Just off the boat, two days on-island."

Emily jumped in. "Katie's a lawyer. One of the best in Texas."

Even though I had no intention of dating Bart, I decided to edit Emily's comment. Collin had explained my mysterious guy-repelling power many times: everyone hates attorneys, especially female attorneys. Plus, there was my McZillion debacle. "On sabbatical. Right now I'm a house remodeler and a backup singer."

"A big-ass half-finished house in the rainforest," Emily said, showing the effects of a few too many Red Stripes. "With a jumbie, whatever the hell that is." I would throttle her later. And Ava for telling her about the jumbie.

"The one up near Baptiste's Bluff?"

"Yes, that's it," I said. Annalise was famous, it seemed.

"Yeah, I know it. I've admired it from afar. My dad's an architect, so I have a genetic fascination with architecture and construction." He shifted his weight from one foot to the other and back. "Hey, I'm off tomorrow. Could I bring you out some lunch? I'd love to look around, or even lend a hand. It's an interesting house, at least from afar."

"Oh, wow, some other time," I tried to say.

"Perfect," Emily interrupted. Forget throttle. That wasn't a painful enough way to die. "We'll be there. It's my first time to see it, too. This is going to be great!"

Ava broke in, back from the bar with three fresh drinks balanced between her hands. "What be great?"

I took two of the drinks from her and gave one to Emily. They were light orange, with something brown sprinkled on their surface. I sipped. Yum. I sipped again. Orangey, coconutty, rummy. Which was fine, because it was late enough for liquor now. "What are these, Ava? They're delicious."

"Painkillers. Go easy on them. Who this, what I miss, and answer my first damn question."

Miss Crankypants. What was up with her?

"Ava, this is Bart. Bart, Ava." Emily used her company manners. "Bart is a chef at Fortuna's's, and he's bringing us lunch at Annalise tomorrow."

Ava's forehead wrinkled. "Bart Something-or-Other? Fortuna's chef? That not what I hear. I hear new guy Bart *own* the place. Am I right?" she asked Bart.

Bart inclined his head. An admission.

Ava steamrolled on. "Who he bringing lunch to? Us? He don't know no us. If a man bring lunch, there ain't no us." She was talking as if he wasn't there, then addressed him directly. "Which one of us you after, Bart?"

Aha. Mirror, mirror on the wall, who's the fairest of them all? I covered my smile with my cup. So that's what had her dander up. Ava had a great deal of confidence about men, but it was hard to blame her. She based it on experience. My resistance to Bart had slipped a little, especially now that I realized I had Ava's goat. The mirror was telling her someone else was fairest in the land, even if only for a moment. I took another slug of painkiller.

Bart's cheeks splotched with pink. "Nice to meet you, Ava."

"Nobody giving me a straight answer," Ava complained.

"He asked me to introduce him to Katie," Emily said. "So . . ."

"Hunh," Ava said. She looked over at me. Grudgingly she said, "Well, she kinda cute." Then Ava grinned. "For a red-haired man-hater. You're a brave man, Bart. I like that. I gonna be there for that lunch. You be needing lots of help."

"Avaaaaa," I said, but the other three were laughing, which turned into chatting, and then into time to go back to the stage, ten minutes late, and only because the manager was standing onstage and tapping his wrist, where he would have worn a wristwatch if he weren't in the islands.

Bart sat with Emily the rest of the night. Two other men joined them, presumably his friends. I sensed Bart's eyes on me, and I kept mine anywhere but on him. He was likeable. Handsome. His sparkly eyes were cute when he looked at me, as if he were interested. In me. Maybe he would be good for me. For my self-confidence. I didn't have to fall in love with him to let him bring us lunch.

So what was this resistance inside me about? It felt almost like guilt. Like I was cheating on my own feelings, feelings for someone dark, sensitive, and difficult, someone far away that I couldn't have.

I let Bart catch my eye, and he smiled at me. It was a nice smile. I'd come to St. Marcos to escape the feelings that were sabotaging my life. I told the reluctant Katie to damn well smile back at him, and she did.

Chapter Thirty-two

Emily's moaning woke me up. Her first morning on St. Marcos was painful because of all the painkillers she drank the night before. She had stumbled from her temporary sleeping quarters on the living room couch and into my bedroom, all of ten steps away, her face white as the powdery sand on Turtle Beach. It was my first night on my new futon, and I'd hoped to sleep a little while longer. I turned toward the wall.

"Help," she said, and flopped onto the futon beside me. "Someone poisoned me."

"Her name is Emily. I'll beat her up for you, if you'd like," I said, my words muffled by the pillow I partially buried my face in. Waves of pain were pounding my head like a mallet to a bass drum. *Yeah, right, painkillers.* "I think she's the same Emily who was too drunk to figure out how to get out of the back seat of my truck last night."

Emily ignored my comment. "Is it safe to drink the water?" she croaked.

"Ugh. Ava," I yelled. "Ava!"

"Ain't no Ava here. Go away," Ava's voice answered.

"Ava, did you get that frog problem fixed? Emily wants some water."

"If Ava here, she'd tell you to hush your mouth. Drink or don't drink. If you hurtin', frogs don't matter."

"Frog problem?" Emily asked. "What does that mean?"

"Infested cistern. I recommend bottled water. Which we don't have." Bottled water meant waking up and driving to the store. Oso whined to go out. The whole universe had aligned against me. Might as well give in to my fate. "Shit." I shoved Emily toward the edge of the futon. "Uppy uppy."

I met Ava coming out the door to her bedroom, and Oso ran into the back of my legs.

"I make eggs. It the only cure," she said.

"I'll run out for bottled water. Do we need anything else?"

"Probably. My head hurt too bad to think," Ava said.

"Serves you right for giving us painkillers."

Half an hour later, Ava and I tag-teamed Emily, who was sitting with her face in her hands at the dining table, her shellacked bed head sky-high and flattened on one side. She had changed from her drawstring Easter-plaid sleep pants and matching white sleep shirt into more plaid, this time darker blues and reds, on her walking shorts. The shirt appeared to be the one she'd spent the night in.

"Eat the scrambled eggs. I not feeling sorry for you this afternoon when you puny," Ava said. How Ava had managed to pull herself together and cook breakfast while I was gone was a mystery. She had her false eyelashes and black eyeliner on, and she was working what the good Lord gave her in a stretchy blue denim miniskirt and matching vest that snapped up the front, opened strategically down to there while the skirt rode her thighs up to there, and nipped in at the waist to emphasize her barely contained bana. I was worn out just looking at her.

"We're not stopping for food," I warned Emily.

"I can't," she wailed.

Ava tsk-tsked. "I told you go easy on the painkillers."

"I should have listened." Emily put her head down on her folded forearm. Her voice was muffled. "It was worth it, though. Sort of."

I set her breakfast down in front of Oso, who had already polished off his kibble. He wolfed the eggs down and wagged his tail, snuffling around the kitchen floor looking for more.

"Time to head out, hangover or not," I said. I didn't feel so hot either, truth be told. I had pulled out all the stops before I went to the store just so Emily wouldn't notice. My hair was in a high, bouncy ponytail. My makeup was light but sufficient to camouflage the dark circles. And my outfit was perky cute: a white sundress with a narrow waist, and some white thong sandals. I wanted Emily to see that the new me had myself in hand, that she wouldn't have to cover for Katie anymore. Hopefully she'd pass that nugget of information along to Collin, too. Plus there was always the chance that Bart would show up today with a hammer and a picnic basket. Meanwhile, this homeowner had work to do. "I have to see if Junior Samples and crew got to work at a decent hour." It was nearly ten.

"I gonna catch up with you later," Ava said.

I turned toward her. "But you don't have a car."

"No big t'ing," she said. "I see you soon-ish."

Ava somehow got around just fine bumming rides. What she did not do was walk. Anywhere. Not that her house was close enough to Town to make it feasible, but still, she didn't use her feet to cover the one mile between one end of downtown and the other if she could help it. It got in the way of her sexy, impractical footwear. Her cork-bottomed white platform sandals were a case in point.

Emily did a mini push-up as she stood, leaving her head and torso on the table as long as she could. She grabbed her purse.

"You have a swimsuit, towel, and sunscreen?" I asked her.

"No, why? Do I need it?"

"Always. You're on vacation. On an island. I'll get you a towel."

Ava grabbed sunscreen off her kitchen cabinet. She had informed me the first time we walked the beaches together that she never went out without it. "I black, but I still burn, and I sure don't want no skin cancer like my grandmother had. Or pruney skin before my time."

"Here." Ava tossed it to Emily.

Emily bobbled it, but managed to hang on. "Thanks."

She walked stiff-legged out of the room, groaning as she did, and returned seconds later clutching a bikini. She stuffed sunscreen and the bathing suit into the beach bag I held open for her. I'd already packed hats and bug spray. We were so prepared we were practically Girl Scouts. If Girl Scouts slammed endless painkillers until two a.m.

Off we went. Or, at least, off Oso and I went while Emily fell asleep in the truck with her head bouncing against the window. Ouch. I had loaded a cooler of bottled water in the back, and I would make sure Emily drank a lot of it. Weren't the tables turned between us today, though, I thought.

I had to give Emily a little shoulder shake to get her attention when Annalise came into view. She rubbed her eyes and swayed, then leaned across me to get a better look out the driver's side window. She gazed at the view across the valley of mango trees and up the manjack-covered hill to Queen Annalise at the summit, surrounded by her royal court of fruit trees.

"Holy shit. I can't believe you live there."

"Just a couple of months and I totally will."

"It's stunning. Wild and beautiful." She turned to me. "And isolated. Are you scared, city girl? I mean, to live out here by yourself?"

I knew that Emily had grown up on a ranch, and I doubted living alone at Annalise would have fazed her. But was I scared? I probed and found no traces of fear. "No, I don't think so. I'm more scared of missing this chance, if that makes sense. I think this place and I are meant for each other."

"Good for you. This isn't at all what I expected. You're going country like me, and I love it. Very courageous."

For some reason, I shrank from her praise. An image of every drink I'd had in the three days since I'd come back popped into my head. My conscience whispered to me, "You're still hiding from something, courageous one." Still, I had kept myself under control. This was the new me, and I was doing fine.

I just said, "Thanks, Emily," and left it at that.

We rounded the corner to the long driveway and pointed the truck's nose toward the house, which from this vantage point looked two-story, her third level carved into the hillside and hidden from the front and side-approach views. Her multi-leveled red metal roof absorbed the sun. The windows on the near side ranged from finished white-paned double glass, to broken versions of the same, to empty concrete squares like the doors. A sheet of plywood covered the middle window to a bathroom in the upper story. Four vehicles were crowding the dirt parking area that would someday soon be a real concrete driveway on the near side of Annalise. Junior's truck was not one of them. I didn't recognize any of the cars, for that matter.

When I made the offer on Annalise, Doug had told me that I needed a contractor with "the right connections." That roughly translated into someone who knew how to get people to approve government permits, come to work, stay at work, work while they were there, and not steal. Usually, anyway. So far, Junior had failed to get people here on time and to be here himself, and we were only on day two. But he could be on Annalise-related business elsewhere. Maybe.

"So does this jumbie thing Ava told me about mean your house is haunted?" Emily asked.

I readjusted the neckline of my sleeveless white sundress. "Not haunted in the Amityville Horror sense of the word. I think she has a jumbie, like Ava told you. It's kind of a voodoo thing here."

Emily laughed. "Voodoo? The tropical sun has fried your brain."

I rubbed the soft spots behind Oso's ears. I'd thought the same thing a few weeks before.

I parked fifteen feet from the row of cars and we disembarked into the middle of a canine convention. They sniffed Oso, soaking in the scents of his adventures from the road. Emily's painkiller pale had subsided and she crooned to the dogs. I knew this because I saw her lips move. I didn't actually hear her. Music coming from inside the house was drowning her out. The sound of men's laughter rose above the music.

Emily and I walked through the side door and into the future kitchen, which of course didn't look anything like a kitchen yet. We were met by the sight of the workers—who were supposed to be plastering the walls with bleach and water—lounging on the kitchen floor smoking ganja. They were the ones plastered, not the walls. They jumped up and stubbed out their joints when they saw me.

Several of them mumbled at once, "Good morning, Ms. Connell, good morning," pronouncing my name with an emphasis on the second syllable. Then they fled.

I saw red, and yellow, and orange. So this was what I was expected to pay for when I wasn't here? Obviously, they hadn't heard me pull up. Not a surprise in the state they were in, and with Sean Paul's "Temperature" blaring out of the boom box.

Emily turned to me and whispered, "They're stoned out of their minds."

"Yeah, and it's only their second day," I said.

Day two! I was getting madder by the second. I knew I should take this up with Junior, not these guys. But where the hell was Junior?

"I'm sorry, Em, but I need to handle this. Would you mind taking a look around by yourself while I make some calls?"

Emily's hair had fallen a bit and no longer had the side-heavy look from the morning. She was again the picture of competence and aplomb. She agreed, already unsnapping her camera case. She would probably tile my patio and still have time to train all my unruly dogs to fetch and roll over. I knew I didn't need to worry about her.

I stalked off and fumed. Junior didn't answer either number I had for him. I left a voicemail on his cell. I kept it brief, but colorfully clear. As I had asked of him, I followed it up with an abbreviated version by text.

I walked back into the kitchen. Emily had moved on, but the workers were back, standing together. The oldest-looking one, who was probably only twenty-five, stepped forward.

"We got a problem with the work, Ms. Connell," he said.

"What's that?" I asked.

"Bees dem in the big room, where we put the scaffolding yesterday. We can't clean there or bees dem get us." He added, "We told your friend not to go there."

"Bees?" I'd heard it all now. I didn't like bees, either, but these were grown men.

"Yah mon, for true." He looked sincere. Or maybe he just looked stoned.

"Show me," I said.

His eyes widened. "You don't wanna go in there, miss."

Yes, yes I did. "We don't have to get close. Just show me. What's your name?"

"Egbert," he said. "People dem call me Egg."

"Lead the way, Egg."

I followed Egg around the corner and into the great room, which had been partially transformed by scaffolding that went thirty feet into the air, its pipes extending in all directions like circuitry in a supercomputer.

"Where are the bees?" I asked him.

"In the fireplace," he said, nodding to the far side of the room. I started toward it and Egg grabbed my arm. He shook his head. Good grief.

"Egg," I said. But he leaned over and picked up a horse puck. As in manure, with his bare hand, and we had no soap and water. I stifled my urge to hurl. He threw it at the fireplace and stepped back quickly.

A horrible humming sound erupted from the fireplace, followed by first a few, then hundreds of bees. Big bees. Loud bees. A swarm of bees moving as one toward us.

Chapter Thirty-three

"Oh, shit!" I said. I ran into the kitchen with the men and we kept running out into the side yard, and well away from the house. I kept my eyes on the door, but the swarm didn't follow us outside.

"Where's Junior? He needs to handle this." I shook my hand in the direction of the bees.

Egg shrugged and looked away. Great.

I walked back in the kitchen-side door to the house. The buzzing had died down. I ventured into the kitchen. No bees. I sucked in a fortifying breath and searched for the courageous Katie that Emily had just accused me of being, and I poked my head in the great room. Only half a dozen bees still stormed the room outside the chimney. I stepped cautiously into the center of the room, searching for a solution. A humming started again and I tensed, ready to flee, but this time it wasn't coming from the chimney. It was coming from every-where—under my feet, from the walls, from the ceiling. Egg appeared at the doorway with two other young men.

"You hear that? You feel that?" Egg asked.

I didn't bother answering. I was worried about my friend. "Emily?" I yelled. "Emily?" No answer.

"You need to come outta there, miss," Egg said. "We getting out of here, you come now."

Yes, I thought. I need to get the hell out. But I stayed rooted in place. I watched, entranced, as Egg disappeared from the doorway. I heard the heavy footsteps of the men as they ran for the exits. The vibrations of the hum were massaging my face.

I wasn't scared. Somehow, suddenly, I knew not to be scared.

Behind me I heard a whoosh, then a roar. I turned toward the sound in slow motion with the walls blurring, my hair lifting and swirling, and saw that the sound was a fire. Flames were consuming the interior of the fireplace and licking outward over the hearth. Now I heard the buzzing again, frantic and loud over the crackle of flame, but no bees swarmed the room.

That's when I saw her.

She was so beautiful. Younger even than I'd thought, maybe not even twenty years old, and as tall as me. Her black eyes burned into mine. She wore her hair in twin cornrows that circled her head like a crown. Her dark oval face was devoid of all expression. She licked her lips, and her tongue was the color of a bing cherry. Without breaking eye contact with me, she tossed another piece of wood onto the fire, the waist of her blousy white shirt lifting with the movement, then she turned on her bare feet with her full skirt swishing around her calves and walked slowly out of the great room. I lost sight of her as she passed behind the wall to the vast entryway. I craned for one more glimpse. I had a perfect view of the path from the fireplace to the front door past the dining room, but I saw nothing but the solid walls of my house.

"Miss?" I called out. "Miss? Where'd you go?"

I ran after her across the concrete floor, thinking maybe she'd passed through the high-ceilinged entryway and into the study. I looked inside. It was empty except for the gungalos on the floor. She had vanished.

I leaned against the concrete wall with my hand on my throat, looking out the broken study window. The inside of my mouth tasted like ash.

Holy smokes.

Chapter Thirty-four

A tongue licked my hand. Oso. I hugged his head to my thigh. "Good boy."

"Katie?"

I whirled around. Was it her?

No. It was Emily. She stood in the front entrance.

"Oh. Hi, Em."

"You look like you've seen a ghost," she said.

I laughed, the sound tinny to my own ears. "Bees. I saw a lot of bees. Did you hear me calling for you? I didn't want you to get stung."

"Your workers warned me. I was out back, by the submarine, or pool, or whatever that giant hunk of concrete is out there. I came back around when I heard the shouting."

"Yes, they shouted all right. From a distance."

"They were saying the house was coming apart. I think they're overly dramatic, and stoned."

I snorted. "I think those two things are related."

"What was the noise? Was it electrical?"

I raised my eyebrows as I said, "No electricity out here."

Emily tucked in her chin. I knew from years of working with her that this was her "perplexed and thinking" face. "An earthquake? The bees?"

"Sort of." My brain worked on a way to explain it that made sense. Nothing was coming to me.

She put her hands on the back of her hips, fingers pointing down. "Are you sure you're all right?"

I palpated my numb forearms with my hands. "Totally fine. Freaked out a little, but fine. Did you see her?"

"See who?" Emily asked.

"I think we had a visit from the jumbie," I said. "She burned the bees out of the fireplace."

"That wasn't you?" Emily's brows knitted.

"Nope."

"No frickin' way." The way Emily said it was an exclamation, not a question.

I walked into the great room with Emily on my heels, giving the fireplace a wide berth. All that remained in it were embers. I saw a chunk of wood on the floor by the hearth, and I picked it up. I backed away, then threw it as hard as I could into the pit. It made a loud thwack. Then, nothing. No buzz, no bees.

Behind me, Egg said, "Bees dem gone!"

"Yeah, I had a lighter with me, so I started a fire, and it burned them out," I said. I swiveled my head and made eye contact with Emily and held a finger over my lips out of Egg's line of sight. She nodded once.

Egg looked at me as if I was speaking in tongues.

"But. . ." he said, staring at me.

"Yes, they're all gone." I wiped my hands on the front of my lower thighs, careful not to muss my white dress. "You guys need to sober up and get to work." Hopefully he would chalk this all up to bad weed and let it go.

"Yes, yes, miss," he stuttered. Now he was the one who looked like he'd seen a ghost. He turned and walked out to join the other men.

"You're going to explain what the hell is going on to me soon, right?" Emily asked, but she didn't really say it as a question.

"Absolutely. I promise," I replied.

We were interrupted by the sounds of vehicles. I hoped it was Junior so I could give him a piece of my mind. Emily and I went out to see.

Two cars. Rashidi was climbing out of his red Jeep. I didn't recognize the other car, a newish black Pathfinder. But I did know the people inside. In the driver's seat, Bart. Beside him, Ava.

So, Bart had made good on the promise to visit. But what the hell was Ava doing with him? I hadn't even taken Bart's number, but somehow Ava had hooked up with him the second she could ditch us. It was ridiculous to get jealous about a man I wasn't dating, wasn't even sure I wanted to date. But he had made it plain that his interest was in me. That was enough to justify pissiness, I decided.

Rashidi now stood beside me, ignoring the dogs that were jostling him for attention. His face mirrored mine. Neither of us said hello. We both just stared at the Pathfinder.

Ava slithered out in her stretchy blue-jean miniskirt and matching vest. Vest shmest, it was a damn bustier. She shouted, "Surprise! Look what I brought you guys!"

Bart got out, and he grinned at me. I wasn't ready to smile at anyone yet, so I didn't. It was my house. I'd just had a paranormal experience. I'd act pissy if I wanted to.

Bart noticed. He spoke to everyone, but directed it to me. "Ava volunteered to be my sous chef." He gestured toward the Pathfinder, which explained nothing. So it was a big black SUV with coolers and bags visible through its back windows and a beach umbrella hanging over the back seat. That told me nothing, and I didn't like it.

"We have a feast, the most amazing feast ever on the island of St. Marcos. We shall dine like the gods," Ava said, throwing her arms in the air over her head.

I heard Rashidi exhale. I still wasn't sure who I didn't trust—Bart, Ava, or both—but I swallowed it for the moment. I didn't want to ruin everyone's day. I would get to the bottom of this later. Soon, but later. And throw a hell of a snit fit if I didn't like what I learned. In with the good air, out with the bad air, I told myself, then adopted a light tone.

"That's great, because I'm starving," I said, and my teeth were barely clenched.

Emily's head had cocked at the tone in my voice. She knew I was pissed. She stepped forward, flicking her blonde hair behind her shoulder, and linked her arm through mine. "I could eat an entire cow," she said. God, how I loved Emily.

"How about you give us a quick tour and then we take this picnic to a beach?" Bart suggested, looking at me.

"A beachable feast," I said, my voice sounding almost normal to my own ears now.

"It is," Bart said. He looked relieved. More than relieved. He looked hopeful.

Hopeful was too much for me right now. He had some 'splainin' to do. I decided to ignore hopeful, and I turned to Rashidi.

"Later today, could you help me find Junior? He's AWOL and his stoned contractors didn't get nada done without him. I need to fire him, pronto." I'd save the bee story for later.

"A pleasure," Rashidi said.

I turned back to Bart. "All right. Let's get this tour started, then."

Forty-five minutes and one grand tour later, we parked two of our three cars along the side of the road at Amon Hall Beach at Rashidi's suggestion, per his intimate knowledge of all things nature on the west end of the island. The beach was narrow and our cars were only thirty yards from the waterline. Coconut palms flanked a small patio-restaurant and bar just to our right as we faced the water. The teak tables and chairs were flipped upside down, the establishment closed. Beyond the restaurant, a hammock swung in the breeze between two sea grape trees whose round succulent leaves shaded the sand below. Rocks broke the surface of the water near the shore and an anchored dock floated a little further out. Two pelicans were cavorting over the dock, and a third one flapped its wings from its perch on its personal party barge.

Emily and I piled out of the truck. A pounding on the window from the back seat stopped me. It was Rashidi. He pointed at his door. I opened it.

"Wah, now I'm a youth again?" he asked. He unfolded his lanky frame and hopped out, his baggy shorts hanging to his knees and his Bob Marley t-shirt wet from sweat and stuck to his chest. "Child-proof locks. Let my people go."

I laughed. "So that's why Emily couldn't get out last night. I'll have to fix those."

"I'm vindicated," Emily said, and pumped a fist in the air.

"You were still hammered," I reminded her.

From our parking spot on the road we heard a loud pop down on the beach, like a gunshot. My hand flew to my mouth, catching a scream. Peals of laughter rolled up to us and I looked down at Ava and Bart, who had already carried a red cooler down to the beach. I saw Ava dancing around with an overflowing bottle of champagne in one hand. She stuck the bubbly to her mouth, leaning over to keep the liquid off her body. It was time for Ava and me to have a do-better talk.

"Are you guys coming or what?" Bart shouted up at us.

Rashidi, Emily, and I joined the party.

Chapter Thirty-five

The water blazed with the reflection of our dancing bonfire. I lay back, grinding sand into my salty hair, plastering it against my skin, which was bare except where my gold bikini covered it. If I closed my eyes just right, the stars became the trail of a sparkler waved across the night sky to light the moon. And if I closed my eyes completely, the effects of an afternoon drinking champagne shot off Roman Candles inside my eyelids. The world on fire, inside and out.

I sat up for another sip of champagne. The bubbles tickled the roof of my mouth, and the liquid left a trail of dryness across my tongue. I sank into my buzz, and it was like floating on my back in the warm ocean; the salt water supporting me, the waves lapping at my feet, the surge of the surf pushing me along in gentle spurts of forward progress. Bart had sprung for the good stuff, and a lot of it. We'd almost drained his case of Möet today. But then, we had been working at it for nearly ten hours.

The beach day would have ended a lot sooner, but Bart had managed to supply a good explanation for the two hours he'd spent chopping veggies and driving around with Ava. He said that he'd assumed she was on an intel mission with my blessing, and he used the opportunity to pump her for information about me. He said she'd grilled him the whole time he was with her. That explained his actions, but not Ava's decision to approach him sua sponte. Of course, Ava herself was the explanation for most of Ava's actions. I sighed. I loved her to death, but her insatiable need to be the object of every man's desire was hard to take, and I couldn't help but think it would get her into trouble one of these days. I drained the last of the champagne from my blue Solo cup and nestled back into my sand pallet.

Just then, Emily snored, loud and glorious, and Oso echoed it. Ava laughed, a cross between a growl and a yelp. A few grains of sand sifted onto my face as she stood.

"I'm going to get in the water one more time," she said.

More sand. Footsteps, receding. Rashidi following her, I thought.

More sand. Footsteps, three of them, coming closer. A body sank into the sand close to mine. Bart. I already knew him by smell. Sharp garlic, sunshine, and the last traces of Halston. I didn't know anyone else who wore Halston anymore. The last time I'd smelled it was on my high school boyfriend. I liked it, though.

And then Bart's head was in the sand, too. Beside mine, but not touching me. I kept my eyes closed.

"Are you asleep?" he whispered.

I paused. I could pretend. Or not. "No," I answered.

"Good," he said. His head was turned toward me. "I have a confession."

I was no priest. Did I want to hear? Listening any longer promised something, didn't it? I could stop him with a word.

He scooted closer, turned toward me, and came up on his elbow.

"Last night wasn't the first time I'd seen you."

That surprised me, and made me just a titch nervous. If he was a sociopathic stalker, he'd fooled me so far. I tensed, ready just in case.

"I was at the Porcus Marinus a few weeks ago, and you were doing karaoke there." He spoke softly. "I was smitten. I went to get a drink while I planned what to say to you, and when I came back you were gone. I thought I'd never see you again."

That didn't sound stalkerish, thank God, although it was scary in a different way. "I was only here on vacation. You almost didn't."

"When I saw you at The Lighthouse, I was one happy man." He closed his free hand around my wrist. "You have beautiful wrists and ankles. Delicate."

Goose bumps rose on my arms. "Thank you."

He released my wrist and began to trace my collarbone. "Elegant lines. Classic. Sexy."

Hummingbirds took flight in my stomach. I wasn't sure whether to end this now or to just let it play out. Maybe if I let it continue, it would wash Nick from my mind.

His fingertips touched my cheekbones, his thumb grazed my eyelids, and his lips closed over mine. Just one lingering kiss. My heart triple-timed. Things I wanted Nick to do. Shit. So far it wasn't washing very effectively.

"I think you're gorgeous. And I like you. I want to have an actual date, just you and me, without the entourage of protective friends."

"They're promoting this more than protecting me." And whatever else it was Ava was up to.

"A little of both," he said.

Laughter from the water. My eyes cut toward Ava and Rashidi. I could see their silhouettes in the moonlight. There was no air between the two of them. I was happy for Rashidi. They'd couple well, and I hoped that he could erase Guy and his death from her mind, and ease her need for other male attention. Ava broke free from his clench, but let him keep her hand. "Come, Rash, let we go." She said it like "Rawsh," with a slightly rolled "r." They walked up the beach toward us.

I rolled out from under Bart's face and sat up. "You guys ready to pack up?"

"Yah, it time," Ava said. She wrapped a fringed white sarong around her waist and tied it, covering the bottom half of her hot-pink string bikini.

Bart said, "Rashidi, would you mind driving Katie's truck? She's had too much to drink, and I said I'd drive her home."

What? Like no one saw through that one. Rashidi didn't respond. Good man, I thought. I opened my mouth to protest, but Ava was already speaking. "I'll drive Rash back up to Annalise, and Emily back to my place. No problem."

"Ava," I said sharply, but everyone ignored me.

Bart's hand found the small of my waist. "You guys run along, then. We want to stay a little longer. We're nearly packed already, and we can carry the rest out in one trip when we leave."

Manipulation was fine as long as I was the manipulator. I wanted to stay, and I wanted to assert my will. How was I to have my cake and eat it, too?

"Sounds good," Rashidi said.

Ava leaned over Emily. "Sleeping beauty, time to continue your nap in the truck."

Emily yawned and stretched. Oso did the same. "I'll just sleep here tonight, if you don't mind."

"Move your bana, sister," Rashidi said. "Grab your towel and shoes and make for Katie's truck."

Emily stood up slowly. Oso jumped up, confused.

"It's OK, boy. You're staying here with me," I said. I patted the sand beside me. "Sit." He licked his lips, walked in a tight circle two times, then flopped back down on his belly. It wasn't sitting, but close enough.

Rashidi, Ava, and Emily were moving away from us within a minute, following their shadows away from the fire toward the truck.

"That was smooth," I said, keeping my face in profile to Bart. "What if I didn't want you to drive me home?"

He reached his hand around the back of my neck and pulled my mouth to his. He kissed me long, deep, and slow, like no one had kissed me in years. I let him, for a few seconds.

"Bart?" I interrupted him.

"Hmm?" he asked lazily.

"I'm choosing to stay, but, for future reference, don't do my thinking for me again."

He looked at me intently. "I like how you said future reference."

"I'm serious."

He adopted a grunt-answering-to-an-officer tone. "Yes, ma'am. In the future I will not think for you." He dropped the tone. "In the present, I am going to kiss you again."

So he did, and he was a good kisser. The sand, the fire, the water, the champagne. All of it was lovely. No fireworks, but something warmed in the center of me. I leaned in and kissed him back. Then it was time to tap the brakes.

"Are you in a hurry to go?" he asked.

"It's more that I'm not in a hurry to get to where you're headed," I answered.

He studied my face in the fireglow. He kissed me once more, but a kiss of finishing rather than beginning. "We don't have to hurry." He stood up, reached for my hand, and pulled me to my feet and into him, his other arm wrapping around me in a squeeze that slid down my back and over my behind. "Although please don't take my patience as a lack of interest. Because I'm very, very interested." He released me, and the night air tickled my stomach where his bare skin had pressed into me moments before.

We rode back to Ava's along the north shore with the windows down so we could drink in every last breath of the night jasmine and ocean air. Bart reached over the console and curled his fingers around mine, our hands resting on my thigh. I didn't pull my hand away. I concentrated on all the things that were right about the moment and willed myself not to ruin it. This could be the start of something good for me. I could choose to be happy. I could choose a different path, an easier path. Bart hadn't even flinched when I'd shared the story of the bees with the group that afternoon, including the appearance and disappearance of my ghostly friend. Not every man would take that in stride. Thinking about the bees reminded me that I had never followed up on my plan to find and fire Junior. Crap. Unfinished business for tomorrow.

Bart still had my hand in his when we pulled up the hill to Ava's house. He made a hard right with just his left hand. Not an easy feat. I peered down the long driveway, then pulled my hand away. Oso sat up in the back seat. From a distance, it looked as if Ava was having a party. Lights were flashing against the night sky.

I sat up straighter. I rubbed my eyes and blinked. I counted cars. Too many? Or were my eyes playing tricks on me? "How many cars do you see, Bart?"

"Four," he said. "Why?"

"I only expected to see my truck. Maybe my truck and Rashidi's Jeep. And I don't even see a Jeep. That flashing light isn't right."

We pulled closer. "They're police cars," Bart said.

Chapter Thirty-six

My champagne haze burned off in a flash fire. "What the hell's going on?" I asked, my voice rising an octave by the last word as I saw two police officers escorting Ava in handcuffs to the car by her front door. She looked up at us, her denim outfit looking tawdry now. The light from my headlights glinted off her wide, round eyes. Red and blue light bathed the entire scene.

"Maybe you should stay in the car. I'll see what's going on," Bart said. He put the Pathfinder in park, but by then I was already out, slamming the door to keep Oso inside as he hurtled from the back seat to follow me. I ran toward Ava as an officer put his hand on the top of her head and another helped her into the back seat. One man's hand was too close to her tush and the other man's hand was too close to the side of her breast.

"Excuse me, excuse me, that's my roommate, what's going on?" I said, too loud, panting.

One of the officers turned to me. "Stay back, miss. Official police business."

"Yes, I understand, but—" I tried to say, but was cut off.

Jacoby stepped toward me out of the shadow behind the cruiser. "I've got this," he said to his fellow officer.

"Jacoby?" I asked. If it wasn't so dark, they could have seen my jaw hanging open wide enough that one of Jacoby's huge fists would fit inside.

He stepped in close to me. "Ava is under arrest for the murder of Guy Edwards," he said in crisply perfect English.

I backed up and he closed the gap between us again.

"What's going on? This is nuts," I hissed. "You know it's crazy."

His eyes bored into mine, the whites shining in the reflection of the red and blue flashing lights. "I'm not sure I know anything anymore," he said. He glanced at the other cops, who were absorbed in whatever Ava was doing in the back seat of the car. "We have two witnesses."

"I don't believe you."

"You don't have to."

"At least tell me what they think they have on her." I closed my eyes for a two count. "Please."

His voice dropped. "Mrs. Edwards confronted Guy about his affair with Ava. Eduardo Chavez set up a meeting for Guy with Ava. Eduardo said Guy was going to tell Ava it was over, so he could save his marriage. Eduardo said nobody else knew where Guy would be."

"Nobody except Eduardo," I said.

"Eduardo said he was helping Mrs. Edwards with the plans for a campaign fundraiser. His alibi checks out." Jacoby looked back at his fellow officers again. One motioned for him to return.

"It doesn't matter, Jacoby. She didn't do it."

Jacoby lapsed back into Local for a moment. "She have motive, she have opportunity." He spat on the ground by my foot. "Sometimes a woman make bad choices, and she pay for it."

"What do you mean?" I asked.

He started walking toward Ava's house. My self control slipped. I yelled after him. "What is that supposed to mean?"

Jacoby stopped, and he raised his arm and pointed at me. "I suggest you don't become part of the problem, Ms. Connell. Now stay out of the way. We gonna search the house."

A search. That changed things. "I'm her attorney, Jacoby. I'll need to review the warrant first." I thought about the promise I'd made to myself. No more criminal cases, ever. These days, never wasn't as long as it used to be.

He chuptzed me, so softly I wondered if I'd imagined it. "You're her attorney? The star of YouTube? How'd that work out for your last client?" At my startled look, he said, "What, you think we don't have the internet in the islands?" He cackled, an ugly sound. "Yeah, I watched you on there. Zane McZillion. He's a pretty good ball player. Nice job, lawyer lady."

I bit down hard and kept biting. "The warrant. May I review it or not?"

"Be quick about it, then."

"I'll be right back. Please don't set foot in that house until I return."

He didn't answer, just walked back to the cluster of officers in the front yard.

The siren on the police cruiser with Ava inside sounded once, then the car made a three-point turn with its lights still on and headed out of the driveway around the remaining two police cars and Bart's truck. Bart was leaning against his Pathfinder with one arm around Emily and the other restraining a whining Oso. I hadn't seen Emily earlier when I'd dashed onto the scene. Her face was pale and she had black circles under both eyes. But she stood up straight as I approached, and stepped toward me, asking question after question before I could answer. "How is Ava? What's going on?"

I let her hug me, then comforted my dog, then filled them in on what was going on. "They're going to search Ava's house, and I need to stay for that. It could last a long time, and I expect they'll tear her house apart. I think you should check into a hotel, Em."

I was much more familiar with what came next than I wanted to be.

Emily pursed her lips, thinking. "I could stay, if you need me."

I couldn't drag Emily any further into this mess. "Thanks, but there's no need. I've got it under control."

Emily accepted my lie. "God, this is awful. Poor Ava."

She didn't ask if Ava had done it. I'm sure she was wondering, what with me bringing her down here and putting her up in the house of an accused murderer and all. But she didn't ask, God bless her. Bart was still leaning against the truck, looking a little out of place as the drama unfolded.

"Ava is in for a tough time," I answered. "No matter how this plays out."

"What do you want me to do about my bags?" she asked.

"I doubt they're going to let us take anything from the house until they're done. Sorry. I can bring you a bag tomorrow, though."

"I'll drop Emily at a hotel on my way home," Bart said, sounding firm and confident.

I grabbed his hand, glad now that I'd stayed loose tonight, that I hadn't torpedoed whatever this was with him. "Thank you. Take her to the Peacock Flower." I looked at Emily. "Text me the details when you're safely in your room, but don't wait up for me. I'll just spend the night here when they're done. I suddenly have a lot to do, and tomorrow will be more of the same. Relax, read a magazine. Enjoy yourself. The spa there is fabulous, and they've got three swimming pools and two beaches." I leaned in and kissed her cheek. "I'll call when I can."

"Do what you need to do." She kissed my cheek back and searched my eyes. Whatever she saw must have satisfied her, because she walked to the passenger side of Bart's SUV.

Bart put his arms around me and pulled me close. He kissed my forehead. "Anything else I can do?"

Take me with you. Go pick up Ava and bring her home. "Call Rashidi. Other than that, no, thank you. You've been great." On impulse, I stood on my tiptoes and kissed him on the mouth, quick and hard. I didn't wait to see his reaction. I spun around and marched into the house with Oso loping to keep up. Katie Connell, criminal defense attorney-at-law, reluctantly resurrected.

Chapter Thirty-seven

Jacoby handed me the warrant.

"Give me five minutes," I said. I shut myself in the truck, leaving Oso to patrol on his own. I didn't want to make this comfortable or easy for them.

Not only was my knowledge of criminal procedure limited, but this was personal. I couldn't evaluate Ava objectively. And I was tipsy, especially now that the adrenaline rush had passed and cottonmouth had set in. I scrolled through the contacts on my phone. Shannon. My former colleague at Hailey & Hart. I dialed.

No answer.

Shit. I could call Collin, but if I did, he would figure out I was in the middle of a cluster-you-know-what. And I didn't know any other criminal defense attorneys. Blue and white collar didn't mix much in the legal scene. I did know one other criminal law expert, though, albeit not well, but this was an emergency. I scrolled through my address book again. The one I wanted wasn't there. I rifled my wallet. A business card. I shined the backlight from my phone on it. Jackpot. I dialed.

"Hello?" It sounded more like "Ullo," with a crack in his voice on the O part.

"May I speak to Mack Duncan, please? This is Katie Connell calling."

"This is Mack. And it's one in the morning." He sounded much more alert now, like he'd sat up. He was probably as surprised to hear from me as he would be to hear from Barack Obama. He'd probably much prefer the president.

It was two a.m. here in St. Marcos, but I didn't think telling him that would help. "I'm sorry to bother you. I didn't know who else to call."

"If you're in trouble, you should call your attorney. I don't play for your team."

"No, it's not like that. I've relocated to the U.S. Virgin Islands. A friend of mine here was arrested on charges of murder. The police are about to search her house, and I'm the only attorney around. I don't know any criminal attorneys to call but you, and I just hoped you could give me the top two or three things to think about as I review this warrant and observe the search."

"You're kidding me, right?" He wasn't laughing.

"I wish I were. God, I wish I were." The line was silent except for his breathing. He wasn't going to help me. "Listen, I'm sorry I woke you. I'll let you go."

"No, wait. That's OK. This is straight up? You're in the Virgin Islands? You're not in Dallas, about to avenge your shame in court against me?"

Means to an end, Katie. I clenched my jaw, then relaxed it and spoke. "I'm on St. Marcos in the Virgin Islands. A few weeks ago, I withdrew from my partnership with Hailey & Hart and sold my Dallas condo. I was living the dream here for all of three days until this happened."

"This runaway caper is about the McMillan trial, isn't it? I can understand. If I'd been in your shoes, I'd've rabbited, too."

"No, it's not that." It was sort of that. "I had already made an offer on my house here."

"Yeah, right." He grunted. "Wait. Isn't that where your parents . . ."

The sentence hung in the air. "Died," I said. "Yes."

Silence again. Now Mack's breathing was softer. I heard a click, like the sound of a lamp switching on.

He finally spoke. "OK, but I'm only doing this for your dad. And as penance."

"Penance for what?" I asked.

"For forwarding the link to the YouTube video to my contact list."

I would never, ever live Zane McMillan down. I cleared my throat. "I'm listening."

"Make sure they have probable cause. Make sure the warrant specifies what they are looking for. Make sure it outlines where they can search. You can stay and watch them but don't interfere. You need to find out when she's being arraigned. That's all you need to worry about now. If they do anything illegal, you can try to get the evidence thrown out later."

"OK. I can do that." It sounded simple when he said it. I'd already read the warrant, and it checked out against his criteria. "Mack, thank you."

"We done here?"

"Yes."

He hung up the phone. Well, I got what I needed out of that. I could lick my wounds later. I lifted my chin and squared my jaw.

Jacoby was standing outside my door. The other officers were lounging against the two remaining sedans. Oso had stationed himself by Ava's front door.

"Time's up," he said through the glass of my window.

I opened my door and climbed out of the truck. "Fine," I said, handing the paper back to him. "I'll be observing."

"Mind you don't get in our way."

"I wouldn't dream of it," I said.

I watched while they stampeded through Ava's house, trampling everything in their path. My status as attorney to the accused combined with my "not bahn yah" status marked me as a double-dog outsider. They seemed to take special pleasure in trashing my neatly packed suitcases. Or maybe I was just paranoid. But they sure acted nicer when Rashidi showed up about halfway through their search, summoned by a call from Bart.

The officers didn't admit it, but I knew they found no damning evidence. They bagged up hair samples and dirty clothes, they removed every cutting implement they could find, they carted out Ava's cell phone and laptop, but there were no war whoops or gloating smiles. No bloody knives. No souvenirs from Guy's dead body. No diary confessions. In an hour, they were done and gone, Category Five hurricane damage in their wake.

Next, Rashidi and I called Ava's parents, waking them up at their home on the island. I hadn't ever met them, but I knew their faces from Ava's pictures. I hated doing this to them at three o'clock in the morning, but they deserved to know. This way, they could choose whether to take action and what that might be tonight.

The call was hard for all of us, one insult after another on top of the injury. What parent wants to learn their child is in jail, arrested for murder, much less the murder of her married lover, a prominent man of their own generation in their small, closed community? As soon as we'd broken the worst of the news, Rashidi dropped off the call to start cleaning up after the search and destroy party. I steered Gill and Anita Butler through a discussion of their daughter's bail and legal representation.

"Ava can't get out until she's arraigned and the judge sets bail. At that point, you can go to any bail bondsman to post it."

Gill spoke. "How much do you think it will be?"

"I wish I knew. I haven't practiced in the V.I. But normally you have to put down ten percent of whatever number the judge sets for bail."

"My business went bankrupt last year. Anita and I were just started to dig ourselves out," Gill said. His voice fell. "We don't have much."

Anita wailed. "We lost everything."

This wasn't good.

"Well, that's something for you guys to talk about tonight, then. Who do you know that might have the ability to help you?"

"No one," Anita wailed again. Then more softly. "No one."

The pain of this conversation was further confirmation that criminal law was not for me, as if I needed more convincing. I told them, "Another decision that needs to be made soon is about who you could call to represent Ava in court."

"I thought you were doing that," Gill said.

"I'm not licensed in the V.I., so I can't represent her in court. I told the police I was her lawyer, but only for purposes of her arrest and the search of her house. She needs to have a top-notch criminal defense attorney, someone licensed here." While my Texas license entitled me to practice law in any state or territory of the U.S. that offered "reciprocity" by recognizing the law licenses from those jurisdictions, the U.S. Virgins was not one of them.

"What about Duke?" Anita asked.

"We could call him," Gill said.

"Duke Ellis one of our dearest friends. And he an attorney on St. Marcos," Anita explained, talking Local and sounding like Ava. Her voice sounded better, more hopeful.

"If you have his number, I could patch him into this conversation," I said.

Five minutes later, we had rousted Attorney Duke Ellis from sleep. Gill told him about Ava and introduced me. I explained to Duke what the Butlers needed him to do for her.

"I've known that girl since she was in nappies," Duke said. His voice was nearly as sad as the Butlers'. "Of course I'll represent her, but only on the condition you allow me to do it as a family friend. And I don't take money from family."

His offer of representation meant that I was free. Freeeeeee! I strapped on a mental muzzle while the inner Katie sang, "I'm walking on sunshine."

"Thank you, Duke," Gill said. "You're a true friend to us and to Ava. What kind of bail do you think the judge will set?"

I could identify a chuptz even through a three-way call. "This is the murder of a senator. They're demigods in this community. It's going to be high. A million or more, I'd say."

Anita started sobbing again. I heard Gill murmuring to her off the phone line. She sniffed and her sobs subsided.

Duke spoke again. "Ms. Connell, I don't supposed you'd agree to help me?"

At first it didn't register that Duke had invited me back to hell. No way on God's green earth, I thought.

"Certainly, Mr. Ellis," I said, because, really, how could I say no with Ava's distraught parents listening in? But the thought of another criminal trial so close on the heels of the McZillion disaster gave me chills and broke my promise to the universe, my parents, and myself. Oh, God was punishing me for sure.

"Excellent, excellent. I'll head to the station now to see about meeting with Ava. Maybe I can find out something about arraignment and bail, too."

We rang off, but he called me back within an hour to ask that I attend the arraignment and bail hearing at eleven the next morning.

A return to purgatory.

Chapter Thirty-eight

Morning came and kicked my ass. I'd slept a measly two hours on my futon before it was time to get up for the sprint over to Walker's office. Walker. Ugh. Two days ago we had scheduled our meeting for ten a.m. today. The only reason I didn't cancel on him was that his office was on my way to the court-house.

Oso jumped up on the futon and tried to bathe me with his tongue. His breath smelled like dead frogs. Gross. That woke me up.

"Stop it. No," I said.

I dragged myself out of bed and to the bathroom. I had to look presentable for court.

I thought about last night while I brushed my teeth, tamed my flyaway be-frizzled hair with some of Ava's pomade, and washed my face. No, it wasn't just a nightmare. It was reality. I was even wearing lawyer clothes today, an outfit I had packed at the last second in my suitcase instead of handing off to the movers for ocean shipment. It was a summery tan pant, shell and jacket combination. Nothing too flashy.

As I put on a dash of neutral lipstick and a smidge of mascara, I fretted again about Ava's bail. Over a million dollars meant the bondsman would require over one hundred thousand dollars. Ava's parents didn't have it. Rashidi sure didn't have it. As popular as Ava was, even if we sent around a collection plate at all the local bars, we'd only come up with a few hundred bucks. No one had asked me, but I was now asking myself. Did Katie have it?

Katie did. I had the hundred thou in cash, but I barely had the collateral. If I put up my money and she skipped bail, I'd be out one jumbie house and the rest of my savings. So, I could do it, but just, and only if it was necessary. If it was the right thing for me to do, and even close to sane, which I doubted. I'd known Ava a total of one month, one *week*, if you only counted the time I'd spent around her. And I was still irritated with her, too, although the events of yesterday with Bart were beginning to feel like ancient history. God, please let someone else come forward, I prayed.

Last night's search had left me feeling violated, and brought out a strong need in me for privacy. I put my makeup back in its zippered bag, and the bag back into my zippered suitcase. I even spun the combination locks for good measure. I shut and locked the house—something Ava never did—and Oso and I headed to Town. On the way, we stopped at the Pirates Bay Deli, a crowded grocery-deli combo store crammed into several spaces in a shallow strip mall, stocked with upscale treats for East Enders and tourists. I needed an extra-large coffee with half and half and Splenda. Oso needed a bag of rawhide bones.

We had to park three blocks from Walker's office this time, way on the other side of the farmer's market, in front of a jewelry store that specialized in silver and gold bracelets with St. Marcos' signature hook clasps. I was carrying my coffee, so there was no way I was carrying a dog. I snapped Oso's leash to his collar. He whined.

"I'm on my last frayed nerve, dog. If you can do this for Emily, you can do it for me."

Maybe it was something in my voice, but he did. In fact, he walked smartly on the left beside me, without pulling, like he was born to heel. The only nice surprise today so far. No, that wasn't true. I was too tired to feel hungover. That was a huge surprise.

I grasped Walker's door handle, twisted it, and gave the door a jerk. It swung open toward me, as if it was still ajar from the last person who'd passed through. I nearly fell over backwards onto my dog. Embarrassment, stress, and exhaustion mixed into my anger. What was I doing chasing down this man a fourth time? How could I ever move on if he was going to hold me prisoner to his lack of concern over my parents' case? If he shined me on again today, I was asking for my money back. Was there someone I could report him to? The Better Business Bureau? The Idiotic Investigators Institute? Something, anything. I was sick of it.

I stepped in the door. "Good morning," I said. I meant it more like, "I'm here, asshole," and to my own ears, it sounded spot on.

Walker didn't bother to acknowledge my presence. He was in the far recess of his Dr. Seuss-y office space, talking to someone just outside of my line of vision. They were standing in a doorway that I hadn't realized existed before. I could hear the visitor's voice. Not what he said, just the deep rumble. Whoever he was, he was above us riffraff who had to use the front door. Well, too bad. There were no alleys or parking spaces behind the buildings, just narrow walkways. So Mr. Special would get a nice long hike.

"Hell-O," I said louder, still standing with Oso beside me, even though I was plenty loud last time and I knew Walker heard me. I was too damn tired to put up with his rudeness. "I believe we have a ten o'clock appointment. Katie Connell here." If nothing else, I'd piss him off, and that would give me a measure of satisfaction.

The back door slammed shut. Walker strode toward us. As he came closer, a growl started in Oso's chest, then died off into a whine. I patted his head.

"Yes, Ms. Connell, we do." He sat at his desk, which now bore neither dust nor stacks of files. Just one file. Mine. I could read "Katie Connell" written on it, but only because he used block printing. I'd never mastered upside down reading. Walker pulled the file toward him and opened it. He scanned the top document. Either that, or he used it as an excuse not to look at me.

I decided to take a seat. Oso decided not to. He remained at attention and kept his eyes on Walker. The fur on his back bristled.

"I'm surprised to see you here," Walker finally said. "What with your friend in jail and all."

I had meant to grab a copy of the *St. Marcos Source* that morning and see what it had to say about Ava. Maybe Walker was about to save me the trouble. I didn't answer him.

He said, "Well, she did the island a favor. That man was as wutliss as the shirt he was wearing when he died."

Everything about what he had just said was offensive. "Wutliss?" I repeated.

"Yeah, wutliss. Worthless. On the take his whole political career, did nothing but screw whatever pretty young thing was stupid and trashy enough to get mixed up with him."

My face burned, my voice sizzled. "Neither of which Ava was. Nor did she do anyone any favors, because she didn't kill the senator." My tone set Oso off again, and now he was growling like a dog twice his size. I let him.

"Your friend is well known, Ms. Connell. As to whether she did or didn't, we'll all see, I guess." He was smiling that crocodile smile again. "Someone needs to give that dog a Valium. Now, I'm ready to deliver my report to you."

"Good." I stroked Oso soothingly. He whined and sat.

"Not a unique theory, by the way, that our police force got something wrong. It's often even a correct one. They're a corrupt version of the Keystone Cops." Not a comforting thought with Ava behind bars. "In your case, though, I didn't find anything that led to a different result than the recently deceased younger Officer Jacoby reached." He thumbed through the pages of my file and pulled a piece of paper out. "The waiter that served them at Fortuna's the night they died? Nothing. The hotel employees—restaurant, bar, maids, room service, front desk—nothing out of the ordinary there, either. The only thing I learned, in fact, was that your parents told the concierge at the hotel that Baptiste's Bluff was on their definite to-do list while they were here, because it was their anniversary and sounded romantic."

"Did anyone tell you they saw my father drinking that night?"

He handed me a restaurant credit card receipt. "No one had to tell me. It's in black and white, here. Three bottles of wine at dinner. The cheapest wine they carry," he added.

I stared at the piece of paper, refusing to let him needle me. The date was right. Other than that, I had no way of knowing whether it was authentic. It seemed impossible, though, that my mother would have allowed—much less participated in—Dad drinking.

"Were you able to find my mother's ring at the hotel?" I asked.

"No." He crossed his arms.

"Can I get a copy of your file with my report?" I asked him.

"This," he gestured toward his mouth with his right hand, then recrossed it with the left, "is your report. And, no, I don't provide copies of my files. If you want to see something, all you have to do is come find me, and I'll show you."

"That's ridiculous. I want both: a report and the file. I'll pay you for your time in preparing them."

He sighed. "Fine. I'll put it together. There'll be a copying fee, then, too."

"And I need it delivered to me at my house." I was done coming to this creepy office.

"Add a delivery fee."

"How much do I owe you then?" I asked.

"I'll bring the bill with me when I come. Your house that big mausoleum in the rainforest?"

Everybody and their long-legged brother knew where I lived, or was about to live. "Yes. Estate Annalise."

"I'll be out there tomorrow afternoon between five and six, then."

"Thank you." I popped out of my chair like I was on springs, tugged Oso, and bounded for the door, desperate to expel the stale air of his office from my lungs.

Chapter Thirty-nine

I parked in the small lot beside the two-story seafoam green stucco court-house and went up the front walk between bougainvillea bushes to the main entrance, where I sent my bag through the x-ray machine and went through the metal detector. The two guards said nothing, just gestured toward a black kiosk with white letters when I asked for directions. I found the room number for the courtroom on the kiosk and took a long flight of stairs past an open-air courtyard. I looked down over its stone picnic tables and small Christmas palms as I made my way up.

I got to the courtroom in time to see Ava led in from the exterior hallway in an orange jumpsuit three sizes too big for her and handcuffs. Her eyes were hollow, and her hair was dull and flattened against her head. She'd pulled it back in a low ponytail. She'd probably gotten less sleep than I did last night.

I slipped in behind her and the guards, then scooted into the second row behind the defense table beside Rashidi. He introduced me to Gill and Anita, his voice soft but carrying. We all shook hands. The anxiety coming off Anita was palpable. Hell, she could probably say the same about me. It was different for Anita than for me, though; Ava was my friend, but she was Anita's daughter. A daughter who looked like a lighter version of herself. Anita was a beautiful woman.

Ava had taken a seat beside a short, slight West Indian man. Duke Ellis, I presumed.

"All rise," the bailiff commanded as the judge entered the room.

We did. The judge was a gray-haired local woman of the Taino body type that Doug had described to me. Her robes made her body look square. She motioned for us to sit after she'd lowered herself into a chair behind her bench.

Ava looked over her shoulder at the four of us clustered together. I shot her a thumbs up. She scrunched her mouth to the side and nodded, uncertain.

In less time than it had taken for the officers to arrest her, the judge led the prosecutor and Ava's attorney through her plea of not guilty and set the bail at 1.2 million dollars. Duke put up a spirited argument in her defense, for all the good it did. After devoting only five minutes to the process, the judge slammed down her gavel and walked out. Wam bam, thank you, ma'am.

Ava remained seated. I saw her shoulders heaving. I glanced at Anita. Hers were, too.

Duke turned around. He noticed me, the stranger to him, and said, "You must be Attorney Connell? Duke Ellis."

I adopted his island convention for addressing members of the bar. "Katie Connell. Nice to meet you, Attorney Ellis." I stood up and leaned across the intervening row to shake his small hand. His palm was callused, and I knew instantly my father would like him.

Duke asked Ava's parents, "Were you able to find a source to put up the bail money?"

Gill and Anita gripped each other's hands so hard their knuckles were white. Gill looked into his wife's face and answered without breaking eye contact. "We weren't. We're going to keep trying."

"It's a big number," Duke said. "I'll do whatever I can to help you find a way to do this."

At that moment, the guards led Ava back out. She looked at us as she passed by in the aisle, her eyebrow raised in a question. Her father said, "Soon, honey. We're working on it." Her shoulders slumped.

"I can cover it," a voice said.

Shit. It was my voice.

"What?" Gill asked.

"Really?" Anita said, a sob in her throat.

Rashidi reached out and took my hand. He squeezed.

"Um, yeah. I have the cash. It will tie up all that I have, though. My house, my entire life's savings, my inheritance from my parents. I need y'all to promise me she won't jump bail." My voice trailed off. Too late to back out, no matter how much I already regretted saying this. I tried to smile, but it was a weak effort.

"I nail her feet to the floor if I have to," Rashidi said. "It a good thing you're doin'."

Now the thank yous spilled out, stepping all over each other to be heard. The walls closed in on me. I stood up.

"Well, alrighty then, I'll just go take care of it, before I go home." My face felt brittle, so I didn't try to smile again in case I cracked it. I made my way out, my gait stiff and jerky.

What the hell had I just done?

Chapter Forty

Oso sat with his head in my lap as I drove from the bail bondsman up to Annalise, careening down the center of the road like a local and steering with one hand while I used my other to deliver a cold Heineken to my central nervous system. If someone came around a corner in the center too fast, I'd probably die. Oh well. Whatever. Dead. Broke. They were about the same thing.

Not broke, I reminded myself. Only at the risk of becoming broke. As long as Ava stayed and faced trial, I was still flush. Ava. The super reliable one. At least I had a friend like Emily that didn't sleep with married guys, flirt with my sort-of-boyfriend, get thrown in jail, and put all my money at risk. And was super understanding to boot. I'd had a couple of text exchanges with her during the day, and she kept telling me that she was having a perfectly wonderful time, with no problems. Sounded awesome. Where could I buy that kind of day? I took another chug of Heinie.

I made it home without dying or spilling my beer. No Junior-mobile, again. Three days: late, absent, absent.

As I opened my truck door, I heard wailing from inside the house. Shouting. The dogs were running around yelping instead of rushing to greet me. Oso scrambled over me and jumped out the driver's side door to join in their melee. I didn't know if I could handle any more stress, and I didn't have any more Heineken. But it didn't seem I had a choice, which felt all too familiar lately. I slammed my truck door behind Oso and ran into the house, calling out as I ran.

Egg met me at the entrance to the great room and grasped my arm, pulling me forward. "Oh, Ms. Connell, Ms. Connell, the scaffolding fall. He coulda die, he coulda die. Come quick."

I wished my parents had raised me a good Irish Catholic girl instead of a lapsed Baptist. I wanted a rosary right now. Something to touch, to hold, to tether me to the earth. I was afraid of dissipating into the atmosphere. I twisted my hair instead, something I hadn't done since I was six years old, but I didn't break stride.

One of the workers I'd met yesterday was lying on a mattress in the center of the great room floor, with about three hundred pounds of metal scaffolding and wooden planks scattered on the floor around him. The tower above him listed perilously. I covered the distance between us in three leaping steps. His co-workers made room for me, and I crouched beside him.

He babbled excitedly, eyes closed. "Come back. You save me. Come back." His eyes popped open. "Did you see her catch me?"

We shook our heads and looked at each other. No one knew what he was talking about.

"Sir, are you all right?" I asked.

"Yah, I fine. I fell."

"I know," I said. "What's your name?"

"Mahatoo. Joey Mahatoo." His voice sounded clear. His answers made sense. Those were good signs.

"Do you know what happened?"

He sat halfway up on his elbows. His co-workers gasped and protested. He looked around me, behind me, everywhere, for something. Then he spoke.

"I hear this creakin' noise, and a scrapin' one. I standin' on the top of the scaffold, on my platform, and then I'm fallin', fallin', but slow-like. I know I gonna die when I hit that concrete, but then these soft arms catch me. Soft and warm, a woman." A surprised look came over his face. "She smell good, too. And she lay me down on the mattress, here. I try to see her, but she gone. And all a'you here instead." He shook his head. "The jumbie save me. The jumbie did it."

Egg touched my shoulder. "No mattress in here before he fell."

I recognized it. "It was downstairs," I said. "Some kids used to sleep on it when they camped out here."

The men talked all over each other. They knew they'd witnessed a miracle, and their excitement bubbled up fast, like a pot of spaghetti right before it boiled over.

"Do you need a doctor? Are you hurt at all?" I asked the young man.

He felt of his own arms and legs, of his head. He stood up, so I did, too. No blood. Not even a scratch. "Nah, ain't nothing wrong with me. I saved by the jumbie."

I didn't doubt it for a second. I wished I could find her, so I could tell her thank you, but there was no sign of the woman I'd seen the day before. I mouthed the words anyway. I walked toward the kitchen. Rashidi was there.

"Did you hear?" I asked.

He nodded slowly, as much in amazement as in answer to my question. "Yah, I come in a minute ago and hear it all. You got a hell of a jumbie, Katie. A hell of a jumbie."

"A hell of a jumbie," I agreed. "And a really crap contractor. Scaffolding doesn't just fall. If it's in proper condition, if it's put together right, it doesn't just fall."

"For true," Rashidi said.

"I wish I had fired him yesterday," I said.

"Yah, best do it quick today."

I'd decided Egg was the foreman, official or not. He was standing nearby, so I asked him, "Where's Junior?"

Egg flinched at the word Junior. "I call him when Joey fall. Junior come soon." He motioned me closer, his voice dropping to a level the other men couldn't hear. "What he doin' ain't right. He workin' a job for some rich doctor. I guess he skippin' out over there instead of takin' care of his business here. He not doin' what you pay him for. But please don't tell him I said so, miss."

"Thank you for telling me, Egg. I won't repeat a word of this to Junior."

I heard an engine outside. Egg's eyes widened. I peered out the kitchen window. Junior was pulling in the drive. Egg hightailed it back to the great room. Rashidi still stood beside me.

"I'll handle this," I said.

Junior was moving his bulky midsection faster today than last time I'd seen him. His face-splitting grin was still there, though. Not for long. I met him outside, trying for less of an audience.

"Ms. Katie, good to see you," he said.

"No, it isn't," I said.

He stopped short. "Wah? Something wrong?"

"Yes, Junior, you know that there is something very wrong. One of your men had a serious accident here today. Joey could have been killed."

"Nah, I hear not a scratch on him."

"No thanks to you."

"Me? I not even here."

"Exactly. And you weren't here yesterday, either, when the guys dem were smoking ganja instead of working. And you were late the day before, when they put the scaffolding up."

He face was blank. "Men dem work better if I let them relax, leave them be."

"If by relax you mean get stoned, then I beg to differ. You have to do some work in the first place in order to work 'better.' And they weren't working."

"I had to go to town for supplies," he said. He held up two paintbrushes, as flimsy as his story.

He wanted me to believe he had gone all the way to town for two cheap brushes he wouldn't need for weeks? I'd had enough. "You won't need those for Annalise anymore."

"Wah?" he said.

I went to my car and got my checkbook out of my purse. I wrote Junior a check marked "payment in full." I held it at shoulder height as I spoke. "When you waste the time I pay you for, that is stealing from me. When you don't supervise your men and they don't work, you're all stealing from me. When serious accidents happen at my house that you could have prevented, you are putting me at risk along with your men."

"It not my fault. The jumbie break the scaffolding," he said.

"Oh, no. The jumbie, if there is one, saved Joey." I handed him the check. "I want you to pack up everything today, and get off my property. Please don't come back."

He studied the check, his lips moving. "This not enough. This not what you owe me."

"This is all you will get from me. You've done no work, accomplished nothing. Please leave."

He glared at me through his clouded eyes. Continental transplants like me always wore sunglasses, but for some reason most of the locals didn't, and many developed premature cataracts. Junior chuptzed loudly and spat on the ground, then walked inside. I heard low growling behind me and turned to see Oso and Sheila, their teeth bared, moving after Junior on silent feet.

Rashidi was right about me needing a pack of dogs. I loved them.

Mere minutes later, Junior and his guys came out in a big hurry and tossed their tools haphazardly into their trucks. Egg looked at me as he passed by, an apology in his eyes.

"I come back for the scaffolding," Junior fumed. "You crazy, and this house the jumbie. You be sorry, lady. You be sorry."

He drove off in a huff and a cloud of dust.

Chapter Forty-one

I spent the night with Emily at the Peacock Flower, as did Oso, who we smuggled in after dark. He and Emily enjoyed the high life together while I zoned out to *American Idol* and my preferred Peacock Flower dinner of fruit and rum punch.

I poured myself another glass as I chewed a piece of pineapple. I wondered where Ava was. I knew her parents had sprung her, because Anita had called me. Ava had, too. They both left effusively grateful messages on my voicemail. My emotions had redlined, though, and I couldn't even handle praise.

And they weren't the only callers I screened. Bart's calls went to voicemail, too, and I left his texts unanswered. I focused everything I had left in the tank on Emily, until I fell asleep with one inch of rum punch in my plastic cup and the TV and lights still on.

The next morning I rose early again, this time to take Emily to the airport. My body was awake but my mind was numb, my heart black. I would deliver an Academy Award performance of "fine," though, or die trying. Oso sat tall between us on the drive.

Emily said, "I'm so glad I came. This has been the best vacation ever. And that includes my honeymoon trip to Banff and to see the Calgary Stampede Rodeo."

My fingers were drumming the steering wheel of their own accord. I stopped them. "You're kidding, right? This has been a nightmare."

She laughed, the sound like breaking glass in my head. "Well, it has been for you and Ava. I feel bad about that, but I know Ava is in good hands. And it was exciting, and it was memorable. Really."

"Do me a favor. When you talk to Collin, how about you use the word 'peaceful' instead of 'memorable'?" An image of Collin kidnapping me and dragging me back to Dallas popped into my head.

"Yeah. I'd better give him the sanitized version." She pulled out her ticket and passport, reading them for, by my count, the twentieth time.

I noticed I was fanning my knees together. I gripped my left thigh and ordered it to stop. Ten more minutes, and I wouldn't have to fake it anymore.

She said, "I hate to bring up a bad subject, but I need to tell you something before I leave."

Perfect. More bad news. "Go ahead." Oso's ears rose and he licked my right knee.

Emily caught her lip between her teeth, then released it. "Nick gave notice at the firm the Monday after you left. By email. From his vacation. It was kind of a big deal at the office, even though he wasn't an attorney. His divorce went through, I hear. But nobody knows for sure why he left."

Holy crap. She should have just handed me an IV drip of Bloody Marys with her news. My truck hit a sharp-edged speed bump too fast and too hard. In lieu of enforcing speeding laws, St. Marcos put speed bumps across all the roads, as if the potholes weren't already enough of a danger to tires. How apropos of the day, of my life. Symbolic even. If I had bought all that karma and chi stuff they pedaled at the Peacock Flower Spa, I'd say mine were out of whack. If I bought into them, which I didn't. The universe just hated me, that was all.

"Ah, so Heathcliff can wander the moors alone now." It sounded flat even to me.

"I'm sorry, Katie."

"I'll be fine." My phone rang. Caller ID said it was Rashidi. His helpfulness, already amazing, had multiplied by ten when I bailed Ava out. He had promised yesterday to pull together a slate of contractor candidates overnight. I didn't want to talk to anyone, but I owed it to him to answer.

"Do you mind?" I asked Emily.

"Go ahead," she said.

I put my headset on and pressed Accept. "This is Katie," I said.

"I got some guys dem for you to meet, to pick your new contractor from," he said. He sounded excited.

"Thanks, Rashidi. You pick one, please. I don't need to meet them." I didn't care, and it didn't matter. Who even knew if I'd have a house to finish? I'd bet one point two million on snake eyes at the Lucky Lady Bail Bondsman yesterday. If Ava crapped out on me, I'd bust.

"Are you sure?" he asked.

"Completely."

"All right. Crazy Grove good to go then. We come to Annalise this after-noon, four o'clock or thereabouts."

"That's his name? Crazy Grove?"

"Nah, it William Wingrove. Grove—short for Wingrove. He go by *either* Crazy or Grove or both."

Locals loved their nicknames. Even the billboards for senatorial candidates gave them: "Vote for Derek 'Lefty' Paul," or "Now's the time for Janeen 'Babyface' Richards."

"Interesting name." I put on my blinker to turn into the airport entrance.

"He gonna do you right, Katie. Everything gonna be fine."

My throat constricted. "Thanks, Rashidi." I reached for my phone to press the End key, but he kept talking.

"By the way, I with Ava. She got out just fine yesterday, stayed with her parents. She said she left you messages. I just wanted to make sure you knew she good and she grateful to you."

"That's wonderful. Thank you again." I pressed End and ripped off my headset.

We pulled into the flat airport parking lot that was the size of an Albert-son's grocery store lot back in Dallas. I cracked the window and left my fuzzy friend and one of his rawhide bones in the truck with the windows halfway down. He'd spent a lot of time in this position yesterday and now today, but he had enjoyed his treats.

"Be a good boy. I'll be right back," I told him. He didn't even look at me. All his attention was focused on the bone.

I walked Emily to the ticket counter. My eyes were burning. I needed to make this quick.

I threw my arms around her. "You are such a good friend, Emily. I love you. I'm going to miss you."

"I love you, too," she said. "You are going to be fine, Katie. I know you will." She patted my back as she spoke.

I kept hearing that word "fine" thrown around, but I hadn't seen it in ac-tion yet.

Emily promised to check on my brother and to give Rich a hug for me. And then she left for Dallas. And it was just like the game of pick-up sticks I'd played with my girlfriends as a kid—when a player removed the wrong stick, the whole pile crashed. Emily was the wrong stick.

I needed to find a soft place to land.

Chapter Forty-two

I figured I had a choice. I could drive straight to Toes in the Sand and drink until I couldn't walk, or to the West End beaches and walk until I couldn't drink. I got in my truck and started driving. I reached the point of no return five minutes later at a traffic light.

Right or left. The direction I turned decided my fate.

I needed expert advice. "Which way, Oso?"

He'd finished his bone, so I got his attention. His tongue lolled, and his tail thumped. No help. I did an eenie meenie miney mo. The answer came out wrong. I turned to the left. I drove until I couldn't go any further without pontoons on my truck. I parked beside a windowless wooden structure with removable wall panels that housed a beach grill, The Rainbow Club. Rainbows, awesome, and please could I have some fairies and unicorns, too? They were closed, and I was the only one in the dirt lot, but then it was only nine o'clock in the morning.

I slumped on the steering wheel and turned the engine off. I thought I would cry when the world went still, but I didn't. The silence was loud. Oso panted. A fly buzzed and bumped into the window. My pulse throbbed hot in the tips of my ears. I closed my eyes and imagined I was invisible. I could hide here forever. Or until Oso and I baked off the bone in this oven of a truck once the tropical sun was high. If it was this bad now, we'd broil by noon.

I opened the door and stuck my feet out into the void, halfway expecting I'd fall to the center of the earth. My feet hit solid ground. I had a two-piece navy blue and white bathing suit on under my new uniform of sundress, so I pulled the stretchy green cotton over my head and tossed it back onto my seat. Years of habit made me reach for the sunscreen, but I stopped. It didn't matter if this redhead burned to a crisp. I grabbed my hat, and I headed for the sand, a leashless Oso behind me.

I walked up and down that beach until the soles of my feet were as smooth as one of the ocean-churned stones. I walked from the rocks at the waterline outside the Rainbow Club down the pebbly shoreline until the sand became grainy again. The beach was narrow here, backed by a two-foot-high sand lip just beyond the surf's reach. Past the sand heading inland, a thick row of sea grapes and the occasional banyan tree hid the curving West End Road from view. I kept walking. I turned around when I had passed an outcropping of tidal pools, their shallow rock tops teeming with marine life. A strand of beach houses started here, and I wanted a beach all to myself, not to share with rental families who were already outside making the most of their vacations. I ignored the cosmic insult of happy couples and splashing children and returned on the path from which I'd come. I banished all the shiny, happy people in the world from my thoughts. Let misery reign, let the tears finally fall.

God, there was so much noise in my head. I walked up and down the beach for miles without seeing, but somewhere along the way, my eyes began to drink in the details. Near the end of the second hour, I noticed the textures of sand and rocks under my feet. I saw the vinegar walker shells and ghostly crabs scamper across the rocks as the water surged in and out. I smelled the ocean as the silky air inside the breeze skimmed across my skin. I watched the water for fish jumping and saw porpoises cruising the shoreline. I heard the rainstick sound of water rushing over exposed coral. By noon, Oso had bailed and was napping under a banyan tree mid-beach as I paced back and forth along the half-mile stretch of sand. Traitorously rational thoughts crept in, right about the time I recognized that the searing pain in my shoulders was sunburn.

Ava said everybody was either running to or running from something when they came to St. Marcos. I had thought I was the "running to" kind of person. Running to Annalise, running to a connection to my parents. I wasn't, though. I was smack dab in the "running from" category with all the other losers. It got worse. I was pretty sure I wasn't running from Nick or from guilt about my parents or even from alcohol, although all three of those were worth running from. No, I was running from me. Me in Dallas, hurting myself. Me here, hurting myself. Wherever I went, there I found myself. Ever ready to wreak havoc on my own life.

Somehow, I had to leave this Katie behind. I had to outrun her self-destructive ways, her bad choices, her crazy leaps. I had to seize control.

That was it. Control. Katie needed to take charge of Katie. She—I—was the only one who could. My fists balled. I looked up at the sky. "Help?" I asked.

When I got no immediate answer, I resorted to my go-to control mechanism: planning. Doesn't God help those who help themselves? Fifteen minutes after I'd started the process, I had decided what I needed to do. Where was a scrap of scratch paper when a girl needed one?

"You can do this," I said.

Crap. My lips split as I moved them to talk to myself. If I didn't want to implement my new plan from a hospital bed, I had to get out of the sun, now. I gathered Oso from his shady rest spot. The sand away from the water was hot, and I ran, wincing, back to the truck. I put my dress on and yelled when the cloth abraded my burned skin.

Apparently, I'd burned the old Katie out like the bees at Annalise. That thought made me smile, which hurt. I pointed the rearview mirror at my face. Not too bad, thanks to my hat. Mostly just my lips. And chest, shoulders, arms, stomach, and back. See? It had happened again. Out-of-control Katie on autopilot, and the result was second-degree sunburn. Well, seven days and a gallon of aloe vera would cure what ailed me physically.

I drove back to Ava's with my foot heavy on the accelerator. When I got inside the house, I surveyed the damage. There, of course, were the ruins left behind by St. Marcos' finest. But there also were my suitcases, sprung open yesterday with clothes hanging out. My Liz Claiborne suit in a ball, with my panties and bra thrown on the floor where anyone could have seen them. Oso's spilled food dish, with ants marching in a line bearing spoils back to their queen. Oso was gobbling up the remains and ignoring the ants. My futon was unfolded and unmade. And, most telling of all, the rum bottles I'd accumulated over the last five days stared at me accusingly from the kitchen countertop. I unscrewed their tops one by one, pouring each one down the drain as I went.

"What you doing?" Ava asked.

I jumped, dropping one of the bottles, and cringed, waiting for the explosion. It bounced.

It bounced.

"What the hell?" I marveled.

"They make them out of plastic now," she said.

What an awesome concept. To be flexible instead of brittle. I held the bottle up in admiration. I emptied it down the drain, too, then took it into my bedroom and set it on the nightstand. A reminder. A souvenir.

Ava followed me. Her long hair was wet, her body wrapped in a towel. "You lost your mind?"

I whirled around. "Yes. I have."

She stared at me. The seconds ticked by. Then she said, "Me, too."

I didn't know which of us started it, but somehow we were hugging each other tight. Ava had one arm around me and was swaying, which pulled on my sunburn. I yelped in pain, then laughed. I felt like a birch tree. Strong. Tall. Rooted. Flexible enough to sway. I could withstand the storms and seasons of my life. I heard ringing. We stopped swaying. Ava cocked her head.

"The kitchen," she said, and sprinted toward the sound with her towel flapping.

"Hello," I heard her say on an outward puff of her breath. "Hello?"

And then she was silent. I guessed she'd missed the call. I was wrong.

"What you saying, Eduardo? What you saying?" Her voice was shrill.

I started toward her. She was pacing back and forth between her kitchen and living room, one hand holding her cell phone to her ear, the other hand covering the other ear. She paced and listened for five minutes, punctuating the conversation from her end by occasionally shouting "What!" and "You're kidding me." Finally, she said, "OK, I got it. I will. Thank you. I understand. Good luck."

She ended the call and the phone slipped from her hand, where it clattered to the floor, shattering into pieces of plastic and bits of electronics.

Chapter Forty-three

"We have to go!" Ava shouted as she ran into her bedroom.

"Where? What?" I said.

She emerged seconds later holding sandals, a skirt, a shirt, and underclothing. She dived for her purse and ignored the ruins of her phone on the tile floor. She grabbed my pocketbook and handed it to me.

"I tell you in the truck. Please, hurry."

And then she was running out the door, barefoot and naked except for her towel. I sprinted after her, still wearing my sundress-over-bathing-suit ensemble, calling for Oso outside. He reached the truck at the same time as me, and I let him in. He scrambled to attention in the middle of the seat, ears forward. Ava was already in. I couldn't move any faster, especially belting in over my sunburn, but she kept saying, "Hurry, Katie. You got to hurry."

I threw the truck into reverse and pressed the accelerator. The tires threw dirt and rocks in the air behind us as I whipped the truck into a turn, then stopped, shifted into drive, and accelerated again. "Where are we going?"

"The Pelican's Nest. You know where it is?"

I did. I had eaten there on a night when Ava was with Guy, on the trip that seemed like a lifetime ago, but was only a month. The restaurant occupied one side of a clubhouse and overlooked through plate-glass windows all along one side the largest marina—and most expensive boats—on the island.

"Now, Ava, tell me what's going on. Please."

Ava drew in a ragged breath and put her hand on her chest. Then she dropped her towel and put on her bra. I hoped she wasn't giving any passing drivers a heart attack. When she had clasped the hook in the back, she spoke.

"That bitch Lisa kill Guy."

"Whoa, whoa, whoa. I'm not following. Who's Lisa?"

"Lisa Guy's wife."

"Oh, my." I struggled to keep my attention on the road. "How do you know that?"

"You know who Eduardo is? Guy's assistant?" she asked, pulling a pink scooped-neck t-shirt over her head.

"Yeah, the one who sold you out to the police, according to the seriously pissed off and jealous Jacoby."

"Right. Guy, well, Guy flipped Jacoby's switch." She bit a fingernail, something I'd never seen her do. I looked at her hands. All her nails were quick-short. "This not about Jacoby, though. That Eduardo on the phone. He said Lisa meeting her boyfriend at the Pelican's Nest any minute now, and we should follow her if we want to know who killed Guy."

Ava had me so confused. "I thought Lisa killed Guy?"

"Well, not her personally, maybe, but she involved." Ava scooched off her towel and stuck one foot and then the other through the leg of her satin thong panties.

"I'm not following you again."

"Eduardo set up my meetings with Guy. You know that. And he set up my last one, too. So, today he call to tell me he overheard Lisa on the phone talking lover-talk, making plans to meet a boyfriend. Well, Eduardo thought that *he* Lisa's boyfriend." Ava shimmied into her stretchy white miniskirt.

Mrs. Guy had dumped Eduardo. Nothing turns a witness faster than getting dumped. The St. Marcos prosecutor was the one whose case had fleas this time. My pulse double-timed in the hollow of my throat.

"Holy moly."

"Yeah, and Eduardo say he told Lisa about me a long time ago, the asshole. Pillow talk. He say she didn't care. But for some reason, two weeks after Guy's murder, Lisa 'confess' to the police about how she just found out Guy had a girlfriend. She tell them she confront him the day he die, and that he told her he dump his good-for-nothing tramp to save their marriage. Lisa tell the police she didn't know who the girlfriend was. She make up some story about how she hadn't told the cops up front because she want to protect Guy's legacy, and that because he had a lot of enemies, she thought it could be anyone. But that she afraid that the girlfriend kill Guy and come after her, too." Now Ava's white gladiator sandals were buckled around each ankle.

I hit the steering wheel with the palm of my hand. Pay dirt. "Did Eduardo tell her who you were?"

"He say he did. He say Lisa made the whole thing up. In fact, he say that Guy and Lisa fight big the same day he die, but it over some bank records Guy find at their house."

"Did Guy catch Lisa spending money she shouldn't or something?"

Ava removed a big-toothed green comb from her purse and started untangling her hair. "I don't know. So, after Lisa tell the police about Guy having a girlfriend, the police re-question Eduardo. They pissed at him because he hadn't told them about Guy meeting with me. He said they threaten to pull his phone records. So he tell them the truth. He say he told them that he would do anything to protect Guy's reputation, and that he certain I didn't kill Guy."

"Well, at least now we know why it took them so long to find you," I said.

"Yeah. That and because we talking about the St. Marcos police." Ava put her comb back in her purse and pulled out her makeup bag. "True."

As we left town heading east, I accelerated. We flew past mangrove-filled saltwater ponds on either side of the road. The vegetation was short and sparse here, the salty ground untenable for most plants. Large stucco houses crowned the hills, but we'd left the Danish architecture behind in Town. We were almost there.

Ava bronzed her cheeks like a housepainter on methamphetamines. "So after all that with the police, Eduardo suspicious of Lisa. And even more so when he hear her cooing on the phone. He confront her about it, all of it, and she fire him. He pack a bag and go straight to the airport to buy a ticket home to Guatemala. And he call me on the way." She shoved the makeup and brush back in her bag.

"So he doesn't *know* that Lisa is involved."

"No, I guess not. But why she tell the police those lies if she not involved?" Ava leaned close to the mirror on the sun visor and quickly penciled black onto the lower rims of her eyes.

And why would she wait two weeks to do it? I had a idea. "Did Lisa know Guy was meeting with you that night?"

"Eduardo didn't say. But why he tell her?" Hot-pink lipstick in hand, Ava slashed color across her lips.

"People in love do strange things."

We pulled into the Pelican's Nest's parking lot, which surrounded the club-house and restaurant on three sides. The far side looked onto rows of docked luxury yachts in the marina. I parked on the broad side of the building, out of view of the front entrance. The parking lot was mostly empty, but to anyone familiar with the ebb and flow of this place, my big dirty truck was bound to be conspicuous.

I asked, "What time was Lisa meeting her mystery man here?"

"Three o'clock." Now that my truck was still, Ava was applying mascara. No time for false eyelashes today.

I glanced at my watch. Five minutes until three. "What an odd time to meet at a restaurant. I'll bet they aren't even open."

A shiny-clean late-model black Tahoe with tinted windows pulled into the lot and parked in front of the entrance. Its driver's side door slammed and a petite woman with perfectly styled short hair came around the front of the car to the sidewalk, her black slingback sandals clicking on the pavement. She wore a blue knit suit with a short skirt and a short-sleeved top with gold piping around the hem and round neckline. She dropped her clutch purse and spun around to retrieve it from the ground. There was a decorative gold button adorning the kick slit in the back of her skirt. As she got closer, I recognized her as the woman who'd handled the Annalise closing. Ms. Nesbitt from the Bank of St. Marcos.

"There she is!" Ava said.

"Where?" I asked.

Ava pointed at Ms. Nesbitt. "That's Lisa."

The wife of the dead senator was Ms. Nesbitt. Bank officer. Sister of Junior. Lisa. Lisa Nesbitt was Mrs. Guy Edwards. Now I got it. It was a very small island. I didn't waste time explaining the connection to Ava.

Lisa walked past the sidewalk leading to the entrance of the Pelican's Nest, and came around the side of the building, headed straight toward us.

"Crap. Lower your head like we're looking for something on the floor," I said. Ava and I both leaned forward and pretended we were searching. I grabbed Oso's collar and pulled him to the floor with us. He whined and struggled against me. "Shhh, boy, want a treat?" I handed him a piece of banana chip from the floorboard, disgusted that it was in my car and satisfied that Oso was cleaning it up for me. To Ava I said, "Don't raise up yet. Keep searching."

"Do you think she saw us?" Ava asked, looking at me from her folded-over position.

Oso was now down on the floor hoovering for more banana chips. He couldn't find anything, so he looked up and licked my face. I pushed him back and resolved to break him of his germy love habit.

"Only if she's standing outside our window staring in. Otherwise, she has no reason to know my truck, or that you and I are connected. OK, let's sit up, slowly, and face each other. Up, Oso," I said, and patted the seat. He complied immediately. The dog was learning fast.

We straightened, and I saw Lisa from the rear as she stepped off the curb at the back edge of the restaurant. She looked all around her, then walked up to a car that was pulling to a stop. Aha. I activated the camera on my iPhone and snapped pictures as fast as I could. "You can look now," I told Ava.

She pivoted, and we watched Lisa get in the back seat of an older-model brown Lincoln Continental. Again, tinted windows. Tinting was technically illegal on St. Marcos, unless you worked for the government or were a thug. Or at least every thug that I saw had them, and they were never pulled over on the side of the road by a cop handing them a ticket. The Continental started forward.

"We're going to have to follow them, Ava."

"Yes, yes, follow them," she said, her eyes glued to the car.

Chapter Forty-four

I'd never tailed a car before. I'd read a lot of Sue Grafton novels when I was in college, though. "What would Kinsey Millhone do?" I asked myself, and almost laughed, but not quite.

The Continental swung around and passed behind us, heading out of the parking lot. I backed out and pulled onto Tamarind Road behind them, away from Town.

"They getting away," Ava cried.

"There's no one else on the road. I have to stay pretty far back or they'll see us," I said. I established a position about two hundred yards behind them.

"OK," Ava said, but she gripped the hand rest and leaned forward. Oso studied her, then leaned forward, too.

The salt ponds gave way to treeless green fields. I knew from Rashidi's lecture aboard the shuttle to his rainforest tour that these were salt marshes, and the greenery obscuring the watery ground was more mangrove, yucca, and sea grape, mixed in with Guinea grass. One mile later, the Continental turned left into a gated community. It stopped at a white wooden guard booth, then the gate's arm rose, and the sedan continued on. I pulled up to the guard booth.

Ava leaned across Oso and me and smiled. "Good day, Bob, how you doing?"

The guard was clad in an official-looking white button-front short-sleeved shirt and khaki shorts. He lit up like a Christmas tree when he saw Ava. "Good day, Miss Ava. I doing well. And how your family?"

"Mom and Dad doing great, thank you for asking. I here today to see Elizabeth Anderson."

"She expecting you?" he asked, picking up his clipboard and a pen.

"Yes. I picking up a costume to be fitted for the community theater musical next month. We doing *Jesus Christ Superstar.*"

While she worked Bob, I kept my eyes on the Continental, which had turned up a hill to the left.

"You always a star, Ava. I be sure to come see you in it." He scribbled on his paper, then hit a button, and the gate opened.

"Thanks, Bob. Goodbye, now!" She waved cheerily.

The Continental was moving into rarefied air now. This hill was one of the most exclusive pieces of property on St. Marcos. There were only three houses at the top, and one of them hogged a section twice as big as the other two. The Continental pulled through the massive iron gate of the compound, a white structure with a giant B in the center. Coconut palms lined the driveway leading up to an oversized traditional West Indian house. Two-story "welcoming arms" bannisters bordered the front staircase, the arms curving down and outward to meet the ground. Arches set into the exterior walls created a breezeway that encircled the entire main house. The stucco was a subdued peach with white accents around the doors and windows, also a nod to tradition.

"Ho, ho, ho," Ava chortled. "If she ain't going to visit the high and mighty Mr. Gregory Bonds himself."

I'd heard the name. "Who's he?" I asked.

"St. Marcos' wealthiest citizen, although not a bahn yah native. He from New York, I think. He made his money in offshore gambling and already a gazillionaire by the time he moved on-island. He own the casino we sang at when you visited, the phone company, and he trying to buy the power company away from the government, too."

"Your future husband," I said. "His limo nearly hit me in Town, once."

"That's him."

I took more pictures and wished I had a better camera than my iPhone. They wouldn't be great, but we'd at least be able to see the car and its license plate number, the house, and, now that she was getting out of the car, Lisa Nesbitt. I managed a few more snaps of her as she walked up to the house and was escorted in.

"That's not him," Ava said.

"What?"

"The guy that let her in a black local. Gregory white. A big beefy white guy with an afro of blond hair, who wear fuddy duddy glasses. Not a good-looking man. Although if he ask me to the prom, I go, since he my future husband," she said.

I kept taking pictures.

"I'm trying to get a shot of the driver, but I can't see him through the window tinting. It looks like he's going to stick around and wait for her. Maybe he'll get out to visit the loo or something, " I said.

"Can we get any closer?" she asked.

"I don't think so. Besides, I think we'd need to be inside the compound to get any better shots than we're already getting from here."

A rap on the glass by my face startled me. Ava and I both gasped. Oso barked.

It was a security guard, although he wasn't dressed the same as the gate guard. This guy was in pressed navy-blue shorts and a navy button-front shirt with a badge on it. Embroidered in white below the badge was "Bonds Enterprises."

I rolled down my window and smiled in what I hoped was a fetching manner. "Good day, sir."

"You got a reason to be here, ladies?" All business. Maybe my fetching wasn't. I didn't go for fetching often. I could have accidentally used my "guilty as hell" smile.

Since fetching hadn't worked, I went for clueless tourist. "No, sir. We accidentally turned up this road and then we saw this beautiful house. I stopped to take a few pictures. It's gorgeous. Someone important must live here. Do you work here?"

Ava didn't say anything, so I assumed this was one of the small handful of men on the island she hadn't dated or who didn't want to date her. Yet.

"You need to move along. This road private property. Get going, now."

He double-tapped the roof of my truck. I looked at Ava. She shrugged.

"Yes, sir. Good day." I didn't bother rolling my window up, just put the truck in drive and did a U-turn.

"Crap," Ava said.

"We have what we came for. Enough to give the police another suspect."

"Not with Eduardo gone," she cried.

"Between the fact that they turned up nothing in their search of your place and these pictures, it's a good start. If they won't act on it, Duke can. Or he can hire an investigator."

And that's when I remembered that Walker was meeting me out at An-nalise. And Rashidi, with Crazy Grove. I needed to hurry.

"Let's stop by the Packin' Male and make some printouts of these pictures. Then we have to meet Rashidi out at Annalise. He's introducing me to the new contractor. And Walker is bringing me his final report."

"Final report? Did he find anything?"

I tried a chuptz. It was pitiful and Ava rolled her eyes and shook her head.

I said, "No, although I'm not so sure he tried. I'm not sure of anything on this island anymore, to be truthful."

Too late, I realized that probably sounded like I wasn't sure of Ava, either. Ava, who was accused of killing her lover. Ava, who two days ago had infuriat-ed me with her behavior toward Bart. Ava stared out the window for a moment while I searched for the right apology. It didn't come.

She whipped her head back to me and in an overly bright voice said, "The Packin' Male it be, then."

Chapter Forty-five

Rashidi and Crazy Grove beat us out to Annalise, but not by much. Rashidi made introductions all around.

"Why don't you let Mr. Wingrove and me speak for a few minutes," I said. "You guys can catch up on things." I wanted to give Ava a chance to talk to Rashidi alone, more than I wanted to talk to Grove alone.

"Good idea," Rashidi said, and he pulled Ava under his arm, guiding her toward the front steps. The dogs followed him, except for Oso. Oso had figured out where his dog biscuit was buttered.

I stayed on the side of the house with Mr. Wingrove. "So, do you want me to call you William or Wingrove?" I asked, not wanting to offend him with overfamiliarity.

"Call me Crazy, miss. It helps with my reputation. Keeps the men dem on their toes."

I liked this guy. We talked about expectations for a while, mine and his. We walked the house together and discussed the work I wanted done. He made some good suggestions and roughed out a timeline and costs for me. He didn't make any pretty promises. Oso sidled up to him and Crazy scratched the dog's head while he talked to me. As we finished, we walked around to the front steps and joined Ava and Rashidi, where they were sitting side by side. Her head was on his shoulder and her arm was through his, and his other hand was covering hers.

"It's a big job," Crazy was saying, "And some of the men dem afraid to work at the jumbie house."

"Oh, come on, now. This isn't a jumbie house," I said. I crossed my fingers behind my back.

Crazy cackled. "Yah, right. What I telling my men dem is the jumbie a good crazy, like me. She really save that boy what fell out here?"

"If one believed in jumbies, then it would be possible to conclude that a jumbie rendered some aid to the young man in question." I winked.

He winked back. "Always good to have spirits dem on your side."

We shook hands on that.

Rashidi and Ava stood up. Rashidi said, "Katie, your dogs have ticks. Bad ticks. Crazy and I gonna take them into town to the vet or they get the tick fever. I shoulda had them treated before I brought them out here." He flashed me his lady-killer grin. "The rainforest ain't for the weak, meh son."

"Yah mon," I answered. I leaned down and parted the fur on Cowboy's back. Urp. A tick. I gave him a push toward Rashidi. "Be my guest, and thank you."

Rashidi imparted one last nugget of information. "I see a blue Silverado truck earlier parked over in the old Rasta village 'cross the road, right before you and Ava got here. I went to check it out and it drove away fast." Rashidi grimaced. "You and Ava need to get on home now, soon as you can. Junior not happy with you."

A ball of nerves formed in my stomach. "Thanks, Rashidi. We're leaving right behind you."

We walked the men back around to Rashidi's Jeep, into which he somehow loaded six dogs and two men. Rashidi saluted us, then he and Crazy drove off, calling out more farewells and waving from their cramped quarters as they drove away.

The wind had picked up. Ava pushed her hair back and held it out of her face. "Walker still coming?"

Damn. I had forgotten about him. "Yes, any time now."

I sagged against the outside side wall of the house, taking care not to scrape the backs of my sunburned arms against the stucco. I was tired to the bone.

I read an incoming text. "Could I make you my world famous Chilean sea bass tonight?" Bart.

I had been keeping Bart at bay for two days. I wanted nothing more than to go back to Ava's place and sleep round the clock. But I'd made more than just a resolution not to drink out on that beach this morning. I had resolved to let this happen with Bart, whatever this was. Starting now. I could drink a Red Bull. Or three.

"I'd love it," I sent.

I calculated the time it would take to finish with Walker, get home, shower, beautify, and drive to Bart's place, which he'd said was in Town.

I sent another text. "Can we make it 7:30?"

Ava spoke. "How it go with Crazy?"

"Good, thank God. I'm so grateful to Rashidi right now, and ready to see the last of that damn Junior."

"Me, too."

Ava reached into her purse and pulled out the envelope of pictures we'd printed at the Packin' Male in between eyeballing the two cute young Puerto Rican guys that ran it. They wore Levi's and white t-shirts with their sleeves rolled up in a 50s style. The store had been hopping, and conspicuously absent of straight men.

I followed Ava around the house to the garage, where I'd parked the truck earlier. Normally, the garage was full of dogs, who liked to watch the road from their spots on the cool cement floor and beg at the door for food, but not now. The truck's back end was sticking out of the garage a few feet. OK, maybe I hadn't parked it in the garage, more like in and out of the garage.

Ava lowered the tailgate, then put her hands flat on it as she jumped and spun, planting her rump solidly. I joined her on her perch, repeating her move but less gracefully. I angled my face up to the sky and let the fingers of the breeze caress my face.

"It's five minutes until six. If Walker doesn't come by ten minutes after, let's head out," I said.

Ava didn't answer. She was rifling through the pictures and muttering to herself as she stared at each one. I leaned in so I could see, too.

"I don't think Guy had any idea Lisa was cheating on him," Ava said as she flipped through the pictures. "He pretty self-important. He sweet, but he saw himself as the one that could, and everyone else those that couldn't."

She locked in on a picture, rapt.

I took in the picture that had Ava's attention. Lisa getting out of the car at Gregory's place. I adopted a terrible accent and said, "I guess that make her the wutliss one."

Ava snorted. "Don't try that accent out in public. People laugh at you. But what make you say that?"

I concentrated for a moment. Nothing came to me. I relaxed my mind and closed my eyes. The answer floated in, soft as dandelion fluff blown by a child.

"Walker told me that Guy was as worthless as the shirt he was wearing when he died. Except he said wutliss, just a lot better than I did."

Ava squinted at me in the late afternoon sun. "He say exactly that?"

"Yes, why?"

"It strange, that all. When I find Guy in his hotel room," she paused, "dead, he wearing a t-shirt from a local band popular years ago. They called Wutliss. His shirt literally say 'Wutliss Crue' on it."

"I thought it was an odd thing for him to say, too, but I guess that explains what Walker meant."

But it didn't, really. Not completely anyway. My scalp started to tingle like it did when my brain was wrestling with a problem.

Ava shook her head slowly, then faster. "I don't think so. I see all the news. All of it. There no pictures of Guy from the room, where he die, I mean."

She shuffled through more pictures, then stopped shuffling to talk again. "The police knew, though. And I think he tight with someone up there. I mean, otherwise, why the assistant chief refer you to him in the first place. Right?"

I didn't answer. I couldn't. I was looking at the picture in her lap. It was one I took of the brown Continental. A good photo, one that showed its ridiculous vanity license plate, NYPD BLEW. The picture was so good, in fact, that it left no doubt that it was the same car as the one pulling in the drive of Annalise right that second.

I grabbed the pictures from Ava. "Look at the car," I hissed. "It's here, right now. Come on."

Ava looked at the picture, then the car, and jumped to her feet. I did, too, and ran around to the driver's side of my truck and opened it. My hands shook so violently that I fumbled the door before I could get it open. I leaned into the cab and shoved the pictures into my purse and hugged it to me. *You must calm down*, I coached myself. I willed my heart to slow its pace, for the heat in my face to cool, for the red splotches I knew were there to disappear.

Ava was right behind me. "What we gonna to do?" she whispered.

"Let's go in the house. Just act naturally. Don't say a word about any of this, about our day, nothing, OK?"

I put my hand on her shoulder to give her a twist and push in the right direction. I could hear the car now as it pulled up the driveway to the house. The engine shut off. The door opened. Feet hit the ground. By then, we were in the kitchen. "Into the great room," I said in Ava's ear. "Let me see who it is."

"Anyone home?" a voice called out. A familiar voice. Whoever it was, he was headed our way.

Chapter Forty-six

"I'm coming. Who is it?" I called out.

His shoes crunched the dirt and pebbles on the concrete floor as he entered the house. Every nerve ending in my body tingled now, and I heard a humming sound in my ears. I swallowed and rubbed my hands on my sundress, the same dress I'd been wearing when I went to walk myself out of drinking, only a few hours ago.

Paul Walker entered the kitchen, his long legs in blue jeans and his protruding gut encased in a white Guys and Dolls Fishing Tournament t-shirt. He was even taller than I remembered. "There you are," he said.

My mind spun. Walker? He was due to meet me out here, but that was his car? The car Lisa had ridden in for the drive to Bonds' house?

I forced my words out. "Right this way. It's not much, but at least we'll have good light and some camp chairs to sit in, in the great room." Oh my Lord, out of sheer force of habit I had invited this horrible man into the parlor like I was some damn Southern belle. I might as well offer him some sweet tea, too, while I was at it. Too late to change course now, though.

He followed me in. "Oh, it's you," he said, surprised to see Ava.

Ava was sitting in one of the two red-and-blue-striped folding chairs. She lifted a hand in a tepid wave. Rally, Ava, I thought. You can do it.

Walker picked his way across the remains of the scaffolding to sit on the stone hearth. I followed him to the other camp chair. When Ava and I turned our chairs to face him, our eyes met. Her pupils were the size of dimes.

"So, you have the final report for me?" I asked.

He waved a green file folder in the air. He opened it and pulled out a stapled sheaf of papers.

"The report," he said.

He added a single sheet to the hand that held the report. "Your invoice."

He lifted the green folder again. "A copy of the file. My notes, documents, photographs, etcetera."

"Great." I stood up and held out my hand.

He didn't pass the documents to me. "If you could pay me for the balance first." He put the report back in the folder, then held up the invoice, forcing me to walk all the way over to him to see it. Every cell in me shrank away from him.

I took the sheet and read the number: $1,274.32. In addition to the five hundred I'd already paid him. The man was a thief as well as a . . . whatever else he was. A person who knew the clothes that Guy was wearing when he died. Who drove Lisa Nesbitt to Gregory Bonds' house. My scalp tingled. Tiny Lisa Nesbitt. Big blond Gregory Bonds.

Wait.

I'd seen his picture in the newspaper, an article about one of his company's acquisitions, hadn't I? The face flashed into my mind, replaced by another face, the same face. A bear of a man with a blond afro sitting at Toes in the Water with Walker. A man who stared daggers at me, a woman he didn't even know. Now my forearms tingled like they were falling asleep. I heard a ringing in my ears. My brain was in serious overdrive. What reason did Bonds have to know who I was, much less to dislike me?

"Ms. Connell, are you going to pay me?" Walker asked.

"Oh! I'm sorry. We've had a tiring last few days. I'm the walking dead."

A crocodile smiled back at me. I had to get him out of here. I propped my purse against my hip and reached in for my checkbook. I dug. And dug. Surely I had it in there?

And that's when it happened.

My purse fell to the floor with a thud, spilling all of its contents out in a tumbling river to Walker's feet. Well, there was my checkbook—along with all the pictures we'd taken at the Pelican's Nest and Bond's house. I buckled to my knees and started gathering them up as fast as I could, blathering, "Sorry, so sorry, what a klutz I am."

Ava bounded across the floor in one step and crouched down to help.

Walker's big hand reached down and picked up a picture that had landed on his shoe. He looked at it, but I leaned toward him and grabbed the other edge of it. I tugged. "Thanks, but I've got it."

He let me win, and I fell backward onto my tush.

Walker stood up. The ringing in my ears reached a crescendo. Above us, there was a loud pop, then a wrenching of metal. Walker peered up into the scaffolding as metal poles rained down on him. Behind him stood the young woman I'd know anywhere, standing tall in her long skirt. Her arms looked ghostly in her loose white blouse as she pointed toward the garage. I could take a hint.

I stuck my arm through my purse handles and scooched backward as fast as I could. "Run, Ava," I screamed, as metal and boards continued to fall. Walker crouched with his hands over his head. Ava sprang into motion, and the two of us scrambled to our feet and ran to my truck.

"Hurry, hurry," I urged her.

I dumped my purse into the seat and grabbed for my keys. I jammed the key into the ignition and turned it so hard I almost snapped it. The Silverado roared to life. I threw it in reverse and mashed the pedal as I put my arm on the back edge of the seat and turned to see my path.

The crunch of my bumper into Walker's rear driver's side door was sickening. We'd only gone five feet, but the impact threw both of us forward into the dash. We were stuck.

"Come on, we'll run," I said.

I grabbed my door handle and wrenched it upwards as I shoved outward. My door slammed into the frame of the garage where someday a door would be, but I didn't care. I leaped out and spun away from the truck—and into Walker's chest. He grabbed me by my neck in his left hand and threw me up against the inside of my truck door. In his right hand, he held a gun. He pressed the cold tip of its barrel against my forehead.

"Stop, Ava," he commanded. "Stop, or I'll pull the trigger and Katie's brains will end up on the inside of her new truck."

"I stop," Ava said. "Don't shoot."

Chapter Forty-seven

"Good decision, Ava," Walker said. "Get in the driver's seat."

Ava stared at him like she was deaf.

"Now, Ava."

The business end of the gun was digging into my forehead. It hurt, but not nearly as bad as his big hand pressing my windpipe closed and his fingers digging into the back of my sunburned neck. I couldn't breathe.

Ava got back in the truck and crawled across to the driver's side.

Walker eased off some, and I gasped for breath. He paid me no attention. To Ava, he said, "You're going to drive this truck to Baptiste's Bluff. Katie's going to drive my car, and I'll ride with her. We'll be right behind you. You and I both know there's no place for you to run, and if you try, first I'll shoot Katie, and then I'll come find you. And I will find you. I won't shoot you, though. We'll have some fun and see where it takes us."

My mind couldn't wrap itself around what was happening. Baptiste's Bluff. He was taking us to Baptiste's Bluff? I could see Ava in my peripheral vision. My keys were still in the ignition. Ava turned on the truck. She put her hands on the wheel. Tears were rolling down her cheeks, but she didn't make a sound.

"Do you have a phone with you, Ava?" Walker asked.

She shook her head.

"It wouldn't matter anyway. There's no cell reception up on these roads."

I did, though. I had a phone. Or did I? Was it in the truck along with everything else I'd dumped from my purse? I tried to think when I'd last used it. We'd plugged it into the USB connector at the Packin' Male to upload our pictures to their desktop so we could print them. I had disconnected my phone when we were done. And I had . . .

"Move it, Katie. You're driving my car."

He released my throat and pulled the gun away from my forehead, but kept it pointed at me as he stepped back. "Get in."

As I slipped into the driver's seat and shut the door behind me, I put my hands down, ostensibly to adjust my body, but really to slip my cell phone out of the loose side pocket sewn into the right hip of my sundress. My mother always told me to avoid unflattering hip pockets, and I was glad I hadn't listened. I lay the iPhone on the seat between my thigh and the door. I thought about calling 911 or Rashidi or even Bart, but I knew I'd lose connection when we were a hundred feet away from Annalise. Rashidi was ten miles away by now, Bart and the police were further than that, and what help could I expect from the St. Marcos police, even if the call went through? But then another thought hit me. Sherry. She had taped Zane McMillan with her phone.

Walker's hand was on the door latch now. I quickly tapped the screen to pull up a voice recording app that I used to use to record witnesses. I pressed Record and the timer scrolled forward. One second, two seconds, three seconds it read, confirming that it was recording. The door opened. I slid the recording volume to max and returned to the home screen, leaving the phone recording, a record for posterity or whoever found my body.

Walker lowered himself into his seat. I put both of my hands on the steering wheel and fought to act normal. When he handed me the keys, I noticed a rivulet of blood running from his temple to his cheek, a souvenir from the scaffolding trick my jumbie friend had played. I pretended to try to insert them in the ignition with my right hand, fumbling them as much as I could, while I dropped the phone back into my hip pocket with my left hand. I did the fumbling so well that I managed to drop the keys.

"Come on," Walker snapped.

I tried again, and this time I turned the car on. Walker was holding his gun in his right hand. He turned his body slightly toward me. He rested his elbow on the dashboard with the gun's muzzle pointed at me. "Make room for Ava to back out. Follow her to Baptiste's Bluff."

I did as he said, trying not to think of the implications of our destination, all the people that had met their death off that cliff, people like my mother and father. Bart was expecting me to show up at 7:30, a full hour away from now. No one would miss us in time to come to our rescue. I didn't want to die.

Ava pulled out, and I fell in behind her. I swallowed hard. My father's coaching returned to me, the times he had earnestly explained to Mom, Collin, and me how to lull an attacker into a false sense of security while you stalled and looked for his weakness. I could get him talking, distract him while I waited for my chance, and maybe even learn something to use to our advantage, anything. Except my brain was having a hard time communicating with my tongue.

"Why'd you kill the senator?" I asked, finally.

"Haven't you figured that out by now?" he responded.

I hesitated. The man had just confessed to killing Guy Edwards. I didn't know for sure why he'd done it, but I'd developed a decent theory in the last few hours. "Because of the bank records that Guy found?"

Walker snorted. "That stupid bitch left them out where Guy could see them. He may not be a rocket scientist, but he was smart enough to know there was only one reason Lisa would keep a rich client's files off bank premises."

"So she kept a phony set of books at the bank, and the real set at home? What, was she helping Bonds launder money?"

"She thought she was helping herself, that Gregory loved her, and that she was securing their future together." Walker drew out the word "loved," turning it into something absurd. "Little mami called big daddy to tell him she'd blown it, and I've never seen him so mad. I think he'll take that bitch out next."

Lisa was a criminal, but she didn't deserve to die anymore than Guy did. Neither did Ava and I, for that matter.

"Who set Ava up?" I asked.

"Nobody. I followed Guy. I knew he was heading to meet some skank because that's what he always did. I didn't know it was Ava, though. I got lucky." He twirled the gun on his finger. "You better hope she's as steady up there as your dad was, otherwise I'll have to shoot you."

Strobe lights went off in my brain. The faulty synapses that hadn't made the connections earlier finally got it right. Of course. My parents had died because they'd seen Gregory with Lisa on the beach that day, the giant blond man and the tiny black woman. Because his connection to Lisa was the link to his laundered fortune. And now Ava and I might die for the same reason. I gasped for air like Walker had gut-punched me.

Walker's laugh was maniacal. "You know what's funny, besides you hiring me of all people to help you figure out what happened to your parents? What's *really* funny is that Gregory had written them off as two stupid tourists. Then your parents had to run off their mouths about it to the wrong person. Which makes them stupid tourists after all, I guess. Full circle. Visitors never get it.

This is a small, small island. Their waiter that night at Fortuna's? Jilly Edwards, Lisa's daughter. And your mother literally points to a picture of Lisa in the paper and says to your father, right in front of Jilly like she's not even there," and here Walker used a simpering falsetto, "Oh my gaw-wad, this is the woman we saw naked on the beach with that big blond man, honey. And she's a senator's wife."

Oh, Mama. My heart broke. My sweet, sweet mother, who had no idea there was evil around her, who saw the beauty and not the danger. Just as she had everywhere in her life. It was one of the things I'd loved most about her. She was positive, she was strong, she was smart, but she was, well, *naive*.

"Yeah, Jilly girl called home. Lisa convinced her it was mistaken identity, but Lisa knew it wasn't. So, Lisa called Gregory. Who called me. Who always calls me."

Chapter Forty-eight

Ahead of us, Ava's car turned right onto the familiar lane I'd ridden down with her one month before. The cliffside was very close now.

"So you just do all Bonds's dirty work and let him keep his hands clean?" I was fighting to keep my voice normal.

"He got me out of a tight spot once," he said, and shrugged. "And he pays well."

Ava pulled over when we broke from the trees.

Walker grunted. "Put it in park, and turn it off."

I did as he asked. The sun was sinking, but no green flash tonight. I looked into the sky of fire, hell above earth. It's not hell, I thought. Hell is this. That's what salvation looks like. I wasn't ready for either salvation or hell, though. I wasn't sure yet how, but I was going to fight until the end. I had to.

"Get out of the car and stand with your hands on the hood."

I did as he told me.

He got out of the car and walked around to my side. "Walk to the front passenger seat of your truck and get in. Go." He shoved me with his left hand and held the gun against my back with his right.

I walked to the truck and got in. Ava was staring at me.

"Are you OK?" I asked her.

"I fine. You?"

"Yes."

"Shut up." Walker dropped himself into the back seat. He shut the door and scooted over behind Ava.

Ava gave a war cry. I saw a flash as she lifted my machete from underneath the bench seat, leaned forward, and whirled her right arm backhand toward Walker, the blade horizontal and inches from my face in the awkwardly tight space. "There's not enough room for this to work," I thought, anguished and hopeful at the same time. Walker's arm shot up and he caught Ava's wrist as she swung. Thud. He twisted. Snap. The machete fell into Walker's lap in the back seat. Ava screamed and rocked forward, holding her arm.

"That was stupid," he said, calm as the eye of a hurricane. "Shut up, put the car in gear, and drive forward."

"I can't," Ava sobbed.

He cocked the trigger of his gun and pressed it into the hollow of her neck below her skull. His voice was slippery and cold. "Yes, you can, dear. Now do it."

Ava carefully placed her broken right wrist into her lap. She tried again with her left hand. "Can you put it in gear for me?" she asked me, her voice breaking over her sobs as she swallowed them.

I didn't say a word, just shifted the car into drive. Using only her left hand, Ava steered. We crested the rise, and the nose of the truck pointed down the short slope.

"Stop," Walker said.

Ava stopped the car. I put it in park.

Ava put her face on the steering wheel. "You a fucked-up bastard."

Walker's face didn't even flicker. But I saw his arm move. I reacted out of years of training and the instinct that had set me apart in the dojo years ago, the inner ear that mattered most, that had drawn words of praise from my sensei. As he lifted his gun and cracked it against her head, I chopped his wrist with my right hand, sending the gun skittering to the floorboard under Ava's feet, and immediately slammed my left arm back in a vicious sword chop to his throat. Ava slumped against the door, unconscious. Walker fell against the seatback. He grabbed his throat, writhing, choking, and gasping for air.

I unclicked my seatbelt and leaned over Ava, unfastened hers, opened her door, and pushed her out to the safety of the grass. While I was extended across her seat, I felt the car begin to move. I sat up and realized with horror that my body had forced the gearshift from park to drive. I wrenched the door handle, threw open my own door, and rolled out. Blue, green, and orange spun around me as I tumbled and rolled, then fell still. I scrabbled toward Ava, not yet believing we were free, and I turned toward my beautiful gold truck to see Walker in profile, frantically trying to open the back door as the Silverado went over the cliff. I heard the scraping of metal on rock, a terrible sound. I saw my parents' faces now instead of Walker's, and I let down the tears that I had held in so long.

I put my face in my hands and sobbed, but only for a moment, then I shook my head, refusing to give in to grief. I clenched my fists and hit both of them into the ground. "I got you, you asshole," I screamed in anguish, in triumph. "I got the bad guy, Dad."

It didn't bring my parents back.

I felt something cold, hard, and narrow against my right fist. I moved my hand and saw the glint of gold in the green grass. I reached under the flattened blades with my thumb and forefinger and plucked the object free. It was a gold band. My heart stopped. I turned it on its side and searched for the inscription.

Hannah.

Seconds passed, maybe minutes. I became aware again, of where I was, of my mother's ring in my hand, of Ava. I stuck the ring on my finger and crouched over Ava, the last of my tears falling on her face as I shook her gently. She groaned.

"Ava, wake up, Ava, it's Katie. Wake up." I smoothed her wild black curls off her face and used my palm to wipe the trickle of blood from her forehead, smearing it more than cleaning it. "Come on, Ava."

Her eyes opened. "Katie? What happen?" She sat up, then held her head. "Oh my God, my head hurt so bad." She took in our surroundings. I saw her remember. "Where he go? Where he?" She tried to climb to her feet, but fell forward on her hands and knees. Her wrist buckled and she cried out, then rocked back on her knees and hugged her arm to her chest.

"It's going to be OK, Ava. He's gone now." I pointed toward the cliff.

She gaped at me. "You kill him?"

"Not exactly. I think the childproof locks did him in."

Ava stared at me like I'd dropped my basket for real. Then she howled like a hyena, laughing until she held her side with her good arm. "I going to hell now, for true," she said.

"For this and all your other sins," I agreed.

She swung her legs around and sat on her bana, then pulled her knees in to her chest with one arm and rested her head on them. "Only one problem. That bastard the only one could prove I didn't kill Guy."

I patted my left hip for the iPhone. It was still there. Please, God, please, I prayed. I reached into my pocket and pulled out the phone. I opened the

recorder and pressed Stop, then fiddled with it until it played back my recording.

"*Come on. Make room for Ava, and then follow her to Baptiste's Bluff.*" I pressed
Stop. I swiped the timeline forward. "*Why'd you kill the Senator?*" I heard my
voice say. "*Haven't you figured that out by now?*" Walker's voice replied. I pressed
Stop again. Halle-freakin-lujah, and thank God for Sherry Talmadge.

"Was," I said. "He *was* the only one who could prove it. Now you've got
me."

Chapter Forty-nine

I speared the earth with the point of the shovel. I shoved it in firmly, then stomped it in further with my foot. When the blade was threequarters of the way submerged, I shifted my hands so I could push down on the handle with all my weight. The shovel levered free of the ground. I lifted a bladeful of dirt, and with a twist of my wrist and arms, heaved it to the top of the small pile I had created. The hole was ten inches deep, ten inches wide. More than big enough now for what I needed.

Sweat trickled down my chest and pooled in my cleavage, dammed off by my bra. I turned to look behind me, up the cleared grassy hill at the imposing yellow hulk of my house in side view. From this angle, I could see the third-story balcony to my favorite room, one I would use as a guest suite before too long. Not so long ago, that balcony was only a jutting concrete ledge. Now it was covered in red pavers that matched those on the patio by the nearly-finished pool. Soon, twisted black metal spindles would support a matching railing. It was nearly a real balcony now. A rock-covered chimney sprouted from the roof above it. Crazy had worked a miracle on Annalise. I'd done my share, too, including staining the mahogany staircase to a deep brown sheen. She wasn't done yet, but I'd move in before summer.

I soaked her in, then returned to my work, down on a knoll that overlooked the long valley full of mango trees. A cluster of cashew trees peeked over the edge of the slope, its fruit red and ripe. I sank to my knees in the dirt. It was cool, in contrast to the hot March air. I needed to hurry.

I scooped a last few handfuls of dirt out of my burial pit, then patted the earth down to create a perfect resting place. My hand dug in the right pocket of my pleated khaki shorts until I found the cold metal I sought. My mother's ring. My grandmother's ring. A ring that I would have worn some day, too, if my mother had lived to give it to me on my wedding day. Assuming I ever got married, which I didn't really foresee. If I had confessed to another woman alive that I was putting this heirloom under nine inches of dirt, they would have called the police for a 5150 pickup. I clutched it, stricken with an urge to keep it, to wear it, to feel it on my finger, but I didn't waver. It was time to put the past to rest. Past time to do it.

I dropped the ring into its grave. It landed with a soft thump, almost a plink. My eyes stayed dry. In the six months since Walker had flown off Baptiste's Bluff, I had shed very few tears, and then only tears of vindication. When the charges against Ava were dropped. When Jacoby told me that the police had officially reversed their finding about my parents' deaths, and posthumously charged Walker with murder, the murders of Frank and Heather Connell, and the murder of Guy Edwards. They left only Michael Jacoby's death unsolved, but it was forevermore under a cloud of suspicion. When Bonds and Lisa were captured on St. John, gassing up his yacht before they tried to make their break out of U.S. territory, I'd wondered how far out to sea Lisa would have made it before Bonds tossed her overboard. The U.S.V.I. police had charged them with conspiracy to commit murder, times three. Word on the street was that the Feds would come after them for money laundering soon, too. I looked skyward and said, "Thank you, God."

I kneaded dirt from my hand. A thin layer formed over the ring. It hurt. It hurt a lot. "You'll always be with me, Mom. You, too, Dad."

My next burial item was easier.

A clear plastic Cruzan Light Rum bottle, empty. The same one I had poured down Ava's sink on the day we almost suffered the same fate as my parents. I didn't need it anymore. I had stayed dry ever since then, and I credited hard work and the influence of a big jumbie house.

Not that I hadn't faced temptations. When your boyfriend owns the hottest restaurant on island and hosts incredible wine tasting parties, temptation is a constant. Bart didn't understand my decision to completely stop drinking, but he hadn't known the old me. He thought I was the next best thing since crème brûlée, so maybe he didn't need to understand. I looked over my shoulder and said, "Thank you, Annalise."

Bart's car motored up the drive now. I couldn't see him, but I heard the sound of the wheels on the dirt road. Spending time up here, I had come to recognize engines by sound: the loud rumble of Rashidi's Jeep, the whine of Crazy's truck as it strained under loads of building supplies, the purr of Bart's well-tuned black Pathfinder. I picked dirt up in both hands, closed my hands over it like a book, then opened them from the reverse side, dumping the dirt in a splat on the liter bottle.

One more item to go. The hardest one. The most secret one. The one no one else had to understand but me. The one I certainly hadn't trusted Ava with. Even though we'd reached an understanding about how we would act toward one another's men after she was so flirtatious with Bart, I knew Ava was still Ava. I didn't feel safe putting this information in her hands, or anyone's. I loved her, but I'd keep my boundaries, thank you very much.

I reached into my left pocket and pulled out the SIM card to my iPhone. The old SIM card, the one for my Dallas phone number. I'd lived on St. Marcos for seven months now, and only this morning had I changed my cell phone to a 340 area code number.

Letting go of my Dallas life shouldn't be this damn hard. I squeezed the tiny black rectangle, and before I even knew it was coming, a sob escaped me.

"Not now. I can't cry now. I can't let Bart see this."

It wasn't letting go of my Dallas life that hurt. It was severing the last link to Nick. A number he knew. A number he could still call, if he wanted. A number he had not called in the months I'd lived here. A number he wouldn't call.

My breath came in sharp gasps now, but I held the tears in. I extended my hand over the hole, SIM card hidden away in it.

"Drop it. Let go of it," I ordered myself.

I sensed a presence to my left. I whirled, feeling foolish but holding the SIM card behind me.

Her. She stood only ten feet away from me, under the farthest branches of a flamboyant in full bloom. Her ebony skin shimmered below the crown of brilliant orange flowers. Her eyes glowed like agates. There wasn't a drop of breeze, but her skirt was flowing out behind her. She shook her head, then held her arms open. I stepped toward her, toward those arms, that embrace.

"Katie?"

Bart's voice. I willed my eyes to track the sound. He stood on the side of the house next to mini towers of biscuit-colored travertine floor tile ready for installation, up the hill from me. He looked taller from this angle, and blonder. He wore a powder-blue t-shirt and navy shorts, and he was fresh, like crisp linen and spring sunshine. He squinted, sunglassless. But he had seen me, and he waved.

"What are you doing?" he called out.

"Hey," I replied, stalling.

I turned back toward my mysterious friend, and saw what I expected. Nothing. Dammit. With my back to Bart, I flung the SIM card into my little pit, and I kicked dirt into it, then rotated my foot longways and used it to shovel more dirt in the hole. The SIM card disappeared. I shoved more. Now soil covered the entire bottle. Another, and another, and then one last time I pushed the dirt in. I couldn't see anything but earth in the shallow, narrow hole. Good enough.

Only seconds had passed. I faced Bart now. He had closed the distance between us.

I said, "Just digging a test hole. I was thinking of planting a banana tree down here."

I held my fingers crossed behind my back. My pulse was so loud in my ears that I wondered if he could hear it. My mind ping-ponged between the hole and its contents and the here and now with Bart.

Bart's arms slipped around me and he pulled me in tight to his chest. I exhaled, and circled his body with my own arms. I laid my head on his chest. His heart thumped at an almost normal pace. He nipped my ear, then whispered into it.

"I thought we would do that together. What are we going to do with you, little Miss Independent?"

Before I could answer, he kissed me, something I had grown to like a lot, and a darn good way to forget about what lay beneath five inches of dirt at my feet. I sank into his kiss for a moment, then pulled back to answer his question.

"I think you'll figure something out," I said, lacing my voice with as much Angelina Jolie as a tall, skinny redhead could muster.

He smiled, and his white teeth gleamed against his island-tanned skin. He looked like California, like the cover of *Men's Journal*, like a man who wanted to lick my toes and eat me for dinner. He grabbed my hand and gave me a tug.

"Yes, I know a few things we could try," he said.

"Wait," I replied.

I pulled my hand out of his and picked up the flat gray rock I had brought to mark the burial spot. I dropped it into position. I wondered if I should have put the SIM card in a ziplock, just in case.

"What's that for?" Bart asked.

I looked straight into his eyes, blue as the Caribbean Sea. "To remind me this spot is too far from the house for the banana trees."

Bart scrunched his forehead, then threw back his head and laughed. "Only you, Katie. Only you."

And I put my hand back into his. I snuck one last glance at the earthen pile, then inhaled soundlessly through my nose. We walked up the hill, away from my buried ghosts, back toward Annalise and the sparkling promise of something new, together.

About the Author

Pamela Fagan Hutchins holds nothing back and writes mysterious women's fiction and Pamela Fagan Hutchins holds nothing back and writes mysterious women's fiction and relationship humor in Texas with her husband Eric and their blended family of three dogs, one cat, and the youngest few of their five offspring. She is the award winning author of many books, including *Saving Grace, The Clark Kent Chronicles, How To Screw Up Your Kids: Blended Families, Blendered Style, How to Screw Up Your Marriage, Hot Flashes and Half Ironmans, Ghosts,* and *Puppalicious And Beyond,* and a contributing author to *Prevent Workplace Harassment, Ghosts,* and *Easy To Love But Hard To Raise.*

Pamela is an employment attorney and human resources professional, and the co-founder of a human resources consulting company. She spends her free time hiking, running, bicycling, and enjoying the great outdoors.

For more information, visit http://pamelahutchins.com, or email her at pamela@pamelahutchins.com. To receive her e-newsletter for announcements about new releases, click on http://eepurl.com/iITR.

You can buy Pamela's books at most online retailers and in many "brick and mortar" stores. You can also order them directly from SkipJack Publishing: http://SkipJackPublishing.com. If your bookstore or library doesn't carry a book you want, by Pamela or any other author, ask them to order it for you.

Books By the Author

Saving Grace, SkipJack Publishing

The Clark Kent Chronicles: A Mother's Tale Of Life With Her ADHD/Asperger's Son, SkipJack Publishing

Hot Flashes And Half Ironmans: Middle-Aged Endurance Athletics Meets the Hormonally Challenged, SkipJack Publishing

How To Screw Up Your Kids: Blended Families, Blendered Style, SkipJack Publishing

How to Screw Up Your Marriage: Do-Over Tips for First-Time Failures, SkipJack Publishing

Puppalicious And Beyond: Life Outside The Center Of The Universe, SkipJack Publishing

Prevent Workplace Harassment, Prentice Hall, with the Employment Practices Solutions attorneys

Ghosts (anthology contributor), Aakenbaaken & Kent

Easy To Love, But Hard To Raise (anthology contributor), DRT Press, edited by Kay Marner and Adrienne Ehlert Bashista

CPSIA information can be obtained at www.ICGtesting.com
Printed in the USA
LVOW12s0912041113

359842LV00004B/10/P